THE
WEDDING
TAMASHA

SUDHA NAIR

THE WEDDING TAMASHA

Copyright © 2017 by Sudha Nair.

For more information, please visit her website:

www.sudhanair.com

Titles By Sudha Nair

LOVE SHOTS SERIES
The Girl With A Secret Crush
Three Of Hearts

MR & MRS NAMBIAR SERIES
Mr And Mrs Nambiar
Ahoy Amrika

STAND-ALONES
Strictly At Work

FREE SHORT STORY
Love Officially
(At SudhaNair.com)

SIGN UP FOR MY AUTHOR NEWSLETTER

Receive an exclusive short and sweet office romance story, LOVE OFFICIALLY, and news, updates, and more, when you sign up to receive my email. Let's keep in touch!

www.SudhaNair.com

1

Shweta froze at the sight of the police officer, her first customer on that cold September morning. She had been busy with her morning chores in the kitchen when the bell on the front door had jingled. The Villa Mexican Café in Edison, New Jersey, had just opened for business, but eight o'clock in the morning was still early for a visitor.

Unless, someone had tipped the police off about her working here without a legal permit…

Through the half-open kitchen door, she noticed the tall, brawny officer making his way towards the counter, his heavy boots thumping on the linoleum floor, punctuated by the squeak of leather.

Her heart thudded.

'Hello, anybody here?' The officer tapped his fingers on the counter, his thunderous voice loud against the quiet of the café, interrupted only by the rhythmic stirring of the salsa pot.

Julie Fox, the sixty-something owner of the café, was stirring the pot of her signature black salsa, something she would never take her eyes off even for a minute. That left Shweta to go to the counter.

Easily more than six feet tall, the young Hispanic cop cut a formidable figure, his eyes narrowed, his hair short and spiked, and his chest so broad, it hid the door behind him. With thick corded forearms crossed over his chest, he looked her over as she approached.

'You work here?'

A chill shot up her spine. Regaining her composure quickly, she put on her best smile. 'Yes, officer, how may I help you?'

'Haven't seen you before,' he said, his voice gruff.

Shweta swallowed. She could feel her legs wobble.

He leaned forward resting his elbows on the counter when, all of a sudden, his walkie-talkie radio sputtered to life and an operator's voice crackled through. Startled, Shweta looked sharply at the equipment he unclipped from his side.

He turned back to her, losing the confident look fast. 'Is *Abuela* here?' he said, his tone urgent.

Grandmother, she guessed from the little Spanish she knew.

Julie came out of the kitchen just then. 'Hey Pete, how's it going? First day?'

In an instant, the tough cop transformed into a docile schoolboy. 'Yes, *Abuela.* Came for your blessings.'

Julie beamed at him. 'Sure, my boy! God bless you! You'll make a fine officer.'

Smiling at his grandmother, he said, 'I better be off now, *Abuela.* I think I got an urgent situation.'

'Will you have *Abuela*'s special sweet bun for the road?'

'No, thanks. I'll see you around. I have to go now.' He tipped his hat, gave Shweta an unexpected, big grin, and turned to go.

Shweta blinked and exhaled sharply after Pete was out of the café, the door jingling behind him. 'I was terrified,' she said to Julie.

'He's my stepdaughter's son,' Julie said, beaming. 'It's his first day! Doesn't he look like a tough cop?'

He had certainly looked tough and had almost given Shweta a heart attack.

Julie returned to her pot in the tiny kitchen behind the counter. The aroma of the rich, dark, smoky salsa with charred peppers filled the entire kitchen.

The salsa was what people flocked to the café for. The special chicken burrito with black salsa and the fish tacos were a hit with the crowds.

The salsa was loved not just by the patrons who visited the café; its popularity, in fact, extended beyond that. By nine every morning, jars had to be lined up for bottling the salsa that would be sold at the Convention Centre.

'Shweta!' Julie called. 'It's time to line up those jars. Quick! Hurry up!'

As usual, Shweta hadn't noticed that the dishes were done. She stopped her cleaning and chopping midway, and hurried to the dishwasher. She wiped each jar carefully and set it beside the matrix of the sparkling, already-cleaned jars she'd formed on the counter. She stacked up the lids right next to them, all ready to be packed as soon as Julie filled them with the salsa.

Julie filled and handed the jars to Shweta who screwed the lids on tight. The jars were still warm as Shweta wiped each one before setting them into a crate that would be placed in a trolley when it was full. There were at least a hundred such jars for sale each morning.

The café had seating for about a dozen people. Though small, it was just enough for Julie and, occasionally, her daughter, Sarah, to manage. They lived in the rooms at the back, and Shweta had been allowed to share the one upstairs with Max. He was their handyman, cook, cleaner and odd-jobs man, all-in-one.

'Where's Max?' Shweta asked, suddenly remembering that he had been missing since morning. Max had recently moved in with a friend and she had begun to miss him already.

Max walked in just then, his head hung low, as if hoping that Julie wouldn't catch him for being late. Max had dark short hair and lean muscles, the type that came from physical labour.

He shambled over to the counter where he took out the rolling pin and started rolling out the tortillas. If Julie had seen him come in late, she didn't bring it up. Max was late every day since he had moved out.

Max began to roll the tortillas thin and round, with perfection, and arranged them on the counter to cook them on the iron griddle. Today, he'd forgotten to switch on the radio and Shweta reached up to the rack above the dishwasher to turn it on. Soft music flooded the kitchen as she went on with her chores. The chicken and beef needed to be cleaned. The pork chorizo sausages needed to be scoured; the lettuce washed, dried and shredded; the jalapenos and peppers chopped. She'd become faster since last week, and was already on to the task of blending the fruit juices before the regular trickle of customers started.

The office crowd started pouring in during lunch hour, the door jingling repeatedly. Shweta stayed in the kitchen, preparing the orders that Julie called out.

Shweta got twenty minutes off for lunch, which was always burrito. She made her way out through the back exit and passed the dumpster on her way to a bench under a tree in the parking lot. She opened her packed bowl and dug in. The aroma of chicken curry emanated from the Kebab Corner next door and Shweta drooled at the mouth-watering smell. She missed her mother's chicken curry like hell. She wished she had the courage to go back home to her family.

The café closed at 8 p.m. As Shweta trudged to her room upstairs, she was surprised to be greeted by the sound of the TV. As she let herself in, she saw Max lying on the single bed, watching a TV show. A pot of soup gurgled on the stove, its rich aroma wafting to where she stood at the door. The room suddenly seemed livelier with Max around and she smiled, forgetting how much her legs ached.

'Sorry, I needed a place for tonight,' Max said, as soon as she entered. 'Soup?'

'Yes, please. And you're most welcome anytime,' Shweta said, overjoyed to see him back, even if it was only for one night. She propped herself on the bed, her legs outstretched, while Max brought two steaming bowls of soup and settled down next to her. They watched *The Lucy Show* as they sipped their soup and laughed at Lucy's madness.

Shweta turned to Max. 'Will you come for lunch on Sunday? I'm making biryani. Then we'll go shopping for a new movie DVD.' She was making biryani after weeks.

Max nodded excitedly.

As they finished the soup and relaxed in front of the TV, Max told her about his spat with his new roommate. She felt worse for his having moved out.

Shweta let him talk. Then she told him all about her encounter that morning with Julie's grandson, Pete, the police officer. Max chuckled at her description of Pete's parting grin. 'Maybe he fancies you!'

She smirked. 'Funny that you scare someone you fancy.'

It was late when they finally settled in for the night. Max insisted on taking his mattress and sleeping under the window across the bed. Shweta fell asleep as soon as her head hit the pillow.

***

Sometime in the night, Shweta woke up to a bad dream. In her dream, she was in a cell, reeking with the stench of piss, strange faces staring at her. Raj was standing at the door of the cell, his grey eyes laughing frightfully at her. She trembled and sat up on the bed.

At the opposite corner beneath the window, the dim night light revealed Max's shadowy sleeping form. She let out a deep breath, thankful for his presence.

Shweta sat up on the bed, unable to get back to sleep. Drawing her knees up and wrapping her arms around herself, she shuddered in the darkness.

What if Raj found her here, just five minutes from her home, or at least what used to be her home until a week and a half ago?

2

Monday was Shweta's day off. She dialled her mother's number at noon, as she pulled out the carrots, onions, and peppers from the mini fridge to prepare the biryani lunch. It was 10 p.m. in India, and her mother, Keertana, may have stayed up waiting for Shweta's customary call. Today it was a little later than when she usually called home.

'Glad you called,' Keertana said. 'I was just about to go to bed, dear.' She sounded happy and excited.

'Sorry, Ma,' Shweta said, as she picked up a carrot and started peeling it.

'I had gone to meet astrologer Kini today, and guess what he said!' Keertana's voice rose excitedly as it always did after she'd met Kini, their family astrologer, a young government clerk by profession, who read horoscopes on the side and always had throngs of gullible believers lined up at his doorstep because his predictions came true. For most, at least. Or so, it seemed.

Shweta smiled. 'What did he say this time? That I was going to pass my driving test?'

Her mother snorted. 'That's not going to happen unless you actually go for the test.'

Shweta laughed. Graduating from her management degree had

been easier. Her mother had guessed right. Shweta wasn't planning on taking the driving test after flunking it twice. Besides, left-hand driving was too confusing.

Her father's voice boomed in the background. 'Ask her if she took the driving test.'

Shweta pictured her father, Prabhakaran Menon, lounging on the easy chair in the porch, puffing away at his pipe for the last time before he went to bed, and listening to his wife's end of the conversation with their daughter. He liked to direct his questions to his children through his wife.

Keertana was just about to repeat it to her when Shweta said, 'No, Papa, I didn't go for the driving test.'

'She says no,' Keertana repeated to Prabhu.

Her father's voice came again. 'Tell her she must know how to drive in America. It's very important.'

'I heard that,' Shweta said to her mother before she could relay it back to her.

'It's been three months since you reached there,' Keertana said, with a sigh. 'And you still haven't learned to drive.'

'I'm okay, Ma. I can manage with Shipra around.' Shipra was her old neighbour, who had a car. Their husbands, both US-educated engineers, worked in the same office in New Brunswick.

'And how is Raj? Is he very busy at work?'

'Raj has gone out,' Shweta lied. Last week, she had told her mother that Raj was travelling. Keertana was happier when Raj wasn't around while they were talking. It pleased her to speak to Shweta without her son-in-law listening in. Only then could she ramble to her heart's content.

Keertana loved to flit from topic to topic. One moment she was talking about some close relative; the next moment she remembered what she was going to say about Kini before. 'Kini's predictions are so wonderful,' she said. 'My friend Neelam was thanking him profusely for finding a good match for her daughter. He found her a boy whose horoscope matched her daughter's horoscope perfectly. I had the opportunity to ask Kini about us too. He said this year and early next year will be exceptionally good for all of us.'

Yeah, right! Shweta thought. Obviously, Kini didn't know enough!

Shweta listened some more to Keertana's chatter before she heard her yawn, and smiled. 'Bye, Ma. I think it's way past your bed time now.'

'Yes, I better hang up,' Keertana said, talking through another loud yawn.

Shweta had just hung up when someone knocked.

'Speak of the devil!' Shweta said, smiling when she saw Shipra at her door.

Shipra came in. 'Hello, ex-neighbour! What have you been up to?' They hugged each other like long-lost friends.

The sizzle from the cooker drowned Shipra's next words. 'Hold on.' Shweta rushed to the fridge to bring out the marinated chicken. 'I'm making biryani for Max today. This cooker is a life-saver. Thank you so much.'

'Don't mention it. It was an irresistible sale. And I know how much you'd miss that kitchen gadget.'

Shweta looked at Shipra gratefully. 'Does Virat know about me being here?'

Shipra shook her head. 'I haven't told him. He met Raj the other day though. Raj told him that you'd gone to visit your parents in India.'

So, Raj was still cooling his heels! Shweta heaved a sigh of relief that he hadn't found her yet. The night that she'd run away from Raj's home, the only reason that she hadn't gone to Shipra's for help was because she knew that Shipra and her husband were out. Running as far away and as quickly as she could had seemed the only option then.

'I'm glad you found this place,' Shipra said, as if reading her mind.

Max walked in just then. 'Hey, girl'

Shweta had told Shipra so much about Max, and vice versa, that it was as if they'd known each other for ages although they'd only met once before. Shipra rushed to give Max a high five and a hug. 'Lovely to see you, Max!'

Max glowed at all the attention he was getting. He inhaled deeply as he walked in. 'Ooh, I can't wait to taste some of that.'

He immediately set about popping some corn in the microwave.

'Popcorn with biryani?' Shipra asked, amused. 'We usually eat biryani with raita, which is slices of raw onions mixed with yogurt.'

Max grinned. 'Or pappadoms. Isn't that also what you eat with biryani? I thought this would work just fine for the added crunch.'

Shweta shrugged. 'We don't have yogurt anyway.'

'Well, then let's give popcorn a try,' Max said, rubbing his hands together.

Soon, the salty, buttery aroma of popcorn filled the room. Max set about laying the plates and spoons.

Shipra looked at Shweta with envy as Max whistled and hummed a tune while serving the biryani and popcorn into the plates. Shweta was damn lucky to have a roommate who cooked and cleaned, she'd cribbed, every time she heard that Max did most of the cooking and helped in the kitchen. 'Will we ever find Indian men like this?'

'Not in a million years!' Shweta chuckled. 'Let's dig in.'

They watched *Chashme Buddoor,* an old Hindi movie, as they ate. Max couldn't stop guffawing at every scene. He loved watching Hindi movies, even though he didn't understand the language. Shweta made sure that she played movies with subtitles when he was around. After the lunch and movie, the three of them decided to go shop for some new movies and spend the afternoon out.

It was late when Shweta got back to her room. As she settled in bed with a cup of hot cocoa, she called up her older sister, Neha, who she'd forgotten to call since she'd come to Julie's.

'Ah, finally, somebody thought of me,' Neha said.

'Couldn't help it,' Shweta retorted.

Neha, her older sister, was a professional yoga instructor and also dabbled in theatre. Her love for theatrics, however, wasn't limited to the stage. Neha loved being dramatic even when she was talking to her friends and family. 'Where were you, my darling? Haven't heard from you in so long.'

'Oh, what a drama queen you are!' Shweta snorted. 'One would think I hadn't called you in months.'

'Well, that's how it feels to me,' Neha drawled.

'How are Mohan and Ria?'

That question about her brother-in-law and niece was going to get Neha talking for a long time, as usual.

'Ria's still in bed. It's only seven-thirty in the morning. She has a project to show at school and she wanted to call and ask you for suggestions. If you have the time, that is.'

'Of course, anytime.'

'And Mohan is busy as always. Last night he was out on an emergency and he only came back this morning, so I haven't seen him at all most of this weekend.' Neha let out a huge sigh and Shweta felt sorry for her and for Mohan's busy lifestyle. Being a doctor wasn't easy, especially because Mohan was also someone who couldn't say 'no'; he'd run to everyone's assistance whether they were family, neighbours, or even acquaintances. She understood perfectly where Neha's frustration was coming from.

The sisters chatted for a little while. It was almost past Shweta's bed time when she hung up.

As she was going to bed, Shweta thought about the conversations she had had with her mother and sister. Staring at the ceiling, she kept wondering how long she could keep up this charade, before finally falling asleep.

3

Max was late again the next morning, and Shweta wondered what had gone wrong this time.

The rush for filling up the salsa jars was already on when he walked through the door, the jingle heralding his dishevelled self with ruffled hair.

His sunglasses were still on as he walked into the café.

'Max?' Julie called out to him.

He ignored her, walking right past to his station and starting on the preparations for the tortillas.

'Maximo Morales,' Julie called out, sternly this time. 'Why are you late again?'

Shweta wondered about Max's drooping shoulders and downcast face. Something was up, what with those shades hiding his dark, beautiful eyes and long lashes. Her ex-roommate looked pitiful this morning.

When Max didn't answer for the second time, Julie let Max's ignoring her pass and continued filling the jars. Even Shweta felt that it was quite unlike Max to be silent. Something was definitely wrong!

Max headed to the console for the radio and turned it on. 'Why so quiet? Why no music?'

Julie rolled her eyes and shook her head.

Soft jazz floated through the kitchen. Shweta was engrossed in the tune when the phone in her pocket started chiming.

She frowned, losing her focus for a moment just as Julie handed her a full jar. It slipped out of her hand, and *thud*, it shattered into a hundred pieces; the salsa sprayed on her jeans and the floor.

Shocked, Shweta's hands flew to her mouth. 'I'm so, so sorry!' she cried, staring at the thick, dark salsa on the floor. She was terrified to meet Julie's eyes.

'You need help?' Max rushed to help her, using a wet cloth to clean her jeans. He started cleaning the floor when Julie stopped him.

'No, we're fine,' she said, urging Shweta to keep going with the leftover jars. She always had spare jars and more salsa than she needed to pack, so they quickly made up for the one that was wasted.

Shweta heaved a sigh of relief when the packing was over. She had to be more careful next time, she thought, as she wiped the mess off the floor. She could get kicked out of her job for this and, at this juncture in her life, it would be worse than a catastrophe.

And now, on to the unexpected caller, Shweta thought, as she remembered the reason for the mishap. Nobody ever called her at this hour.

'I'll be back in two minutes,' she called out to Julie who was heading towards the front with the trolley of crates.

She opened the exit door at the back that led to the dumpster. A cold draught of air felt shockingly refreshing as it hit her face.

Shweta fished out the phone from her pocket and checked for the missed call.

Ma?

Panic struck. Could it be that her father had had a heart attack again? With trembling hands, she called back. Her mother's phone beeped with a busy tone.

Shweta disconnected and fidgeted by the dumpster, all sorts of terrible thoughts running through her head. The stench from the dumpster quickly overpowered her and she moved further down until she could inhale the aroma of spicy Indian chicken curry from the Kebab Corner. Much better! Her stomach rumbled although lunch was still an hour away. She sighed at the thought of the usual burrito for lunch and glanced at her phone again.

Nothing.

Suddenly, her phone chimed again. Startled, she almost dropped it before picking up the call. 'Ma?'

'Where are you, my dear? How many times I've tried to call you!' Keertana said, her tone anxious.

Shweta's heart dipped. 'Many times? When? What's wrong? What happened to Papa? Is everything ok?'

Her mother tsk-tsked. 'Nothing's wrong except you're talking faster than a jet. Slow down. Papa is absolutely fine.'

Shweta let out a sigh of relief. Her mother probably thought nothing about the scare she'd caused from thousands of miles away in India.

'Are you there?' her mother's voice cut into her thoughts.

'Yes, Ma. Why did you call?'

'There is good news! Didn't I tell you Kini told us that there would be good news?'

'What news?'

'Simbu and Lekha have decided to get married.'

'What? When?' Her brother was getting married?

Keertana continued, 'This December. Simbu called us just a little while ago. Your Papa and I haven't been off the phone since. You'd better plan your tickets in advance. Can you be here by early December and let Raj join us closer to the wedding date. I can't believe we're going to have another wedding this year...'

This was going to be a nightmare. 'Ma, how can you have two weddings in one year? That's crazy.'

'That's what Simbu wants. And why delay it now? Lekha and he have been together for two years. It's fair to give them the wedding they've been waiting for, right? Can't believe I'll see you again in

December.'

Shweta scowled. 'You don't get it, Ma. I just got here a few months ago. It costs a lot to fly back and forth. Can't you ask Simbu to make it next year during summer? That way, all the cousins and their kids can also join, during their school holidays.'

Keertana hmphed. 'Don't be silly. And as if that's up to me. Simbu says Lekha's tired of waiting. And if your father says okay, it means okay.'

Shweta walked back to the dumpster not hearing any of the rest. Her head spun with many terrible thoughts. Most of them being: December. December. December? The word struck a cacophonous gong in her brain. And it was impossible to shut it off. It was September already. She wasn't prepared to return to India so soon.

'Can you come as early as you can?' Her mother asked again.

* * *

The next morning, in India, Prabhakaran Menon, or Prabhu as he was known, was sprawled on his easy chair, his legs propped on a foot stool, his glasses perched over his nose, and a pipe stuck between his lips. A curl of smoke spiralled upwards from the pipe.

He was peering into the *Economic Times* when Keertana brought in his customary tea at 7 a.m. Abruptly, he put the paper down with a frown.

'What are you so unhappy about today?' she asked.

He pulled his pipe out and folded the newspaper. 'The market is still down. My equity is not doing well and I'm worried about the upcoming marriage expenses.'

Keertana's brow furrowed. 'Who knew we'd have two marriages in the same year? In any case, Simbu should be able to take on some of the wedding expenses himself. He's a boy, after all, and he's been working for a long time now.'

'What are you talking about?' Prabhu took his feet off the footstool and planted them on the ground. 'Ask my son to pay for his wedding?! Are you out of your mind? As long as I'm alive and doing well, that's never going to happen. First we let him marry a girl of his choice and then we make him pay for it! Impossible!' Prabhu yelled, glaring at Keertana.

She pulled a chair close to him. 'Think about it. You're not keeping so well these days. Expenses are mounting. The medicines and...'

'Nonsense,' Prabhu said, rising from his chair. 'My father made sure all my six sisters were married off well, and with dowries, and my marriage was held in the grandest style, by the standards of those times. If my brothers-in-law heard of this, what would they think?'

'Oh, sit down,' Keertana said, tugging at his hand. 'The doctor has asked you not to take on too much stress. Why are we fighting over nothing? If you're not comfortable, do whatever you like. But I'm a little overwhelmed by the suddenness of everything. It seems like only yesterday that we got Shweta married. It's hardly been three months. Shweta was right. Simbu should have waited a little more.'

Prabhu settled back into his chair. 'He's waited enough,' he said, reaching for his pipe again. Seeing that the flame had died, he began to pinch and fill in more tobacco from the pouch and stretched to reach for the match. 'He's waited so long for Shweta to get married. You think his girl, Lekha, is going to wait forever?'

Keertana pulled the match from his hand, leaving him bewildered. 'How many times has the doctor told you to cut back on smoking? You're going to ruin your health. At least think of the wedding in a few months. Do you want to go back to the hospital?'

'One heart attack is not the end of the world. People I know have implanted six or seven stents and are still fine. I'm sixty-five, too old to be dying young.'

Keertana rose from her chair. 'I wish we'd talk about something other than death and bad finances. It makes such a terrible start to my day. I'm going for a walk, and after you're done with your papers, I think you should go for a walk too or do a bit of yoga. Neha's been asking me if you're practising what she taught you.'

Prabhu grunted and buried his face in another newspaper. Keertana hmphed and walked away.

* * *

By then, in the US, it was closing time at Julie's café. Shweta had been on her feet since morning and had had absolutely no time to think any more about her mother's call. The mad rush at the café wound down at closing time. However, Max, usually the last to leave, was nowhere to be seen.

Just then there was a commotion outside. Shweta and Julie ran out to see what it was.

Max and a man were in a heated argument in the parking lot. Suddenly the man threw a punch at Max's face; it landed on his nose.

'Argh!' Max screamed, clutching his bleeding nose. Before he could see it coming, another punch hurtled towards his jaw. Max turned around and socked the man's eye. 'It wasn't me,' he cried, locking arms with the man.

The man kicked his knees and Max collapsed on the floor. Before he could pick himself up, another hard blow landed on his ribs. Max doubled over and curled into a ball, groaning with pain.

The man was about to lift his leg to kick him again when Julie shouted, 'Stop it or I'll call the police.'

As Max writhed on the floor in agony, the man yelled, 'You deserve it!' He kicked him one last time in the stomach and bolted down the alleyway.

Julie and Shweta ran towards Max and lifted him up, grabbing him by the shoulders from both sides.

'We should take him to the hospital,' Julie said.

'Hold on, I'm good,' Max said, hobbling inside with their help. 'I'm not going anywhere. I'll be fine by tomorrow.'

'Get my keys, we're going to the hospital,' Julie said firmly.

4

Back home from the hospital, Shweta helped Max settle down on the bed in her room. She grabbed some ice and gently pressed it on his nose. Luckily, the doctor had said that he hadn't broken any bones and just needed to get some rest. But Shweta could see that he was in pain.

'Was it Alex?' she asked, propping an extra pillow behind him to support his head.

'We had a fight over his money. He thinks I stole it,' Max mumbled.

She raised her voice, unable to contain her anger. 'I don't understand why you left this place!' She pushed her hair out of her eyes. 'I've been watching you get hurt and you still keep going back. This is called abuse, Max. When will you ever come to your senses? How many times have I told you not to... .'

'Shweta, please, stop clucking like a hen...Ow!' His hands moved up to grab his jaw and he grimaced with pain.

She stopped shouting immediately and hung her head in shame. He'd done the opposite for her, she reflected, talking to her kindly and making her feel at home when she'd first arrived, confused and anxious after running away from Raj's home. In the brief time that they'd lived together, they'd grown so thick. Telling herself that she now had to be softer when he was hurting inside, she got up to make some ginger tea.

Setting Max's tea by the bed, she took her cup and stood by the window, throwing open the glass panes. The cold breeze blew against her face. Lights twinkled in the distance. She took a long slow sip of her tea, enjoying the sweet and spicy flavour that rid her of her stress.

Feeling better, she let out a deep breath and returned to Max, ready to apologize for getting mad at him.

'I'm not going back,' Max said, suddenly.

She glanced towards the desk and noticed his bag underneath it, but that didn't mean much. 'I hope you mean it, Max. I really hope this time it will be for good.'

'I mean it! I gave him a black eye,' he said, lifting his hand and showing his bruised knuckles.

He looked like such a sweet puppy when he said that. 'I'm sorry,' she said, and leaned in to plant a kiss on his cheek. 'I missed you.'

'Ow!' Max's hand went up to his cheek.

'Sorry!' Shweta smiled. 'That bad?'

He nodded sheepishly.

She put her arm around his shoulders. 'Drink up and let's watch a movie tonight. You pick. I can't wait to celebrate, now that you're back.'

Max emptied his cup and gave it back to her looking more cheerful already. Once again, Shweta was reminded of how cute he looked despite the swollen nose and how she loved everything about him, including his love of colour and his discerning eye for style, which was apparent from his pink striped shirt and trendy tan pants. But most of all, she was glad he was back. She placed the empty cups back on the kitchenette counter and went back to join him.

Now that Max had gathered himself and was going to spend a peaceful night with her, Shweta realized she'd really been looking forward to a movie and some company tonight. She headed to the second-hand TV on the wall beside the front door and switched it on.

Then taking the two DVDs she and Max had picked up at the sale last weekend, she showed them to him, giving him the choice. She held the *Queen* DVD in her right hand and the *Lunch Box* one in the left, waving her hands excitedly.

He pointed to her right hand and picked *Queen*.

As Max settled under the sheets, Shweta told him all about her mother's call that morning and that Simbu planned to get married in December. 'I'm not ready to tell them about Raj. Mum would be devastated and Dad would send me right back to him.'

'So, your brother's getting married and you don't want to tell them about Raj. Then what are you going to do?'

Shweta wished she knew. She'd hoped to hold off telling them for as long as she could but now with the wedding, they were bound to find out. 'I don't know, Max. I'm really at my wit's end.' She wiped her clammy hands on her jeans before she inserted the disc into the player and settled back beside him, sharing the fluffy, warm duvet with him.

'You could make up a story about Raj, no? Say he's busy or something?' Max said.

'But for how long? They're going to find out sooner or later when they call him for the wedding.'

'Then make sure they don't call him directly.'

The thought, though unlikely, gave her some hope. 'I don't know if it'll work.'

She picked up the remote, clicked on play and leaned against the headrest. Max had taken both pillows to prop himself up.

In the middle of the scene in which the friends of the lead actress decorated her hands with the mehendi, Max turned to Shweta. 'You know?'

'What?'

'You look like her.' Max slapped her hand playfully.

She angled toward him. 'Who, Kangana? No way!' She pinched his arm. 'Not at all!'

'Yes, you do,' Max said, looking at her in all seriousness. 'You both have the same hair.'

'Ha-ha.' Shweta snickered and ruffled Max's hair.

Max pulled her hand out of his hair. 'Stop it! You're pretty. Like her.' He jerked his thumb at the TV, stressing on the pretty as if to bring his point home.

Shweta stared at him, curious. 'Ok, come, out with it! What's this really about? I can't tell when you're being so nice. Spit it out.'

Max levelled with her gaze. 'I meant it! You are pretty. But there's something else…'

'Yes?'

'I want to go to India with you.' His words came out soft yet deliberate.

'Are you serious?'

'I've always wanted to go on a Himalayan trek. It's been a dream. This is the perfect chance.'

'You can't be serious?'

Max gave her a pleading look. 'And I'd like to watch a real wedding, not just these faux Bollywood weddings in movies.'

Shweta shook her head, unable to believe that now, on top of everything else, she'd have to explain Max to her family.

'I can't, Max. It's a terrible idea. I'm in trouble as it is, and then to have you with me…my father would hit the roof.'

Max took her hands in his. 'Look, I'll leave if they don't like me, or…we'll make up another story about me, ya?'

This was getting more complicated by the minute.

But Max was already rubbing his hands together. 'Yay! I can't believe this is happening. Thank you, Shweta. I love you for accepting me. I'm so happy I'm going. Now all I need is a passport.'

Passport!

How in the world could she have forgotten? 'Oh. My. God.' She dislodged the clip from her hair and buried her head in her hands, rocking to and fro. 'Oh my god!'

Max touched her shoulder. 'What happened?'

She raised her head, fear sweeping through her, her feet feeling numb. 'I don't have my passport.'

Max shot her a surprised look. 'What do you mean? What happened to your passport?'

'I left it at Raj's house. I forgot to take it with me.' She pulled her hair. 'Oh God, what am I going to do?' All she'd wanted when she'd asked Julie for employment was to leave for India when she'd earned her flight money. And she hadn't once remembered her passport!

Shweta felt the ginger tea rise back up her throat. She felt like she was going to puke.

5

'What do you mean you can't come?' Neha's voice pierced Shweta's eardrums.

Two days after she realised her goof-up with the passport, Shweta had thought it was a good idea to call her older sister and see if there was a chance she could implore her to impress on the family the need to postpone the wedding. Neha was better at handling such complicated situations. But for that, Shweta knew she would have to first convince Neha to see the problem from her point of view.

Obviously, that plan had backfired and Neha had started yelling instead.

'Come here and sit down if you want me to braid your hair.' Neha seemed to be multitasking, talking on the phone while getting her daughter, Ria, ready for school.

Ria's chirpy voice floated through the speaker. 'Who are you talking to?'

Shweta heard her say, 'Shweta,' and then scold Ria. 'Sit still, silly girl. Keep your head straight.'

'Hi, Aunt S,' Ria said, before she groaned in pain, 'Ah!'

Shweta smiled, thinking of her adorable little niece. 'Hi, sweetie!'

'Sit still, I say!' Shweta heard Neha admonish Ria again. 'So, you were saying, Shweta? Turn your head this way, Ria.'

Shweta let Neha continue to be distracted by Ria's antics. She heard Ria groan again. 'You know what I'm saying, Neha,' Shweta continued in a wheedling tone. 'Tickets cost the earth. Coming once a year is okay but in six months? That's extravagant. And I can't have Papa pay for our tickets. Can't Simbu postpone the wedding to next year?'

Neha tsk-tsked. 'Look, Shweta. Simbu's waited so long. He's nearly thirty. As it is, your wedding took so long. Now what if Lekha calls off this wedding altogether when he asks her to postpone it again? He and Lekha have waited for over a year. In fact, all of us are tired of waiting. Even Mohan thinks it's high time the love birds got married.'

The mention of her brother-in-law Mohan put a dent in Shweta's argument. Mohan was like an older brother to her and she didn't want to let him down. Shweta scowled.

'Have you called Ma?' Neha asked. 'Papa and she are over the moon.'

The whole point of calling Neha first was to get Neha to ask Keertana. But it didn't look like it was going to work. Shweta heard Ria groan again. 'Why are you hurting the poor child? Should I call you later?'

'No, I'm done. Ria, have you taken your water bottle and pencil box?'

Shweta heard Ria say good-bye to her mother and then to her. 'Bye, Aunt S. Call me over the weekend.'

Shweta heard Neha let out a deep breath followed by the bang of a door. 'So, what were you saying?'

'Mmmm…about having another wedding so soon…'

'Oh, come on, Shweta, you have to be out of your mind! Ma was telling me that the Nambiars have already sent her some sample wedding cards over e-mail. Things are moving quickly.' Then she changed the subject. 'How is Raj? Shouldn't December be a good time for him too?'

Shweta wished she could say 'No.' Or tell her that he wouldn't come. Or that she didn't know where he was or what he was doing.

In the meantime, Neha got busy with something in the kitchen.

Shweta hung on, as she heard sounds of a spoon and the opening of the microwave at the other end.

'Mmm…,' Neha finally got back to Shweta after a long slurp of her drink. 'Ah, at last I get to sit down and drink my tea in peace. What were you saying again?'

For a moment, Shweta wished she could come clean, tell her sister everything. Maybe Mohan could even do something to help with the passport. 'You know Neha, I have to tell you something… .'

'Ok, I know what you're going to say,' Neha interrupted her. 'How you want to start working and buy tickets with your own money. How you don't want to be so dependent on your new husband or your father. Blah. Blah. But brothers don't get married every day.'

'No, it's not that.'

'Hold on. What, Mohan? Coming! Sorry, got to go, Shweta. Call you over the weekend. Ria said she wanted to discuss something about Talent Day at school. She said you might have some ideas. So, call later. Bye now.'

Before Shweta could respond, Neha had disconnected the line.

Shweta stared at her phone for a few moments.

Then suddenly she picked it up again and dialled. There was only one person now who she could talk to about this.

'Hey,' Shweta greeted Shipra as soon as the latter answered her phone. 'Can you pick me up tomorrow afternoon? We need to talk.'

'Well, perfect!' Shipra said. 'I've been wanting to go to the Middletree Mall for some quick retail therapy. Meet you at three outside the café.'

Shweta hung up and exhaled. She could request a little break after rush-hour at the café and probably do with some retail therapy herself to unclog her mind.

* * *

'You what?' Shipra's eyes darted alternately between Shweta's face and the road, on their way to the mall.

'What could I do? What would you do if you were running away from your husband?' Shweta squinted at Shipra. 'Would you run for your life or think about gathering your belongings?' Shweta had had to make a split-second decision and she'd started running towards the nearest mini strip mall, hoping to find some place to hide until she could call Shipra to pick her up. All she'd grabbed were her purse and phone, and she'd blocked Raj's number as soon as she'd remembered. The rest Shipra knew.

'Ok, I rest my case. I would've just run too. But we could have gone back in a few days to get your things. In fact, we should go now. He can't refuse to give you your passport.'

Shweta thought about that for a moment. 'Hmmm… But I don't want to give him any ideas if he still has my passport and hasn't destroyed it. Wouldn't it be better if we got it back ourselves?'

'But how are you going to get it back without going to him?'

'That's exactly what I'm thinking. I don't want to go near that geezer again. I'm still a little frightened of him. I mean, I'm still terrified thinking of that night. No, I won't go to him if I can help it.'

'Then what do you propose to do? Steal it?'

'Come to think of it, that's not a bad idea.' Shweta grinned, thinking of carrying out a Bollywood-style heist.

Shipra looked at her as if she was mad. 'Are you out of your mind? You know that'll be a criminal act, right?'

'I've seen worse criminal acts. Think, trying to kill your wife.'

'Tell that to the cops!' Shipra smirked. 'You have no proof. But if you get caught breaking into the house, he can have you arrested. Have you thought of that?'

Shweta sighed, thinking of the worst that could happen. Yet something told her she should at least give it a shot. 'Is there a way we can get an extra key to the apartment?'

'He hasn't left the spare key with us. There's no way except a break-in.'

'I'm thinking if there is a more sophisticated way…'

'A sophisticated way to rob someone?' Shipra snorted.

'Hey, it's my passport. I wouldn't call it robbing, just…fixing a few errors from the past.'

'You are a riot, Shweta, but while you're thinking about it, can we stop at Maria's sale? I think a little window shopping will clear your muddled brain. Plus I think you could do with another pair of jeans. I'm tired of seeing what you're wearing. How can you survive with just one pair?'

Shweta laughed. Shipra had been the one to take her shopping when she had absolutely nothing but the clothes she was wearing. Shweta, however, didn't really care that she had only one pair of jeans that she washed every Sunday. That she was safe and alive was enough. 'I'm really not in the mood to shop but I guess just looking won't hurt. And I have to get back to work in an hour.'

'Done.'

Fifteen minutes later, they were at Maria's and checking out the jeans on the rack.

'Should I try this on?' Shipra asked Shweta, showing her the jeans that she'd picked up.

'Sure, I'll just sit down for a bit,' Shweta said, gesturing to the stool near the changing room. 'I'm tired already. I can't seem to find anything I like. Everything's either too expensive or I don't like it.'

'Ok, be back soon.'

Shipra came out of the changing room in a few minutes, twirling around to show Shweta the fit. 'Doesn't this one look great?'

Shweta nodded. 'Pretty smart, I think.'

Shipra jumped in excitement. 'I love it.' She looked at Shweta quizzically. 'Aren't you going to get anything at all?'

'I'm not in the mood to shop. Besides if I were going to India, it'd be much cheaper to get a pair there. But without the passport, it's doubtful. Even if I tried to apply for a new passport, I might not get it in time for the wedding. That means I not only miss the wedding, but also draw the ire of my entire family for what I've got myself into.'

Shipra squeezed her shoulder. 'Listen, let's try not to jump the gun. We'll find a way to get your passport back. Cheer up now, okay? Let's go get a cup of coffee.'

Shipra paid for the jeans at the counter and the two of them walked into a Starbucks outlet a few stores away. Shweta still had a few minutes left before she had to get back to work.

They got their coffees and sat facing the centre of the arcade where a group of kids was laughing and running around a small water fountain.

Shipra laughed as the kids dodged and screamed with glee at the water spraying from the fountain, but Shweta's mind was elsewhere. Her insides were knotted with worry; she couldn't stop thinking how she was going to get her passport back.

6

Shweta called Raj's apartment superintendent on Tuesday morning and reported a leaky tap. It was the first step in her ploy to enter Raj's house—*her* house—without a key.

Shweta was sure her plan to get the superintendent to use his spare set of keys would work. It seemed like the only opportunity she'd get to look for her passport at Raj's house without his knowledge.

Since Shweta didn't have a car *and* she didn't know how to drive, it fell on Max's shoulders to find an excuse to borrow Julie's pickup and drive her to Rivendell Way, her old apartment, that morning.

'What if this doesn't work?' Shipra looked concerned, as they stood outside Shipra's door, waiting for the superintendent to turn up.

Three hours later there was still no sign of the superintendent. Shweta and Shipra waited until lunch hour and then just as the girls decided to call it quits to break for lunch, heavy footsteps sounded in the hallway.

The superintendent, a short, stocky guy with a tool belt hung low on his hip, swaggered towards them and nodded in greeting. 'What's the problem with 101?'

Shweta gushed at him. 'Hi! I'm from 101. I'm sorry I came out to talk to my neighbour and got locked out. There's a leak in the bathroom.'

'Did you make the complaint?'

Shweta smiled effusively. 'Yes, sir. And this is my neighbour, from 102,' she said, pointing to Shipra.

Shipra smiled at him and nodded in agreement.

'No problem.' The superintendent pulled the huge ring attached to his belt and found the spare key to the apartment. Turning the key into the lock, he opened the door and stepped in purposefully. 'Which way?'

The girls entered right after him, Shipra leading the way for the superintendent.

Shweta paused at the doorway and looked around with nostalgia. More than three weeks had passed since she'd left this house. The curtains in the living room were drawn, giving it a dingy look, and the carpet looked like it hadn't seen a vacuum cleaner in days.

Shipra allowed the superintendent to step into the bathroom, then glanced back at Shweta and gestured to her to hurry up. As the superintendent and Shipra stood in the bathroom to check on the leak, Shweta headed to the bedroom, peeking into the kitchen on the way. Messy dishes sat in the sink and crumbs of Raj's breakfast littered the counter. It was apparent that he hadn't bothered cleaning up.

'Which tap?' The superintendent's voice boomed from the bathroom. 'Everything looks fine here.'

'It's the shower,' Shweta called out quickly. 'After I close the shower tap, it still leaks.' She turned towards the bedroom, passing the bathroom on her way. She heard the spray of the shower. It was lucky she'd remembered that leaky shower tap. She hoped it was still problematic. She quickly made her way to the dresser in the bedroom where the passport had been before she'd left.

While the superintendent hammered on the tap to pry it open, she rummaged in all the drawers only to find papers, files, and Raj's cheque books. Her passport wasn't there. In fact, neither was Raj's. It was obvious that both passports had been moved, she noted with despair.

She heard the superintendent chat with Shipra while he checked the leak. 'You've been here long?'

'About two years,' Shipra said. 'What about you?'

Shweta returned to her search. 'Think!' she told herself. *Where could the passports be?* She turned to the wardrobe and noticed that none of its doors were locked, thankfully. Shweta opened each one and checked behind the clothes and inside the drawers, but her passport was nowhere.

Long after the superintendent had left and the girls had searched every inch of the house, the passport still couldn't be found. Dejected, Shweta and Shipra were heading out, when Shweta suddenly remembered something. 'Wait, there is something else too that I really want back.'

She disappeared back into the bedroom and returned with a slim, black square case. 'At least I found this. It may not be my passport but it's my second most valuable possession.'

'What is this?' Shipra asked.

'It's my movie hard disk,' Shweta said, slipping it into her jeans pocket.

Shipra looked horrified. 'What if he realizes it's missing?'

'He'd never notice because he never watches movies. Besides, this disk contains a treasure trove of all my favourite movies. I'm definitely not leaving without this. I don't care if he finds out.'

They headed out, pulling the door close as it locked automatically behind them.

Shipra insisted Shweta stay for lunch. There was still time before Virat or Raj returned from work. 'I've tried a new chicken recipe.' Shipra said, looking at her excitedly.

'Love to.' Shweta realized that she was famished. It was well past lunch time.

Shweta's mood lifted as soon as she entered Shipra's tastefully decorated home. The transparent cream curtains swayed against the tall glass doors to the porch. Curios, lamps, and potted plants dotted the nooks in the living room. The dining table showed off a colourful runner across its middle.

Shipra had made aromatic basmati rice with the chicken curry and had fried some potato wedges.

The girls sat down to eat and polished off the chicken and rice on their plates, Shweta licking her spoon clean. They put away the dishes and settled down by the bay window with glasses of cool lemonade, thinking of what to do next.

The discussion continued with Max when he came to pick Shweta up around 4 p.m., but they couldn't come up with any new ideas to get back her passport.

The thought of her missing passport plagued her all through the week and into the next week at work.

7

'Is everything alright at home?' Julie asked Shweta one morning after she'd mixed up her third order at the café, the week following her misadventure at Raj's.

Shweta had spent a terrible week, tossing and turning for several sleepless nights and fumbling during the day. Her mother had called to say that Simbu's wedding was going to be held in Chennai, and Lekha's father had already arranged the wedding hall, the hotel for the guests' stay, and the catering. Shweta's father had wanted her passport details, and she'd steered that conversation away by saying that she'd book her own tickets. How in the world was she going to tell him that she didn't have her passport *or* the money for the tickets?

Shweta's face paled at Julie's question.

Julie peered at her. 'You and I are going out for lunch today,' she said sternly.

Shweta nodded and threw a questioning glance at Max as soon as Julie had turned. Max simply shrugged.

It was after 3 p.m. that they stepped out of the café. 'We'll be back soon,' Julie called out to Max, leaving him to handle everything. Shweta glanced at Max one last time before following Julie outside.

Shweta and Julie made the short distance from the café to

Rosette's Deli, a block away, on foot. The weather was mild for September but the warm sun cast a beautiful yellow glow on the sidewalk and the trees lining the stores. The traffic outside was normal for this time of the afternoon, when the lunch crowd was probably back at work or wherever they needed to be.

Over a lunch of soup and salad, Julie eyed Shweta's plate and chided her on her appetite. Shweta, who'd otherwise have given anything to vary her lunch from the usual burrito, was suffering from a sudden lack of appetite since last week. She had refused the salad and was now struggling to finish the soup. Julie looked at her with a frown.

After they'd put away their finished bowls, Julie came straight to the point. 'Okay, let me hear it. What's been bothering you?'

'Nothing,' Shweta said, not wanting to meet Julie's eyes.

Julie wasn't buying it. 'Either you tell me now or I'm firing you.'

Shweta threw her an anxious look.

'I'd rather you be honest with me.' Julie was good at tough talk when necessary and she wasn't easy to shake off when she'd made up her mind. 'Look, I know the orders are getting mixed up. Something's not right and I can't make my customers suffer for whatever it is.' Julie watched Shweta for a moment and switched to a mellower tone. 'Besides, although I've only known you for about a month now, I just know it's not like you at all. So, do you want to tell me what this is about?'

Shweta had no choice but to pour out the story, from the discovery of her missing passport to the break-in and the resultant failure. After she finished, she waited for Julie's reaction.

Julie was silent and thoughtful for a few moments. 'Okay, the way I see it,' she said, 'you've lost an important document *and* you don't have much time. If I were you, I'd call my parents and get this sorted out with the husband. After all, you're not his prisoner. He can't do anything to keep you if you wish to leave.'

'I wish the decision were so easy, Julie. I really want to keep my parents out of this.'

'But why would you take such a big risk?'

Shweta hung her head. She didn't have an answer to that. All she wanted to do was sort this out like a big girl, and not drag her parents into her mess.

'Your parents got you married to a person you didn't know,' Julie continued, narrowing her eyes. 'He could be bipolar, from what you've described. Do your parents know their daughter is in trouble?' She leaned forward and took a deep breath. 'You remind me of my daughter, Sarah, and the time she got into trouble. She wouldn't come home until I promised I'd forgiven her.' Julie paused, as if thinking of those days. Then she became serious again. 'You should tell your parents. They could contact the embassy and get you out of here.'

'That will be my last resort, I promise. I have so many things to consider before I make that choice. My father just had a massive heart attack at the beginning of this year. Now he has Simbu's wedding to worry about. I'd like to not have them worry about me too.'

'I understand your situation, Shweta. I do. But involving your family is the only way I can think of. You can stay with me until then but I can't help you much with your current situation and I can't let customers be affected either.'

Of course, Shweta understood. Julie had done so much already. Shweta touched Julie's hands gently. 'Thank you, Julie. You've done way more than I could have asked for.'

Julie settled the bill and they rose to leave. Ahead of them, outside the deli, a cold breeze blew dry leaves on the ground into a circle. Julie's hands were stuffed into her pockets and the two fell into step, walking slowly back to the café.

'I'm so glad I met you outside the café that night, Julie,' Shweta said, rubbing her hands to keep the chill out of her fingers. 'I don't know what I'd have done if I had to spend the whole night out on the street. As I hurried down here that night, the first person I saw was you, and I just took a chance.'

'And, I took one look at you, Shweta, and I wanted to help. Of course, I'll admit, I really needed another hand in the kitchen too. And

I figured you'd do just fine. So, I wasn't really being a saint. It was a little selfish of me too.' Julie gazed at Shweta with a smile.

Their shoes crunched the dry leaves as they walked. Shweta was lost in thought for a few moments. 'To think that I didn't even have any papers or a work permit! You could have gotten into trouble for employing me.'

Julie shook her head and laughed. 'Of course, we both knew this arrangement was temporary—only until you could buy your ticket. And I knew you were anxious when you said you didn't want to serve customers.'

'I got worried that day when Pete walked in. I thought he was from the immigration and he'd been tipped off about my case.'

Julie laughed and took Shweta's hand. 'Oh! I'm sorry Pete frightened you. He did look like a tough police officer, didn't he?'

All of a sudden Shweta came to an abrupt halt. The mention of Pete's uniform and comportment had triggered a crazy idea. She tugged at Julie's hand firmly. 'Wait! Of course, I never thought about Pete! Why didn't I ever think of him before?'

Julie looked at her, puzzled.

Shweta squeezed Julie's hand and looked directly into her eyes. 'Julie, I think there *is* a way you can help and I really think it's a good idea.'

Julie had no clue what she was talking about but in Shweta's mind, a plan had already begun to take shape.

8

Biryani soon became a regular weekly affair, ever since the arrival of Max and the rice cooker. Shweta called Neha after she made the biryani, on Skype this time, because Ria had wanted to talk to her about her school's Talent Day.

Out of the corner of her eye, she noticed Max lift up the rice cooker's lid and inhale the aroma. He gave her a sly wink and served himself some biryani.

'Some for you now?' Max mouthed.

Shweta shook her head.

Neha started with a barrage of complaints as soon as she knew Shweta was on the line. 'First of all, why haven't you called in so long? Ria's been asking about you every day and so has Ma. You've become so inaccessible now. It's no wonder they say that once you're in America, you forget your family. And it's not like you have to be in America to forget your family, really. Look at your BIL. He's forgotten that he has a family. What is the matter with these men? By the way, did you see Lekha's picture? Doesn't she look gorgeous? Simbu is so lucky. I hope he keeps Lekha happy. And, look at Mohan…I'm so tired of his schedule…'

Only Neha could talk endlessly and never tire of it, Shweta

mused. And all this, when only a little more than a week had passed since her last call.

The sounds of Ria's footsteps interrupted their conversation. The next moment, Ria pushed her mother aside and settled into the seat in front of their laptop. 'Aunt S, I don't need help anymore.'

Shweta was glad to see her niece. It wasn't often that she made Skype calls because first, it wasn't too convenient on her phone, and second, she didn't want her folks to guess the change in her surroundings. Right now, Ria blabbered on, unmindful of Shweta's baffled words. 'Why don't you want my help?'

'Niru came and showed me how to make and flip a humongous omelette. It was so cool.'

Wait a minute! 'Niru, as in, Savitri Auntie's son, Niru Karthik? But I thought he was in Dubai!'

Neha nudged Ria to reclaim her space in front of the laptop. 'Ria, show Shweta the cookies you baked today.' She turned to Shweta. 'I told her to take the cookies for her contest but she's so taken up by what Niru showed her that she wants to practise that instead.'

'What's Niru doing in Bangalore?' Shweta asked. 'I didn't know he had returned from Dubai.'

'Someone's keeping tab of Niru's movements,' Neha teased.

Shweta acted offended. 'I was just curious about that idiot, that's all.'

'You know, you guys still behave like kids. By the way, he's moved to Chennai and I heard that he's got an Italian girlfriend.'

'Oh.' Shweta feigned nonchalance although she would have loved to hear more. Niru was Simbu's classmate and an ex-neighbour back in Bangalore. Every piece of gossip about Niru was exciting, even now, after she'd lost track of his whereabouts since the last few years. She hadn't seen him after he'd left to get a culinary degree from New York. The last she'd heard, he was in Dubai. And now, he had an Italian girlfriend and was in Chennai. Good for him!

'He said something about starting a new restaurant in Bangalore.'

Neha winked.

Shweta gave her a mock disinterested look.

'And…he asked about you.'

Now Shweta's antennae were up, and she didn't care to hide it. 'Really? What about me?'

'Oh, the usual! Which part of US is Shweta in? What does her husband do? Does she have a job? The same old.'

Why did she think Niru would come up with more interesting questions about her?

When she hung up, the memory of Niru kissing her on her eighteenth birthday, just before he was to leave for New York, came out of nowhere and Shweta felt her cheeks become hot. That evening, she remembered, while she was digging up some paper cups from the niche in the backyard of her house, Niru had walked in through the back door and seen her. He teased her as usual, after giving her a card and a box of chocolates. She couldn't remember what their banter was about. Something about being the only unkissed virgin he knew. Shweta had flared up at the insult and dared him. One thing led to another and he'd pulled her in for a brief kiss. And then she'd giggled. He'd pulled back immediately, looking hurt, and had openly avoided her after that. She pushed those thoughts away. She was glad Neha had hung up.

Done with her call to her mother as well, Shweta heaped some biryani on her plate and settled on the bed with Max, this time determined to finish *Queen* in one sitting.

Her thoughts, however, kept drifting back to Niru more times than she could help.

9

'Her husband will see right through this,' Pete said. 'Besides I don't have the authority to…well, flaunt my authority. It's against the law!'

Shweta had begged Julie to ask Pete for help. Julie, in turn, had pleaded with Pete. 'Just think you're doing it for a friend. You know her life depends on it. Without the passport, she can't go home.'

It took all of Julie's persuasive powers to get Pete to agree to a visit to Raj's house.

Pete agreed on the condition that he'd do it during off-duty hours and that Shweta and Max would drive separately in Max's pickup instead of going with him in the squad car. He was anxious even as he agreed to do it. 'This can cost me my job, *Abuela*! I don't know why I'm doing this.'

So, one late evening, after about ten days had passed since the break-in, Pete, and Max and Shweta, drove up to Raj's house separately after Pete's regular shift had ended. Shweta was instructed to keep her head down and not say anything until specifically asked to. The lights in Raj's house were on. Only Pete and Shweta made their way to Raj's house and rang his doorbell.

Raj took a few minutes to open the door. He was wearing an old T-shirt and shorts; his chin had grown a thick stubble. His grey eyes registered surprise when he saw Shweta standing next to Pete. Pulling off the glasses perched on his long hook nose, he stopped just short of yelling, 'You!'

Pete flashed his badge. 'I'm Officer Peter Rodriguez,' he said. 'Are you Mr Raj Valsan?'

Raj turned to Pete. 'Yes, sir, I am.'

'We have a complaint from Ms Shweta Menon regarding a lost passport and we have reason to believe that it is in your possession. I need you to hand it over to me, please.'

Though not as tall as Pete, Raj was huge and menacing. His open mouth turned up at the corners, baring his pointy canines. 'I don't know what you're talking about, officer. Are you pressing charges against me?' Shweta thought she detected a slight trembling in Raj's high-pitched voice.

'Mr Valsan, anything you say can and will be used against you in a court of law. Do you or do you not have this lady's passport?' Shweta didn't dare look up. Instead, she stared at her feet and hoped that Raj would hand over the passport, and she could be out of there.

Pete waited for a reply, standing there, his legs apart, fixed on the ground, his arms crossed over his chest.

Raj stammered, 'I…I…haven't seen this woman in at least two months, officer. I…I'm being charged falsely.'

Shweta's head shot up; she stared at Raj in astonishment.

Pete bore down on him. 'I repeat my question, Mr Valsan. Do you or do you not have this lady's passport with you?'

To her surprise, Raj said, 'You can search my house, if you do not believe me, officer. It's not here.'

Shweta snuck a glance at Pete in alarm. Searching Raj's house was not part of their plan. Pete would have to make a quick decision. Shweta had assumed Raj would give in to the threat, but it definitely seemed like he had decided to stand his ground. Shweta wondered what Raj was up to when he knew as well as her that the passport wasn't in the house.

Pete remained silent for a moment.

Although she'd been told not to speak, Shweta knew that she had to take a chance. It was her fault she hadn't told Pete about her previous failed attempt. If she didn't tell Pete now, he'd be setting out on a wild goose chase. She cleared her throat. 'It's not inside the house, officer. I already looked. He's hidden it somewhere else.'

As soon as the words were out of her mouth, Raj turned to glare at her.

Pete caught on quickly. 'I see. Is it true that this lady is your wife, Mr Valsan?'

Raj's grey eyes fixed Shweta with an icy stare. 'Yes, officer.'

'Is it true that both of you came to the US on May 16 this year?

'I don't remember the exact date but I think so...'

'Is that a "yes" or a "maybe", Mr Valsan?'

Shweta couldn't understand where Pete was going with this new line of interrogation but she'd just have to trust him.

'Yes.' Raj nodded vigorously, obviously not getting the new direction of questioning either.

Pete continued. 'Do I have reason to believe that your wife left your apartment on the night of August 29?'

'I have nothing to do with that evening,' Raj said anxiously. 'We had an argument and she went away of her own accord. I had nothing to do with it.'

Pete twitched his right foot and moved his hand to his Glock. It was a very casual move but Raj noticed it too. He blinked. Pete looked Raj straight in the eye and paused before bearing down again. 'Are you in this country legally, Mr Valsan?' His words were slow and deliberate. The air tensed. Raj cast an imperceptible glare in Shweta's direction, as if he hated her for this mess. His fingers started up a nervous tremble. He rolled his hands into fists and moved them out of sight.

'Yes,' Raj said, after a pause.

'May I see your passport please, sir?' Pete's voice acquired the thunderous quality that Shweta remembered so well. He'd obviously caught on to the delay in Raj's reply. She held her breath.

As Raj turned and stepped into his house, Pete and Shweta

followed.

The house looked like it had the last time she'd seen it, probably a little worse.

Raj didn't go into the bedroom, as Shweta thought he would, although she'd already looked there and was pretty sure the passport wasn't there. Instead, he went towards the sofa and pulled up his office bag lying by its side.

He carried his passport to work? Shweta thought that was strange. She didn't remember Raj ever doing that before but maybe he'd wanted to be more cautious after she'd run away.

Raj unzipped the bag first, then an inner pocket, fumbled, and pulled out a passport, pushing something else out of the way. Shweta was certain there was something else in there besides his passport. She hoped Pete had seen it too. With reluctance, Raj handed the passport to Pete.

Pete held out his hand and took the passport, his eyes never leaving Raj's face. A film of sweat glistened on Raj's nose.

Shweta shut her eyes and prayed for a miracle. All her thoughts centred on how far they'd come with this charade, and the miracle that Raj had cooperated so far. If only she could get what she'd come for, she'd make a trip to the Aiyappa temple in Parsippany and offer a coconut in thanks, she prayed.

Pete flipped open the passport and his hands stopped on the first page. He looked up quickly at Raj before scanning the remaining pages for the next few moments. 'Interesting,' Pete remarked. 'Is this the only passport in your possession, Mr Valsan?'

Shweta held her breath.

As if he'd been relieved from all suspicion, Raj nodded. 'Yes, officer. This is the only passport I have.'

'In that case, Mr Valsan,' Pete said, stressing on each word, 'this isn't your passport.' He waved the passport in front of Raj's face.

Shweta's hands flew to her mouth as soon as she heard this. Could it be? Could it be that in his stupidity he had pulled out the wrong passport? That could mean only one thing.

The passport that Pete held in his hand was hers!

Shweta felt a bubble of excitement rise in her chest but she held her breath.

'Since I have what I need and since this lady here,' Pete said, turning to Shweta, 'is kind enough not to press further charges, we will keep this and take our leave, Mr Valsan. Good night!'

Raj looked dumbstruck but he did not say a word as Pete and Shweta turned around and walked out of the house. Shweta did not once turn behind to see the reaction on Raj's face.

Once near the car, all three of them whooped in excitement. Max and Shweta congratulated Pete on his brilliant performance and Shweta was confident, like she'd already told Pete before, that Raj would never guess that he'd been set up, and think to seek redress for unlawful questioning by an off-duty police officer.

When they got back to the café, there was a beautiful surprise. Julie had a wonderful dinner planned in celebration. They ordered pizza and Julie opened a bottle of wine.

'I just knew all of you were pretty smart. If Raj hadn't agreed, I'm sure Pete would have made him see sense the hard way,' Julie said, over slices of pizza.

'I don't think so, *Abuela*. I think we just got lucky,' Pete said, and they all laughed. 'And I did it all for this pretty girl,' Pete teased Shweta.

Shweta blushed and said another "thank you". She still couldn't believe her luck.

'But I do think you'd be safer back home rather than working at *Abuela*'s without a work permit on your passport. I can get into trouble for this, you know.' Pete held her gaze.

Shweta understood and nodded. 'I will be careful until I get back, officer,' she said, tipping her wine glass to his.

It felt like the longest yet happiest night in recent times to Shweta. She relaxed and enjoyed the easy conversation and laughter that flowed into the night, along with refills of wine and more servings of pizza. However, Shweta never got a chance to thank Pete again, although he'd stayed over with Julie that night, because he was gone before the café opened for business the next morning.

10

By the end of September, Mohan had arranged for Shweta's flight ticket to India for December 1. It was on the assurance that he would let her pay him back at the earliest, even though he had absolutely refused to let her pay at first.

Her father had been unable to contact Raj for some strange reason, her mother had said. It gave Shweta some peace, whatever that strange reason might have been.

Julie invited Shweta and Max for a Thanksgiving dinner at her place on Thursday. Since it was close to the date of Shweta's leaving for India, she also called it a send-off party for her.

It was Shweta's first Thanksgiving in the US and she was touched that Julie had thought of including her in the family celebrations. Julie's daughter, Sarah, and husband, Tim, were already at the house when Shweta arrived with a box of homemade rice pudding for everyone.

Sarah was checking the turkey in the oven. Julie was standing over the sink, washing carrots and tomatoes for the salad, when Shweta entered the kitchen.

'Hi, need some help?' Shweta asked the two women. They glanced over and smiled as she placed the dessert on the counter. 'I brought some Indian dessert for everyone,' she told them.

'Oh, that's so sweet of you, Shweta,' Julie said. 'I'm sure everyone would like to try a new dessert. And, if you could serve the mashed potatoes and the gravy into the two bowls I've laid out, that would be great.'

Shweta went over to the opposite counter and began putting the potato and the gravy into the bowls. She took the bowls to the dining table, which had already been set with six places. Two tall candles burned at either end and a pumpkin centrepiece added a festive look to it all. Tim stood near the record player, checking out Julie's song collection. Shweta returned to the kitchen.

'Here.' Julie gestured to the carrots and lettuce by the side. 'Could you peel the carrots and shred the lettuce while I dice the tomatoes? We'll be getting the salad ready soon.'

Sarah stepped out into the living room to join Tim and check when Pete would join them.

'So,' Julie said when they were alone. 'I hope you don't mind my asking. Have you told your parents about everything?'

'No, I haven't,' Shweta said, starting on the carrots. 'I've decided to tell them in person, not over the phone.'

'That's certainly a good decision. But I really hope Raj hasn't beaten you to it. You should be the one telling your parents first.'

'Surprisingly, they haven't been able to contact Raj, so I hope I'll be the first to tell them.'

'And, what are you going to do in India after the wedding? You won't be coming back, I presume.'

Shweta finished slicing the carrots and started washing the lettuce. 'No. I plan to start working again. I have to pay my brother-in-law for the flight ticket. And I want to be independent. If I get a job outside the city, I'd like to live on my own.' Shweta sighed, suddenly overwhelmed by the thought of it all.

Julie looked at her and smiled. 'You don't think all that is possible?'

'It's not going to be easy, I know, but I want to start afresh, build my life again, and be self-sufficient.'

'And what about your marriage?'

'I don't know yet.'

'Well, it's going to be a tough decision.' Julie stopped what she was doing and turned to Shweta. 'Do you think your parents will want you to remain in the marriage?'

'I…frankly, that's the last thing on my mind. I mean, living alone here has taught me a lot. I never thought I could take care of myself. I always lived with my parents and then with my husband. I always thought I needed someone to be with me, take care of me. But life here has taught me to be independent and strong. So, whatever I do next will be for the right reasons, not for the sake of convenience.' Shweta laughed. 'And only for love.'

Julie smiled, tears brimming in her eyes. 'I'm so happy I could help you. If there's anything you need, advice or a patient ear, do let me know.'

'I will, Julie. I promise.'

Shweta shredded the lettuce into the salad bowl while Julie threw in the tomatoes. Sarah came in to help when the turkey was ready. She eased the turkey out of the oven and carved it. Soon everything was on the table. Pete walked in right then, just as everyone had gathered around the table.

He looked striking in plainclothes; Shweta thought he looked cute and that was probably because she wasn't afraid of him anymore. Pete greeted the family and hugged everyone. When he hugged Shweta, she was amused to see that she had to stand on her toes.

After the toasts to good health and a great Thanksgiving, everyone dug into the food. Julie had excelled at the all-American Thanksgiving meal prepared especially for her son-in-law, Tim. The pumpkin pie and Shweta's sweet rice pudding rounded off the meal.

Pete came by to drop Shweta and Max off at the door, as they were leaving.

'I thank you for again from the bottom of my heart,' Shweta said to Pete, her eyes growing moist. 'If it weren't for you, I wouldn't be going to my brother's wedding after all.'

* * *

Three days later, on Sunday evening, Shweta bid a tearful adieu to Julie. Shipra and Virat drove Shweta and Max to Newark.

Shipra was teary eyed when their car drove into the departure area.

'We'll keep in touch,' Shweta said, squeezing Shipra's hand. 'You should visit me in India.'

Shipra nodded. 'And don't forget to email or WhatsApp. I'm going to miss you so much.'

The girls hugged, before Max and Shweta finally waved goodbye to Shipra and Virat.

As she and Max walked towards the check-in, Shweta couldn't believe it was actually happening. She was finally taking a flight to her home in Bangalore. She had plenty to think about on the trip back home—the family reunion, the wedding, and all the fun she'd have. The worries about facing her family and starting right back from where she'd been six months ago also bothered her, as did the crumbling of her 'happily married' charade.

As she took her seat, Shweta decided that she'd focus on the excitement and ignore the anxiety.

11

The stopover at London was a nightmare. The airport was so huge that the walk from the exit terminal to the re-entry terminal to board the connecting flight took over two hours. Shweta and Max made it just on time. The second leg of the journey - London to Bangalore - was longer than the first.

Their flight landed at 4 a.m., and it was almost six o' clock by the time they got home. Shweta had asked her parents not to come to the airport to pick them up. She and Max drove down in an airport taxi to Shweta's parents' small duplex in a gated community on Sarjapur Road.

Shweta's father was standing at the doorway when the taxi pulled into the drive. His trademark handlebar moustache was curled up, but his pot belly seemed to have reduced since she had seen him last. Her mother was watching his diet, Shweta concluded. Max and Shweta got out and lugged their suitcases up the narrow steps to the door.

Shweta looked at her father's unsmiling face, so unlike him. 'How was the flight?' was all he asked, his tone indifferent.

Shweta felt Max move closer to her as if he was a little nervous. Then he held her hand. She smiled awkwardly at her father. 'Okay.'

'Why is he behaving like he's married to you?' Shweta's father switched to Malayalam in a gruff voice. His eyes were literally falling out of their sockets.

Shweta shrugged her hand free and made quick introductions. 'Max, this is my dad, Prabhakaran Menon. Papa, this is my friend, Maximo. We call him Max.'

Max held out his hand.

'Call me Prabhu,' her father said, shaking his hand in a humourless way as he stepped back to let them in.

Her father went across the room looking for his pipe and matches. Her mother was not to be seen. 'Ma?' Shweta called out, wondering where she was.

Her mother called from the kitchen, 'Coming! Just getting some breakfast ready for you. You must be very hungry.'

Wiping her hands on a towel, her mother headed towards them, beaming. Shweta hugged her tight for a few moments and then made the introductions. 'Max, this is my mother, Keertana.'

'Oh, you didn't tell us you were bringing a guest,' Keertana gushed, seeming quite taken in by Max's looks.

'Won't you introduce your guest properly, Shweta?' Prabhu asked, returning, pipe in hand.

Keertana cut in, 'There's time for all those stories later. Sit down at the table. Breakfast will be ready in a minute.'

Prabhu nodded and gestured towards the table. They left their bags at the door and walked in, Max admiring everything about the house, from the lights on the ceiling to the swing on the porch outside the living room. 'Beautiful house!'

'Thank you.' Another gruff reply from Prabhu.

Prabhu sat at the head of the table, while Max and Shweta took their seats on either side. 'You said he was a friend,' he said to Shweta and turned to Max. 'How did you two meet?'

Max opened his mouth to reply but Shweta cut him off. 'Oh, that? I meant he is a friend's friend. When he heard about Simbu's wedding, he wanted to come too because he's so fascinated by Indian weddings. He also wants to climb the Himalayas before he returns to the US.'

'Go up the Himalaya mountains? That's a wonderful reason to visit India.' Prabhu struck a match and lit his pipe. Inhaling deeply, he let out a few puffs before pulling it out of his mouth, and continued. 'And Simbu's wedding. Yes, you are most welcome. But have you made arrangements for your stay?'

Shweta gave her father a surprised look. Why was he being so rude?

Just then Keertana walked out of the kitchen bearing a large tray. 'What sort of a question is that, Prabhu? Of course, he will stay with us until the wedding is over. We can put him up in Simbu's old room upstairs.' She turned to look at Max. 'And when we go to Chennai, we'll put you up with us at the hotel. I hope that's all right?'

'Of course, ma'am!' Max gave her a brilliant smile. 'I am grateful for your hospitality.'

'Well, that settles it,' Keertana said with finality, threatening Prabhu into silence with a glare. She laid out the plates, served idlis and ladled sambar into bowls. 'Enjoy your breakfast,' she said to Max. 'You too,' she said to Shweta, smiling. 'You may not have seen the face of idlis since you left.' She bustled back to the kitchen to bring out the tea.

Although they'd both eaten on the flight, the last couple of hours of waiting and traveling to the house had left Shweta famished. She began to eat.

'Are you an American citizen?' Prabhu's question came out of the blue, just as Max was stuffing a piece of idli into his mouth.

'Yes,' Max said, his words muffled. He swallowed quickly and continued, 'My parents were immigrants from Mexico. But I was born in the United States.' He returned to his food.

'Have you met her husband, Raj?'

Max looked up, surprised, and shook his head. 'No. I've only heard of him from Shweta.'

'In India we consider marriages very sacred, so being with another man is unacceptable.'

Shweta's cheeks burned.

'It's the same in our culture,' Max was quick to reply. 'I don't think you should worry about me. I just came to see an Indian wedding.'

Prabhu looked taken aback for a moment but retorted quickly. 'I'm glad to hear that.' He rose from his chair. 'I'll leave you two to your breakfast. It was nice to meet you.' With an abrupt nod he left the table, leaving Shweta and Max to eat their breakfast in peace.

Shweta heaved a sigh of relief. Now that her father had left them alone, she had time to look around her home. It did, in fact, look beautiful. Her mother's delicate hand-knit crochet curtains hung across the two tall bay windows in the living room, billowing softly in the cool Bangalore morning breeze. The lamps, with wicks lit, in the prayer niche in the corner of the dining room cast a soft glow on the beautiful brass Ganesha and Krishna idols placed inside. The jasmine-scented incense sticks in front of the idols swirled out fragrant vapours into the air, lending a calm aura to the house.

After they chatted for a while with her mother, over tea, Shweta took Max upstairs to show him his room, once Simbu's room.

The huge mahogany bookshelf was still full of Simbu's collection of second-hand books and his old engineering textbooks. His basketball hoop and guitar lay in a corner, and his knick-knacks littered the desk by the window.

Max went up to the window and gazed outside. 'Lovely view!'

Shweta walked up to him. The mango tree inside their compound was up to the height of the window they were standing at and bore a few mangoes. The hibiscus and rose bushes on the other side were in full bloom. The narrow road stretched in front of the gate, offering a view of the row of houses on the opposite side.

'I'm sorry about my father's behaviour,' she said, squeezing Max's hand.

'Don't worry. I'm not offended.' He deposited his bag beside the desk. 'I'm loving this room and your home,' he said. 'And there's not much that can deflate my delight at being in India finally.' Swirling around, his hands spread out, he lifted Shweta in a bear hug and twirled her around until she squealed and begged him to put her down.

'I'm glad,' Shweta said, out of breath when he finally released her. 'Now, let me show you the rest of the house.'

They headed back downstairs in the direction of the garden.

The swing on the porch beckoned and Shweta sat on it, feeling like a child again as she kicked her legs high to gain momentum. It was as if she'd never left home, and she wished it were true. She'd decided she was determined to have a good time, no matter what. And right now, that meant being happy for Simbu.

12

Shweta sought Keertana out in a little while after breakfast. 'Ma, there's something I want to talk to you about.'

Shweta had decided she was going to tell her mother everything and not hide the truth anymore. Keertana was in the kitchen making lunch. Her long thigh-length hair was twisted into a bun and she was peering into the pan on the burner, frying onions. Roundels of lady fingers lay on the chopping board beside the burner.

Keertana added the chopped lady fingers into the pan, mixed them in once, and turned around. 'We've still not been able to reach Raj. Papa said he was going to try calling him again today. Why didn't you ask him to call us? Is he coming? It wouldn't look good if we didn't invite him personally.'

'I couldn't tell you all this over the phone.'

'What happened? Is everything okay?' Keertana's eyes grew concerned.

'I...I...'

Just then, Prabhu strode into the kitchen, fuming. 'Why didn't Raj come?' he asked Shweta.

Her father's menacing look struck Shweta with fear.

'Or are you telling me he doesn't even know about the wedding?'

'Prabhu...'

'You keep quiet, Keertana!' Prabhu's voice boomed, cutting her off. 'Don't try to defend her. I want to hear the truth. This time, directly from her.' He glared at Shweta.

Shweta swallowed. 'I don't know where Raj is, Papa.'

Keertana looked at Shweta. 'But you were just telling me...'

Prabhu trembled with anger, shaking his finger at Keertana. 'Were you a part of this drama too?'

'Me? What are you talking about, Prabhu? Tell me what happened.'

Prabhu stuffed his pipe into his mouth and paced the floor, taking a couple of quick puffs. He stopped abruptly and pulled it out. 'Ask Shweta. The queen of suspense here is not saying a word and making a fool of both of us.' He waved his pipe in Shweta's face. 'Tell me!'

Shweta felt her palms go cold, and a shiver swept up her spine. 'He's...he's...I left his house,' Shweta said. Her voice was so soft that even she couldn't hear it.

'Why are you muttering?' Prabhu thundered, his jowls shaking.

'I left his house,' she said, and her lips trembled.

Prabhu's eyes flashed with anger and Shweta did not dare to meet his eyes. 'That's what his mother, that blabbering idiot, said, and I couldn't believe her. She gave me Raj's new number and when I called him Raj said he had no clue where you were. He said you were in jail, most likely, and he couldn't reach me because he had lost his contacts.'

'But why were we not able to reach him?' Keertana asked.

'He said he'd lost his phone too and I gave him a piece of my mind. Told him it was his duty to contact me if my daughter was missing. Told him to come here and take you back. I don't care what your differences are. I'm not having this nonsense in my house.'

Keertana touched Shweta's hand. 'Is it true, Shweta? You could have told us, couldn't you?'

Shweta's throat had dried up, the words refusing to come out. She could feel the tears welling up in her eyes. She looked from her mother's face to her father's. 'I can't, Papa...I'm not going back.'

'You what? Then what do you intend to do? Stay here? What will people say? This is no way to behave. I don't expect my children to come running back to us every time there is a fight. That is not how we brought you up.'

Shweta's sobs were stuck in her chest. She could barely breathe.

Keertana tried to intervene. 'Prabhu, let's hear her out. You're not letting her speak.' She turned to Shweta. 'Shweta, tell us what happened. Why did you leave?'

Shweta stared at the floor, not wanting to meet her parents' eyes. 'He became violent and...and...'

Prabhu scoffed. 'Next, she'll say he tried to thrash her and kill her.'

Yes, that's what he did, and he abused me. Is that the kind of husband you want me to go back to? Shweta wanted to scream.

'Wait, I want to hear what she has to say,' Keertana intervened.

'You're supporting this childishness?' he yelled. 'There will be some misunderstandings, some fights. But these issues must be sorted out. Running away cannot solve anything.'

'Calm down, Prabhu,' Keertana pleaded. 'This screaming isn't good for you. Now that she's back, we'll sort this out.'

Prabhu turned to Shweta. 'Grow up, Shweta!' His voice grew a tad softer. 'A husband and wife will have arguments, especially in a new marriage. When you don't know each other, it's normal. Nobody runs away at the first sign of trouble.'

Keertana tugged at Shweta's hand. 'How did you live alone? How did you take care of yourself?'

'Some friends helped me,' Shweta said.

'Another lie,' Prabhu roared. 'I'm sure that boy Max knows exactly what she was up to.'

'I worked in a café with him.'

'So he's a waiter, and my daughter served as a waitress too?'

'Papa, there is dignity of labour in the US. There is nothing cheap about working in a café.'

Prabhu slapped his palm on his forehead. 'How could you have lied to us every time we spoke? Aren't you ashamed?'

'She must have been scared, that's all,' Keertana said.

'I didn't raise you to be such wimps.' Prabhu countered.

'I'm not going back,' Shweta said between sobs. 'I won't stay here if you don't want me to, but I'm not going back to him,' she blurted out in one breath, tired and hurt by the arguments, and the allegations her father was making.

Keertana's hands flew to her face in horror.

The smell of burning abruptly ended the conversation. Keertana turned to check the pan on the burner, and gasped, 'Oh no! I've charred the vegetable.'

Raging, Prabhu waved his pipe in Shweta's face again. 'Are you planning to marry that Max? Is that why he's here?'

'No, Papa,'

'No, don't answer that. I've decided to handle this problem my way.'

'But…'

'This matter is closed for now,' he said with finality, and strode out of the kitchen.

Shweta's eyes were filling up fast. She looked at Keertana, pleading. Keertana, her eyes clouded too, could only gaze back at her daughter, helplessly.

13

Lunch that afternoon with her uncommunicative father and withdrawn mother proved to be an ordeal. That over, Shweta and Max went to their separate rooms upstairs to get an afternoon nap because they were so jet-lagged.

Shweta had just changed and scrambled into bed when she heard a knock at her door.

When she opened it, she saw Neha, who screamed in delight and hugged her. 'Welcome back, my dear. How was the flight? Did you sleep well?'

'I was just turning in to catch an hour of sleep, at the least.'

'Never mind. Now that I'm here you can sleep later. I just finished my classes and lunch, and got here as soon as I could.'

'What about Ria?'

'Oh, Ria is at school and she'll be here in another hour. I've asked her bus driver to drop her off here. Mohan said he'd drop by in the evening to pick us up.'

There was another knock on Shweta's door and both the girls turned around to see who it was.

Max stood at the door, smiling, and Neha was so surprised to see him that she just gawked.

Shweta made the introductions. 'Neha, this is Max. Max, this is my older sister, Neha.'

'Who is th...this?' Neha stammered, giving Max the once-over.

Shweta grinned as Max waved at Neha. 'This is Max, my roommate from Edison.'

Neha shook her head as if to dislodge the confusion. 'Your roommate?' She squinted at Shweta. 'You didn't tell me about a roommate?'

Shweta laughed. 'I'm sorry. It's not what you think.' She gestured towards Max. 'Max is a good friend.'

Neha gave her a look and Shweta knew she had a lot of explaining to do. 'So, what do you do, Max?'

'I work at a café.'

One look at Neha, and Shweta could tell she was completely bowled over. Max's voice had a deep baritone. Neha's eyes fluttered and her 'Oh!' touched a higher pitch than intended, ending in a squeak.

It was one thing to see Max and quite another to see *and* hear him. His James Bond-like looks and voice seemed to have a strange effect on women of all ages.

'Are you married?' Neha prodded.

Max shook his head and laughed. 'No.'

Shweta gave her sister a pointed look.

Neha cleared her throat and said, 'Never mind, I'm married.' Then to Shweta, she broke into a dialogue from a Hindi film, '*Main ek chutki sindoor se bandhi na hoti toh...*'

'Oh, come on now, Neha, you're making him uncomfortable.' Shweta laughed, looking at Max who seemed to be, in fact, enjoying the conversation. 'By the way, Max, Neha loves acting so you'll often hear her rattle off dialogues from Hindi films.'

'Oh, theatre is just a hobby.' Neha was grinning.

'And, by the way,' Shweta added, 'Neha is a professional yoga instructor by day and a stage performer by night.'

'We're only amateurs.' Neha waved her hand, deflecting the praise. 'I'm part of a small theatre practice group and we do a few plays every year. Yoga, though, is more serious business.' She stood up smiling and held out her hand to Max. 'Where are my manners?! Nice to meet you, Max.'

Max shook it. 'Nice to meet you too!'

'Neha is an excellent yoga teacher,' Shweta said, 'I remember you saying you'd love to try yoga, Max. Would you be interested in joining Neha's class?'

Neha's face lit up. 'Of course,' she said, without waiting for Max's reply. 'I have three morning batches. At 6 a.m, 7.30 a.m, and 9 a.m. You can come to any one of them. No charge for you. In fact, Ma comes to my first batch with her friends from this place. I can ask her to bring you along. The women will be thrilled to have someone new in their class.'

Max brought his hand up to his chest. 'Thank you.' Then he made to leave. 'I think I should leave you two alone,' he said. 'Just came to ask if Shweta had an extra pillow. I couldn't get any sleep with the light in my room.'

'Here.' Shweta threw her pillow to him. Neha stared at him as he caught it.

He waved goodbye to the girls, closed the door behind him, and left.

Neha let out a soft sigh, still staring at the door. She slumped on the bed and stared at the ceiling. 'My God, what an Adonis!' she said dreamily.

Shweta shook her head, laughing. She thought it'd be fun not to tell Neha about Max's gender preferences and let her find out by herself. 'What if Mohan sees you drooling over another man, Neha?' she teased.

Neha scowled. 'Oh, don't talk about Mohan. He doesn't have time for me at all. He's always so busy with work. I hardly see him, even on the weekends. Do you know how long it's been since we took a vacation? We had a big fight about it this morning.'

That reminded Shweta about her row with her father just before lunch. She pulled up her knees and buried her face in them. A moment later Neha touched her arm.

'Enough about me,' she said, 'tell me about you now. I met Ma briefly as I was coming upstairs to meet you. She looked terribly upset. She said she had a headache and was going to lie down. Something happened here?'

'Papa spoke to Raj just before I left and found out that I had left him.'

Neha gasped and sat up. 'What do you mean you *left* him? When? Why didn't you tell any of us?'

'I'm sorry, Neha. It happened suddenly and I was in shock. I thought I'd tell Ma and Papa later but Papa came to know before I could tell him and he went ballistic. We had a big argument just now, before lunch.'

Neha bit her lip so hard, it turned white. 'What did Papa say?'

'When Papa began to question me,' Shweta said, 'I felt like a deer caught in the headlights. You know how I clam up when I feel threatened!' Shweta buried her face in her knees. 'I wish I could make it all just go away as if it were a bad dream. How can I tell Papa all of this? He'd never understand or believe me.'

'But what exactly was the problem? Why did you leave?'

'The truth is Raj has severe anger issues. In a fit of anger, one day, he smashed every Corelle plate we had and charged at me with a piece of broken glass. I was afraid for my life. I…I couldn't live...in fear. I don't want to go back to him. I want to end this marriage.'

Shocked, Neha squeezed Shweta's hand. 'But why did he lose his temper?'

'It was something silly. We had an argument. One thing led to another and he started throwing the plates on the floor.'

Neha looked Shweta squarely in the eyes. 'You've got to tell Ma and Papa. But I would give it more time. Let Papa speak to him. Let's hear what Raj has to say in his defence. If it was one incident, does it call for a big decision like this?'

'No, it wasn't the first time. He's always had bipolar issues but refused to take medication even though I'd begged him to see a doctor, many times. He'd get into a frightful rage at times and later he'd forget everything.' Shweta swallowed, remembering the harrowing time she'd gone through, like it was yesterday.

Neha took Shweta's hands in hers. 'I want to hear it all. Tell me what happened, from the beginning.'

Shweta began to sob, as she recollected every little detail, and Neha waited, consoling her sister until she had calmed down.

Shweta wiped her tears and haltingly began. 'One time, I locked myself in the bathroom for four hours waiting for him to calm down while he kept beating at the door in his rage. Another time, he yelled at me in the middle of dinner at a restaurant, and drove back home leaving me stranded there. I didn't know what to do. Finally, he came back for me after an hour and didn't speak to me for a week after that.'

Shweta paused to wipe her nose. 'His mood swings are terrible. I can still remember how he charged at me that night.' She shivered as she recalled that moment. 'He cut his foot on a piece of broken glass as he tried to come at me. He was bleeding and had to rush to the bathroom. I was so afraid that I ran away at the first chance I got. I thought I'd make it to the closest strip mall just fifteen minutes away and call for help. I ran as fast as my legs could carry me.'

Neha squeezed her hand. 'I probably would have run away too. But why didn't you call one of us? Why did you take the whole responsibility on your shoulders? Why did you lie?'

Shweta rose and walked to the window. She needed some fresh air...

Shweta could never forget that night. She'd seen Julie locking up. It was a restaurant that Raj and she used to frequent. All Shweta could think of at that time was to find a place to hide.

Julie had smiled as Shweta went up to her, out of breath. 'Are you here about the ad for the kitchen help?'

Silently saying all the prayers she could remember, Shweta had nodded, a ray of hope shining through her.

'You have experience?'

She nodded vigorously to that too. 'But I have no place to stay.'

Julie took her up to the room above the restaurant that she'd let out to Max. That night, Max had made her feel so welcome. He made her some hot soup and let her have the only bed in the room while spreading his own mattress on the floor.

Shweta had lied to Julie about her experience, thinking that it would be a good idea to stay there and let things cool down before she called her parents. However, Julie had soon realised that Shweta didn't really have any experience in the kitchen. But when she heard what Shweta had been through, she'd been kind enough not to kick her out.

Shweta turned around to face Neha. 'I was worried about Papa's last heart attack, and about Ma. I didn't want to lie, but as things turned out, that became the only thing to do. I didn't want to go back to Raj even if Papa forced me to. And I knew that if I was away long enough, Papa or Raj would be powerless to do anything about me.'

Shweta crossed her arms and let out a deep sigh. 'If Simbu's wedding hadn't turned up unexpectedly, my plan would've worked. But as it stands now, Papa has threatened to fix my marriage with Raj.' She looked at Neha's face beseechingly. 'Tell me, what should I do now?'

Neha wrung her hands in silence.

'Aunt S!' Suddenly, Ria's voice floated up the stairs, breaking the silence in the room. The thud of her school bag preceded another 'Aunt S' call.

Neha rose and touched Shweta's cheek lightly. 'Look, let's not worry about this for now. I'm pretty sure Papa will be too busy with the wedding to do something now. I'll talk to Mohan and see if he can think of something. Now, I'll go down and speak to Ma and send Ria upstairs to meet you. Meanwhile, you better make sure she doesn't know you've been crying.' With that, Neha left the room to go downstairs.

Shweta gathered herself, wiped her eyes, and headed to the bathroom to wash her face.

Her seven-year-old niece, after all, was a very sharp girl.

14

Ria dropped her school bag on the ground and bounded into Shweta's room, her bobbed hair bouncing around her cheeks. She ran straight into Shweta's outstretched arms and squeezed her in a hug.

'I'm so glad to see you again, Aunt S. You look exactly the same. Except, I think your hair's grown a bit longer.'

Shweta laughed. 'And it looks to me like someone got a new haircut,' Shweta said, brushing Ria's silky hair. 'And new glasses too!'

Ria smiled and nodded, tucking her hair behind her ears.

'Oh, and you've lost your front teeth too. Aw, you look so adorable!' Shweta grabbed Ria into another embrace and tickled her. 'Let me see if the tickle still works.' She laughed as Ria doubled over with mirth. 'Does it, huh?' Shweta stopped tickling and held Ria by the arms. 'Okay, so what else has been going on with you?'

Ria giggled. 'Nothing, except watching new videos.'

Shweta widened her eyes.

'Only after ten sums of maths and one page of English grammar every day,' Ria added quickly.

Shweta chucked her under the chin. 'That's like a good girl!'

'Did you get me a gift?' Ria jumped up and down, excitedly.

Shweta winced inwardly. How could she have forgotten?!

'Well…' She racked her brain for an excuse. 'So sorry, dear. I think it's at the bottom of my suitcase. I'll pull it out as soon as I can.' She patted the bed so Ria could sit beside her. 'Tell me all about your videos. What do you watch?' This was a good time to find out what to buy for her niece.

Ria's eyes sparkled as she recounted the fun DIY videos. 'There are also loads of drawing and sketching tutorials online.'

They continued to talk about school and Ria's new friends. It was just like old times again. Ria wanted Shweta to comb her hair and to try on her aunt's make-up and nail polish. As they laughed together and did girly things, the doorbell rang. Shweta and Ria bounded downstairs to see who had come.

Mohan, her brother-in-law, a cardiologist at Sakra Hospital, walked in with a bright smile. Lean, tall, with close-cropped salt-and-pepper hair, he looked a bit tired yet overjoyed to see Shweta.

Mohan ruffled Shweta's hair and peered into her eyes. 'How's my big girl doing?'

Shweta and Mohan chatted about her flight and his work, before he headed towards the kitchen to greet his mother-in-law. While Mohan, Keertana, and Neha talked in the kitchen, Ria ran upstairs to take her drawing book and pencils from her school bag to show Shweta her artwork. They settled down at the dining table. Ria's drawings gave Shweta the perfect gift idea for her. Bits of conversation from the kitchen floated out into the dining room. It was obvious they were talking about Shweta. Though Ria's ears pricked up at whatever little she heard, Shweta managed to keep her engaged in chatter as she sketched in her drawing book and they both waited for Keertana to bring out the evening tea and snacks.

Just as Keertana brought out the tea tray, the doorbell rang again. This time, it was their neighbours, Prasad and his wife, Bindu. Smartly dressed in a crisp cotton kurta, and with well-styled jet black hair, Prasad stood beaming beside Bindu, who wore a pink net saree and a huge pink bindi. Prasad and Bindu were called the evergreen couple because they never seemed to age. Prasad was her father's childhood friend and over the years, they'd become close family. They were always the first to come over when any of the children were visiting. Shweta rushed towards Prasad and bent to touch his feet, and hugged Bindu.

Prabhu, who had been in his room since lunch, came out reluctantly. A round of greetings followed and everyone headed outside to sit in the porch and enjoy the cool breeze along with their tea.

Keertana brought the tea tray out to the porch. Bindu helped carry the tray of pakodas and chutney. The women settled on the low porch wall and the men took up the lounge chairs. They were joined by Mohan and Neha, who sat on the swing. The tea and snacks put all of them in good spirits.

As the conversation flowed freely and everyone savoured their pakodas dipped in chutney, Max sauntered downstairs. He paused midway, looking at the crowd on the porch with surprise. Seated nearest to the porch entrance, Shweta caught his eye and waved to him to join them.

The conversation stopped when Max stepped on to the porch. Shweta introduced Max to Prasad, Bindu, and her brother-in-law.

'Hello, young man!' Prasad shook Max's hand warmly and invited him to join them for tea and soon engaged him in a conversation about his visit to India. Shweta's father ignored Max and talked to Mohan instead.

'I hope Kini is right about Shweta, that things will get resolved with her husband,' Keertana said as she poured Prasad a second cup of tea and added the milk and sugar.

It was strange that her mother should mention this in front of the Prasads. Did it mean that they knew about it too?

'I don't want to hear what Kini has to say. When has he been right?' Prabhu said, butting in. 'There isn't a single time that things have gone smoothly. First it was the delay in Shweta's marriage, now this latest problem. I don't want to ask Kini if these problems will be resolved or not. I'm the father of the girl. It's up to me, not some astrologer, to decide what to do for my children.'

A silence fell on the group and the discussion stopped just as suddenly as it had started. Keertana excused herself awkwardly and headed to the kitchen to get more tea and snacks. Bindu followed her. Max too made a lame excuse. Prabhu returned to his conversation with Mohan.

Neha asked for another cup of tea and Mohan, who was nearest to the kettle, stopped his chat with his father-in-law to help her. Shweta couldn't help but notice how Neha played footsie with him while he poured her tea. This was the kind of marriage she'd wanted. Although Neha was always complaining about her busy husband, Shweta thought she was the luckiest wife in the world. Mohan adored her; it was evident even from the way he served her tea.

Prasad turned to Prabhu. 'I heard Lekha's parents have contracted Bindu's uncle, Nambishan, for the wedding sadya lunch. He's a much sought after wedding caterer in Chennai. Looks like the wedding preparations are making good progress. Let's hope the continuing rain does not cause any problems.'

Prabhu shook his head. 'Lekha's father is sure everything will be fine.'

'Where have the newlyweds decided on a honeymoon?'

'I haven't gone on a vacation in so many years,' Neha cut in. 'I wish we could go off on our second honeymoon.' She looked at Mohan, pouting.

'I've been extremely busy,' Mohan said, apologetically. 'But I promise to make up for it soon.' He flashed a smile at Neha who rolled her eyes.

'Even Keertana and I plan to take a foreign trip after the wedding,' Prabhu said.

Shweta got up from her seat and decided to check where Max had disappeared. She headed inside and seeing Max and Ria busy at the dining table, joined them.

Ria looked delighted to be in Max's company. He 'aww'ed at her sketches and even taught her how to shade a horse's tail with fine, straight pencil strokes, much to Ria's amusement. Neha and Mohan also joined them at the table.

Suddenly, the voices from the porch grew louder.

'Are you out of your mind, man?' They heard Prasad shout.

'I just want to know what the hell happened between them.' Prabhu's voice matched Prasad's.

Shweta looked at Neha and Mohan in dismay. Max tried to distract Ria by explaining something to her while Shweta strained her ears to keep track of the heated conversation on the porch.

'But these matters are to be dealt with in private and not in the middle of an important wedding. I thought you had more sense than this. What's happening to you?' Prasad said, sounding livid.

'I'm discussing this with a fool like you, that's what it is.' Although Shweta had heard them argue before, it had never sounded like this.

'How dare you call me a fool? *You* are a fool. An utter, complete fool. First you marry your daughter off to a stranger, and then instead of going there and sorting it out, you invite him here and that too to your son's wedding. Utter nonsense!'

What! Raj was being invited to Simbu's wedding? Shweta thought with alarm.

'Wasn't Mohan a stranger to us when he married Neha?' Shweta heard Prabhu yell back. 'You can say what you like but I know I can fix this. Raj will come, he'll see all these celebrations, and it'll be like old times. He'll give up this stubbornness and take Shweta back with him. And that's what I want.'

Shweta clasped her hands tight. She hoped Raj would be too busy to show up.

A chair scraped. 'You want to send your daughter back to that monster? What kind of a father are you?' Prasad cried.

Another chair scraped. 'A concerned one,' Prabhu shot back. 'Fights happen in all families. If couples started to separate for every small fight, do you think any of us would remain married?'

'But this was not just a fight,' Prasad shouted. 'And you know that!'

Shweta wondered how he'd known that. Had Neha hinted to Keertana, and Keertana rung Bindu to tell her? The news had indeed spread unbelievably quickly.

'I want to talk to Raj and hear what he has to say,' Prabhu continued. 'Shweta is my daughter and I will do what I think is right for her. I have six sisters. No one has divorced children! How will I face my family? What will I tell them? That I was incapable of raising my daughter right? You can say whatever you like because you don't have children. You don't know how it feels.'

A painful silence descended.

Shweta could imagine how hurt Prasad must have felt at that. It was a fact that even though he didn't have children of his own, he cared for Prabhu's as if they were his own. He had always thought of Shweta as his own daughter.

Prasad's voice resumed, sounding hurt. 'I may not be a father, but Shweta is like my own child. I would have handled this differently. Get the boy's family and talk to them, I'm not disagreeing to that, but at least find the right time to do it. You're ruining Simbu's wedding too.'

'Bindu!' he then called out to his wife who was still in the kitchen.

Bindu rushed out of the kitchen and hastened to the porch. 'What happened? What happened?'

Keertana hurried out too. By the time Shweta and the others headed to the porch, it was too late. Prasad and Bindu had left.

Keertana shook her head and sniffled noisily into her saree. It was all she could do to stop the tears from rolling down her cheeks.

With the altercation between Prasad and Prabhu, the mood of the evening had taken a turn for the worse.

Shortly after, Neha announced that Mohan, Ria, and she were leaving too. After they left, Prabhu stomped out for a short walk and Keertana returned to the solitude and peace of her bedroom.

Shweta went to her room and threw herself on the bed. She had had enough of these fights herself!

15

Shweta hoped her father would act normal again at least while Max was with them but he continued to be grumpy from the moment he woke up.

Keertana woke him up before she left for her yoga class with Max, every day. And from then on, he'd sit in his favourite spot in his easy chair by the bay window, his legs propped up on the footstool, his three daily newspapers, pipe, and books arranged perfectly on the small table at the side, until she returned.

When the maid came in the morning and began breakfast preparations in the kitchen, Shweta would finally make her way downstairs to get her cup of tea and return to her room quickly, deliberately avoiding her father. Then, she'd emerge only when Max and her mother got back from their yoga class and called her for breakfast.

Her mother enjoyed serving breakfast in style after the children were grown up and she had more time on her hands. She'd bring out the teapot, milk jug, sugar pot, cups and saucers on a tray, and use glass serving dishes.

That morning she had made aromatic upma, peppered with diced capsicum and carrots. The green and the orange sprinkled on to the white of the upma made it a visual delight. She glanced at Prabhu's face as she served him, waiting for his approval. It was only when he looked satisfied that she smiled and sat down to have her breakfast.

In the last few days, things had taken an unexpected turn in Chennai. Heavy rains continued, flights were cancelled, and the airport was closed for a few days. The TV in the living room was on and aired the latest news about the floods in Chennai. The situation was horrible in several parts of the city.

'Will the wedding be moved to Bangalore?' Keertana asked Prabhu, passing the upma around.

Everyone, from Shweta's parents to her relatives in Bangalore, was concerned about the wedding. Her parents hadn't been able to contact Lekha's family since the last few days. Lekha's parents had later messaged to say that their locality was okay so far. But power outages, water contamination, and food and medicine shortages were choking the rest of the city. TV reports covered one devastating flood incident after another, but all they could do was wait and hope that conditions would stabilise before the wedding.

'We still have two weeks to go,' her father said, and switched off the TV. 'Lekha's father seemed positive that things would settle down soon.'

Taking her cue from him, her mother urged them all to enjoy their breakfast in peace, filling them in with talk about neighbours and family.

Shweta had come to enjoy these long tea sessions that spanned over an hour at breakfast, when Keertana filled everyone in on gossip she'd heard on her walks with the neighbours, family news gathered from her various telephone conversations with relatives, and the affairs of the planets and stars and reports of their positions and their effects on their current lives, gleaned from astrologer Kini. These days, she also regaled them with tales of how the women oohed and aahed at Max's flexibility in doing the various yoga postures they were taught in class.

Prabhu enjoyed these titbits very much and although he wasn't really talking to Shweta and Max. He'd ever so often offer a quip or two about this person or that, or whatever his impressions were at that moment.

Some days later, Max booked his tickets to Delhi for a date after the wedding. From Delhi, he had arranged for a guide to take him on the Himalayan trek. He was so excited about the trip that even Shweta was pulled into his infectious excitement. But first, they were counting down the days to the wedding and all the excitement that lay ahead.

One evening, Keertana knocked and peeked into Shweta's bedroom.

Shweta was at her desk, browsing on her computer, and she turned around in the swivel chair in surprise. Her mother, who'd never come up to her room in long, held a few shiny pieces of silk in her hand.

Shweta rose and went to see what they were. 'Wow!' she said, feeling the delicate raw silk. They were clutch-style purses with zari and brocade clasps. 'Where did you get these? They look absolutely exquisite.'

Keertana's eyes gleamed with pride. 'I stitched them. I'm giving these as gifts to your aunts and cousins.' She unclasped one of them to show Shweta. It had a zip pouch dividing the bigger open pouches. 'It can hold a mobile phone and house keys, money, and a lipstick or something small too. It took me a while to think of this idea but I feel that it has turned out beautifully. What do you think?'

Shweta turned it around and marvelled at the invisible seams. 'These are absolutely gorgeous, Ma.'

'Well, I guess these are good to go then, right?' Her mother beamed. Then abruptly, she peered at Shweta. 'Look, don't mind your father's moods. I spoke to Kini yesterday. He says things will be fine soon.'

Shweta rolled her eyes. *Where was Kini when she was getting married? Why didn't he warn them about such a match?*

'Don't worry, my dear,' her mother continued. 'He says that

Saturn has moved into the seventh house so there will be some marital problems, but everything will get resolved soon.'

Her mother was pretty good at using astrological predictions to explain every occasion; it was what some would call 'looking at the bright side'. If something went well, it was because Kini said so; if something didn't go well, it was because the planets had moved to a bad position.

'Resolved?' She looked at her mother incredulously.

'I think once you have a baby everything will be fine. This is just temporary. I'm sure it will be sorted out. Papa will speak to Raj.' Her mother's voice was gentle but Shweta had had enough.

'Arrgh! Please stop it, Ma.' This whole arranged marriage business was ridiculous. Visits to astrologers, religious poojas at home, temple visits—the works—she had done it all. And what now? She was back home after a failed marriage, in just six months. She felt like shit. She wished Keertana wouldn't say her current situation was temporary. For Shweta, this marriage was over. She was done waiting for planets and stars to keep up their game.

Keertana touched her shoulder. 'Let's forget about all that.'

Shweta exhaled and went back to her chair.

'What were you doing here all by yourself?' her mother asked, trying to change the subject. 'You should go meet Neha sometime. You haven't gone to her home yet.'

'I forgot to buy Ria a gift and I wanted to get her something so she wouldn't think I'd forgotten. That's what I was looking for online.'

Her mother laughed. 'All this online stuff makes no sense to me. In fact, I don't even know what to do with a computer! I wanted to buy a book but your father's too busy to do it for me. He does all his trading online but I can't even order myself a book.'

'Tell me which one and I'll order it for you. But first, look at what I've decided to buy for Ria.' Shweta showed her the pictures of the Faber Castell colour pencils and thick drawing sketchbook she'd wish-listed on an online portal. She looked to her mother for approval.

'These look expensive,' Keertana said. 'Look dear, if you need money, please let me know. I can ask Prabhu.' She paused and waved her hand when Shweta started to protest. 'I won't tell him that it's for you.'

'Don't worry about me, Ma,' Shweta said quickly. 'I had some balance in the bank when I left.' Unlike the heroine in *Queen*, she had left her bank account untouched when she left for the US. 'That's why they say every girl should be financially independent.'

Her mother nodded. 'That is why both my daughters are educated enough to find jobs.'

Shweta wished her mother had thought of herself too. Why had she never thought of doing something besides cooking and looking after her family? 'Wouldn't it be great if you could earn too?' she asked her mother. 'If only to buy a few things without needing to ask for cash…'

'Me?' her mother said, surprised. 'What can I do to earn money now? I wish my parents had let me complete my graduation but those days were different, and I was the fourth girl child. They were in such a rush to get me married.' Keertana smiled as she reminisced.

Shweta shook her head. 'There's no reason you shouldn't try something new just because you've never done it before. Now look at these purses.' Shweta picked a purple one with green brocade lining. 'If you made some more of these, maybe one day we could sell them online. These would make such beautiful and practical gifts for women. Don't you think that it's a brilliant idea?'

Keertana didn't look convinced. 'I don't think I can make these consistently. I'd get bored after making a few. I'm just doing this for the wedding.'

Shweta gave her a pointed look. 'If you got orders for another friend's wedding, would you not make them for her?'

Keertana shrugged. 'I guess I would. I'd love to be able to do something like this for my friends.'

Shweta clasped her hands together, already excited about the prospect. 'That's it then! After this wedding, I'm going to do some marketing for you and we're going to get orders. When the orders start picking up, you're going to have a small business of your own.'

Keertana chuckled and rose from the bed. 'You and your ideas! Don't count your chickens before they hatch, they say. I'm not doing anything until after the wedding and then, we'll see,' she said, with finality.

'You better watch out for the orders, Ma,' Shweta teased her.

Keertana laughed and headed to the door. 'Come for dinner now, quickly. It's almost ready.' She paused at the door for a moment. 'And when you meet Neha next, ask her why she looks so lost these days. I think she's feeling left out, what with Mohan's busy work timings. You sisters are close. See if she'll tell you what's been bothering her lately.'

'I'll find out. Don't worry, Ma.' But when Keertana had left, a thought crossed Shweta's mind. She knew that Neha was upset with Mohan's work timings. Was her mother overly concerned or was Neha really unhappy? She resolved to find out.

Bindu and Prasad didn't come home again, but on Sunday, which was her parents' usual Rummy Day at Prasad's home, Keertana persuaded Prabhu to go over. 'They're like family,' she said, 'and this is not the first time you both have exchanged heated words.'

He sulked and kept dragging his feet, but finally went along with her and was in a much better mood when they returned.

16

Ayurvedic massages seemed to be the next thing that Max wanted to try out, so Shweta booked him into a retreat for a few days until the wedding. Meanwhile, there was lots of shopping left to do for the wedding, and her mother had been nagging both the sisters for days so they could all go together.

Shweta woke up one morning a few days before the wedding and saw Prabhu pacing the porch. It was very unlike her father. He usually read the paper in the living room in the mornings, and was never out of his easy chair until Keertana returned from her yoga class.

He stopped, filled his pipe with a few strands of tobacco, struck a match to it, took a long drag, and resumed his pacing. Holding the pipe deftly with his right hand, he let out long, thick curls of smoke and stared ahead, lost in thought.

When Keertana returned from her yoga class, she was surprised to see Prabhu already seated at the dining table.

'Did you finish reading your newspapers early?' she asked him.

'Didn't feel like it today,' he said, massaging the bald patch on his head vigorously. 'Things at the stock market didn't look too good yesterday. Thought I'd finish my breakfast and sit down to check the rates. I'm thinking of a new investment to help pay back some debts soon.'

Keertana shook her head and walked to the basin to wash her hands. Then she went to the kitchen to ready breakfast for the three of them.

* * *

Out of the blue one day, Shweta wondered whether she'd run into Niru now that she was back, and he was visiting Bangalore sometimes. She'd thought he might call at her home to see her or she might bump into him on the street. After all, he lived only two houses away on the same street. But to her surprise, and relief really, neither had happened.

Her family still had wedding cards to distribute to their neighbours before leaving for Chennai. So when it was time for the visit to Niru's home, she joined the party, more curious about him than anything else. Had he changed? Did he look any different?

Niru's house was a lot more traditionally furnished than Shweta's. A carved teak seating, wood-panelled columns, and Tanjore paintings gave the house a very rich yet simple look. Niru's father had passed away a few years ago. His mother, Savitri, welcomed them.

The Karthiks were close family friends, like Bindu and Prasad, and Niru's mother jumped straight into questions about the wedding. The two families discussed Simbu's current job, how he had met Lekha, her family background, and the current problem in Chennai.

'Will the wedding venue have to be shifted?' Savitri asked, concerned.

Over the last few days, the situation in Chennai had continued to be tense. Prabhu too had been worried after he heard the latest TV reports that fresh fruits and vegetables were a problem to find, medicines had run into scarcity, and diarrhoea and water-borne illnesses were spreading rapidly throughout the city.

Prabhu threw his hands up in the air. 'God knows! It's really up to the Nambiars now. They think it will settle down soon. We'll worry about it when we have to fly down there.'

Savitri turned to Shweta. 'You look so lovely after your wedding, Shweta.'

Shweta grew hot under her cheeks. Her mother threw a nervous glance in Savitri's direction, making it obvious to Shweta that she hadn't told Savitri.

'What about Niru? How's he doing?' Keertana butted in.

Shweta heaved a sigh of relief as the conversation moved from her marriage to Niru.

'Niru's doing well,' Savitri said. 'He wants to start a restaurant of his own. He also supports an NGO that provides lunch to the poor once in a week. You know, I was worried about his future when he said he wanted to go to catering college. But now, I'm so glad I let him do what he wanted. He's happy and that means a lot to me.'

Niru might not be at home at the moment, Shweta assumed, remembering guiltily how she'd teased him about his chef dream.

'Have you found a girl for Niru yet?' Keertana asked Savitri.

So, the idiot was still single, Shweta thought as Savitri replied, 'What to do, Keertana? We can't choose a girl for our sons these days. They want to be left alone to decide who to marry and when.'

Shweta amused herself with the thought of what his mother might think of his Italian girlfriend. Maybe she'd die of horror!

His mother actually became a little emotional after that. 'He refuses to consider any girl I suggest.'

'Don't worry, Savitri,' Keertana consoled her. 'He'll get married when the right girl comes along.'

Shweta offered to make tea to escape this little family drama. She'd been to their kitchen several times as a young girl. As soon as she'd put the kettle of water to boil, the two mothers came inside and huddled in a corner of the kitchen. She was sure her mother was discussing her.

As Shweta looked around the kitchen to focus on anything but the discussion between the two women, the oven sitting in a corner on the kitchen counter caught her eye. Back in the day, Savitri was the only person in the community who owned an oven. Only because Niru was so keen on learning to cook.

As she added tea leaves to the boiling water, images of the cake batter she'd once tried to make at Niru's home popped into her head.

'Is it sweet enough?' he'd asked her, after she'd finished folding in the flour.

She had dipped a finger in the batter to check and he'd pulled her finger into his mouth. 'It's fine,' he'd said, making her blush as she pulled her hand away clumsily. The baking session had led to increasing visits from Niru to her house on the pretext of meeting Simbu. Or maybe she was still holding on to the imaginations of a blossoming teenager with a crush on someone. On a more sensible note, so many years later, it was hard to imagine that Niru would have wanted anything to do with her. Anyway, all he'd ever done was mock and tease her.

'Is it sweet enough?' a voice spoke behind her, just like he had. She turned around, startled to see his mother asking about the tea. It felt like déjà vu.

Shweta poured the tea into cups and carried it out to the living room. More conversation followed, tea was finished, Prabhu gave Savitri the wedding card, and they all left.

When they returned home, Shweta had an argument with Keertana, sure that she had discussed her marital problems with Savitri. 'Why did you have to tell Savitri Auntie about my marriage? This is so unfair. You could have waited until this wedding was over. Now she's going to go around telling the whole world.' By whole world, she meant Niru. She didn't want him to know. But her mother didn't need to know that.

'But she's my best friend, Shweta. If she hears this from somebody else, imagine how hurt she'll feel. Don't worry. I've asked her to keep it quiet until after Simbu's wedding. She's not going to tell anyone.'

But Niru was definitely going to hear about it, and that was what put Shweta off. The way Niru had teased her about marrying a stranger and his words, now almost true, were still fresh in her mind. 'And what if this man you're marrying is an axe-murderer?'

'Get off your high horse, Niru. Not everyone is afraid of getting married, like you,' she'd retorted, acting braver than she'd felt.

She'd sensed his uncomfortable silence, confident that she had touched a nerve.

Now, she cringed, he'd gloat at this new juicy bit of information about her.

Well! Shweta chuckled. She had something to tease him back with, his Italian girlfriend who he hadn't introduced to his mother yet.

17

Niru was used to crazy busy and crazy long days, like the one today, thanks to the water crisis in the kitchen and the inability to source the dozens of eggs for the cakes. It seemed like Chennai was reeling under the pressure of not-to-be-missed wedding dates despite the flooding and unpredictable weather.

When he left the hotel, where he was currently helping out a friend from his New York days to run his first restaurant, it was late. It was later still when he finally got on the metro and reached his apartment.

He was sure his best friend Simbu shouldn't be getting married here at all under the current weather conditions, but Simbu had seemed happy to go along with the preparations being made by his fiancée's parents. Simbu had asked Niru to cater for the pre-wedding parties. And he could not refuse his best friend or let him down, come what may.

But, there was also the slight complication of meeting Simbu's little sister, Shweta, at the wedding. To be laughed at by one's first crush at sixteen was bad enough but to discover that no one came close to her kind of indecisive, lazy, yet simple nature, was hard to digest. Not only did she never judge him but she was also game for whatever fun her brother and he were up to. He'd never find that kind of an adventurous and trusting girl even if he searched the whole world. That was the girl he'd left behind when he went to study in New York.

She was also partly the reason that he'd been off girlfriends for a while. No one could match up to his Shweta. When he'd heard that she was getting married he'd been crushed that he'd lost his chance. He had wanted time to work on a career, settle down, earn well enough before asking for her hand. But unfortunately, he had been too late. If only he'd asked Shweta to wait for him then. If only, he'd had the guts.

Later, he'd met Lisa, who was a head-turner, but she was nothing like the crazy, uncomplicated, happy-to-be-herself Shweta, who could make him laugh just by entering the room, with her noodle-like curly hair standing upright like she'd been electrocuted, or her ability to make a disaster out of any cake recipe.

And he'd thought he had moved on until his mother mentioned Shweta again the other day. 'Shweta had come here and was asking about you.'

He'd felt a sharp pang in his heart. 'Has her husband come too?'

'Things don't seem to be going too well,' his mother said.

Well, she had married a stranger for God's sake. Niru had been too mad to attend her wedding. He knew he was still mad at himself for having let her go. Memories of the past were never pleasant.

His heart beat faster now though, at the thought of seeing her again. He shook his head and let out a deep sigh.

Pacing the two-bedroom apartment that he shared with a bachelor roommate, he made a call to his agent in Bangalore. By the time he'd hung up, he had closed the deal for the house he'd been considering for his restaurant. His dream was beginning to take shape. Soon he'd have a place to call his own. The two-storeyed house he'd zeroed in on had looked perfect to be remodelled into a café with plenty of adjoining art and reading space.

* * *

'Do you know, an old woman living alone was found murdered in her Jayanagar home yesterday? They say that she had been dead since about three days,' Keertana said, peering over her reading glasses at Shweta as she approached the kitchen table. Today was when Shweta, her mother and her sister had finally decided to go shopping for the wedding saree. Shweta was annoyed to see her mother still in the kitchen.

'Such gruesome news, Ma,' Shweta said, shaking her head. 'Have you nothing better to read?'

'I worry about people living alone. I wonder how Savitri copes.'

'Niru could marry his girlfriend and come live with her,' Shweta said with a sly smile.

'Don't be silly. He doesn't have a girlfriend or Savitri would have told me.'

Shweta stayed quiet. Keertana had always had a soft corner for Niru. 'Come eat with us, Niru,' she would say, or 'Niru, can you tell me if my bread tastes okay?' or 'Niru, will you help me with this hummus dip?' It was always Niru this and Niru that. Keertana had been fond of Niru for as long as Shweta could remember. Even more than she was of Simbu. But Shweta was pleased enough that she had a secret weapon against Niru now.

Keertana sighed as she folded the newspaper and put it away. 'Your Papa says reading the newspaper every day will drive away my ignorance. As if! With such horrible news to read every morning I'm sure to die of shock rather than ignorance.'

'Did you get the book you were looking for?' Shweta said, suddenly remembering that her mother hadn't given her its name.

Keertana sighed again. 'I asked your father but he was too busy with his stock buying and selling, and watching TV, to care. Now, I don't think I will have it in time for the trip. What will I do in Chennai? We'll be there three days ahead of the wedding and I will have some time on my hands.'

Today, if possible, Shweta decided, she was going to teach her mother how to shop online. It was high time her mother learned how to use the internet. For now though, she made a mental note to get the book's name and order it as soon as they returned from the market that evening. She'd already ordered the sketch book and colour pencils for Ria; they were due to arrive any time.

'You should get ready now,' Keertana said and rose to go to her room. 'We have so much shopping to do, and now that the Nambiars have sent me Lekha's horoscope, I want to show it to Kini too.'

'But what's the point of showing it to him just days before the wedding?' Shweta was exasperated with the Kini talk her mother brought up every time.

'Just for my satisfaction. What's the harm? He's seen Simbu's horoscope already.'

It raised her hackles again. 'Exactly! See, that's the problem. Kini wouldn't hurt your feelings so he'll massage the truth, present it to you on a platter, and watch you lap it up.'

Keertana glared. 'Show some respect, Shweta. Is this how you talk?'

There! She'd pulled out the respect card at the drop of a hat like every other time she'd wanted Shweta to keep quiet. Anything Shweta wanted to say, any opinion of hers was always smothered by the respect shroud. Would anybody ever let her speak her mind in this house?

'Simbu's marriage better not go my way,' Shweta said, sobering down. But even as she said it, she knew Simbu's marriage was not going to be like hers at all. Simbu and Lekha had known each other for over two years. Shweta, on the contrary, hardly knew Raj before the wedding; they'd met only three or four times before they were married. Why had Kini okayed their horoscope? Hadn't he known what was to follow?

'Why are you wasting time now?' Keertana asked. 'Go change quickly. Neha will meet us directly at the store and we mustn't be late.'

When Shweta went to her room and opened up her suitcase on her bed, she realized that she'd thrown the only pair of jeans she owned for a wash. She rummaged in all the drawers and found a pair of Neha's old leggings.

Bereft of any other options, she put them on without a second thought and turned a deaf ear to the scolding her mother gave her about her shabby attire, all along the way.

18

Shweta and Keertana reached Kalaniketan, the saree lover's paradise, just as Neha's car turned into the parking lot.

Shweta noted that all the shoppers had dressed up as if they all wanted the salespersons to know their taste in clothes, so they could provide them the best to add to their collection. Shweta now looked embarrassed at her own attire; her mother and Neha more than made up for her by looking perfectly dressed.

Although Neha and she would probably never wear their sarees after the wedding, they were a prerequisite for the occasion. These days, Neha said, new-age silk sarees, the lighter version of Kancheevarams, were in.

After being shown an umpteen number of colours and patterns, the women picked up sarees that were all in double colour combinations. Neha picked a blue saree with a yellow border. Shweta decided the sisters could go for border-colour coordinated sarees, so she picked up a pink saree with a yellow border.

Keertana picked out a beautiful blue and gold Kancheevaram with a peacock motif in gold silk thread on the border for herself. She also bought a few dozen, colourful, faux silks with beautiful thread zari borders for her friends and relatives.

Since they were the groom's family, they didn't have to buy jewellery by the kilo, but they had to buy the bride's ring, the auspicious gold thaali pendant—the sign of a married woman—and the accompanying gold chain.

They stepped into the Alukkas store next door. It was interesting, Shweta noted, how clothing and jewellery shops hustled for adjacent spots. It was convenient for shoppers and guaranteed business for the stores - a win-win for both!

Luckily, Lekha had already sent her ring finger measurement and it was easy to buy a ring for her. Since Simbu was going to arrive only close to the wedding date, Shweta texted a picture of the rings they liked. They bought the one he approved and went on to look at the pendant designs.

Malayalis wore a leaf-shaped pendant as the thaali, but even that had a few designs to be selected from, so Simbu was sent another bunch of pictures and he picked one among them.

As she was looking at the thaalis on display, Shweta touched the thaali she was still wearing around her neck, thinking of the time they'd spent selecting one for her. She had chosen a lightweight pendant in the shape of a leaf with 'Om' etched on it in indigo blue and a matching gold lightweight chain.

'What do you think? That was quick, wasn't it?' Neha nudged her, bringing her out of her reverie.

She nodded and they stepped out. Shweta couldn't help thinking how the whole wedding shopping experience felt depressingly surreal.

* * *

They were so famished by the end of their saree and jewellery haul that the sisters felt like going for a buffet meal. Shweta was salivating just thinking about it. While their mother wanted to go home and check on their father's lunch, the girls headed to Chokhi Dhani on Inner Ring Road, a restaurant that served a smorgasbord-style seven-course Rajasthani meal fit for a king and his army.

It could have been a fourteen-course meal, for all Shweta knew.

The dishes just kept coming to the table. First the sweets, then the snacks, and then the flat breads with at least six sides. Rice followed, more sides were offered, and finally there were desserts. Shweta was sure she'd skipped a few things that came to the table. Every morsel of the gourmet spread was so delicious; she couldn't get enough of the aroma of fresh food cooked in ghee. She had eaten so much that towards the end she could barely look at the plate.

After the meal, all Shweta wanted to do was to go home and sleep. But it was almost time for Ria to get back from school so Neha suggested they go to her house first, and then she could ask her driver to drop Shweta back.

In the car, all the way back home, Neha was quiet. Shweta, slumped in the back of the car, was quiet too. They probably resembled alligators basking in the sun after a heavy meal.

Neha sighed. 'Can't believe we're doing this all over again! It feels like only yesterday that we did this.'

'Hmmm.' Shweta nodded, thinking the exact same thing. She looked sideways at Neha. Something was different about her sister lately. She hadn't been very enthusiastic about the shopping either. 'What does Mohan say about the wedding?' she asked, trying to find out what was wrong, without offending Neha. A full stomach and a half-asleep brain made this the best time to broach the subject but Shweta's own fuzzy brain was refusing to help her do this properly. She knew she made a pathetic interrogator, but this felt like a good opportunity. She just had to go about it cautiously.

Neha didn't have a clue about what Shweta was getting at. 'He's okay with it,' she said, simply. 'Too extravagant for his tastes, of course, but he can't stop Papa from spending whatever he likes.'

'How's his practice? How's it going since he joined Sakra?'

Neha scoffed, looking exasperated just thinking about it. 'He's at the hospital in the morning, at the clinic in the evenings, and God-knows-where every weekend. I'm getting tired of his work schedule. It's eating into our family life.'

'Hmmm...' Shweta knew she should be doing something more

than hem and haw. 'Why don't you talk to Mohan about his busy schedule?'

Neha turned and leaned towards Shweta, eyes narrowed. 'You know what, Shweta? He's not telling me what it is but he doesn't have time for us. His patients are more important than we are. I'm just tired.' She stifled a sudden sob.

Shweta clasped Neha's hands. 'It's very unlike Mohan...'

The rest of her sentence was broken off by the slamming of brakes. Their car came to a screeching halt behind a Volvo bus, which had rammed into a car in front and abruptly halted ahead of them. They gaped in shock at the huge red bus, with the dawning realisation that they had been inches away from the crash. Miraculously, there was no vehicle behind them. Their driver slowly steered to the right and they passed the hit car, its back completely caved in, its driver already in a furious argument with the bus driver.

They were five minutes from Neha's house when Shweta suddenly remembered she'd not got Ria's gift. 'I'll drop in another day,' she told Neha. 'Can your driver drop me right after he drops you?'

Neha blinked in surprise. 'You've come this far and you won't come home?'

'Not today. I'm expecting a courier,' Shweta said. 'And I'd promised to help Ma shop for a book online so I better not be too late.'

On reaching home, Shweta was relieved to know that Ria's package had arrived. Then, without wasting another minute, she sat her mother down at her computer, and showed her how to select and order the book she needed from Amazon. That done, she ticked off one more item from her to-do list for the day.

It was almost dinner time but since she felt stuffed after the heavy lunch, Shweta decided to skip it and call it an early night. After her mother left her room, she changed, propped herself on her bed, and decided to watch a movie. She flipped through the options and finally settled on *Titanic*. Everything about that movie was so magnificent that it felt new even though she'd watched it a few times before. However, she didn't remember what happened after Leo and Kate stood on the stern of the ship; when she woke up, it was already morning.

19

Armed with the colour pencils and the sketch book, Shweta called at Neha's house in HSR for lunch on a late Sunday morning. She knew Neha would be free from her classes by mid-morning, and Mohan would also be home.

The smell of frying fish greeted her at the door as she waited for Neha or Ria to answer the doorbell.

A quick patter of feet sounded and seconds later the door opened.

Ria rushed out to hug her even before she could take a step forward. 'Aunt S!' Ria screamed before she turned back and announced to Neha, 'Ma, Aunt S is here.' She noticed the packages in Shweta's hand and jumped in delight. 'For me?'

Shweta nodded, laughing. 'Sorry, it took so long for me to get these to you.' She saw Ria's eyes brighten as she pulled out the gifts from the package, even before she'd let Shweta enter the house. 'Do you like them?' Shweta asked.

Ria bubbled over with excitement, her mouth open, as she tore open the packages, uncovering the large sketch book and the pack of colour pencils. 'I love them. Come in, Aunt S.' She dragged Shweta in by the arm, shut the door, and bounded off inside with the gifts.

Shweta looked around the two-bedroom, ground-floor apartment. She loved the extended, cobblestoned balcony that gave it the feel of a private porch like the one in her parents' villa. A few potted plants, bamboo shoots and a new tulsi plant adorned one corner. A rocker, two outdoor chairs, and a sturdy cast iron table completed the outdoorsy garden look of the medium-sized porch. Shweta noticed a solved Hindu crossword page spread open on the centre table and smiled, remembering how Mohan loved to finish the crossword every day.

The clang of a pan took her to the kitchen. But instead of Neha, she was surprised to see Mohan standing by the burner, turning the fish over very carefully to make sure he didn't inadvertently crumble the fillets.

Shweta stepped closer and noticed four big pieces of pomfret sizzling in the pan.

Mohan glanced over and gave her a big smile. 'Hey! Just in time for lunch.'

'Hi!' Shweta replied and peeked into the utility area beyond the kitchen looking for Neha. She waited for Mohan to finish flipping the fillets before asking, 'Where's Neha?'

'She had a migraine attack this morning. I've asked her to lie down. She's in her room.' Mohan moved on to open the rice cooker. Shweta watched in amazement at the ease with which he moved around the kitchen. 'Will you have something to drink?' he asked her.

'When did you learn to cook?' She'd known him for over a decade, and in all those years she never knew Mohan could cook, she realized with surprise.

Mohan laughed. 'One has to be an all-rounder,' he said, and winked. 'Plus, since you were coming today, we couldn't let you down.'

Shweta came around to the counter and noticed the covered dishes, wondering how he had managed to cook all of them without Neha's help. She lifted the lid off one. 'You didn't have to go through all this trouble for me.'

'I wanted to make sure I hadn't lost my touch,' he said. 'We lived in the hostel back in my student days and my chilli chicken was always a hit, you know.' He put a wok on the fire and poured some oil into it. 'Need to fry some pappadoms. No meal is complete without them, no?'

There was a tug in her chest. Pappadoms were her favourite too but Raj strangely hated them. How can one eat all this fried stuff and stay healthy, she remembered him saying. It was only after returning to India that she'd been eating pappadoms to her heart's content.

She watched with amusement as Mohan pottered about with a napkin hanging out of his pocket, wiping his hands on it ever so often. 'Did you have clinic this morning?' she asked. Did he look tired or was she imagining it?

'No, I'm free on Sunday mornings, but I've taken up something in the evenings. It's keeping me super busy these days.'

'You've started working too much. You should take a break.'

Mohan turned around and peered at her. 'Has Neha been complaining about me?' Turning back to the wok, he checked the heat of the oil by throwing a small piece of a pappadom into it.

Shweta made a face. 'You think I'm concerned about you only because of Neha? You, of all people, should know enough about good health and sleep. I see dark circles under your eyes. You look so drained. Shouldn't you be taking care of yourself too?'

He laughed, brushing her off. The oil had become hot enough and he eased a pappadom into it and watched as it fluffed. With a tong, he deftly pulled it out and laid it on a napkin to soak up the extra oil.

'I can help you with that,' Shweta offered.

'No, I got this, dear. But, can you please take these serving dishes and set the table? And the plates and spoons, please?' He paused and caught the concern in her eyes. 'Don't worry about me. I'm fine, really.' He ruffled her hair. 'But my patients need me too.' As she turned to do as he had asked, he called out, 'But I promise, I'm taking the family on a vacation soon. Because, God knows, I do need a break. Maybe after Simbu's wedding.'

'Speaking of the wedding,' Mohan continued, after Shweta had set the plates and spoons on the dining table and had come back for the serving dishes. 'Neha was telling me about Raj.' He turned around to look at her. 'Have you thought about what you're going to do afterwards?'

'I'm asking for a divorce,' Shweta said, trying to sound nonchalant.

'If you're absolutely certain,' he said as he held her gaze, 'you can seek an annulment since it's within a year of your marriage. I will speak to Prasad Uncle's lawyer friend, and we can get it started as soon as possible.' He peered at her. 'Immediately, if possible, so that we're ready when Raj comes to the wedding.'

Shweta held her breath. First of all, she didn't believe that Raj would come to the wedding. But even if he did, was it really going to be over that quick and easy?

Mohan caught on to her anxious look and said, 'I never said it'll be easy but we mustn't wait too long, especially if you've made up your mind.'

'But what about Papa?' she said, her anxiety mounting.

Mohan breathed out, easing out the last fried pappadom from the oil. 'There's nothing wrong in preparing for the worst even if we might not need *all* the preparation, right?'

Shweta nodded. 'By the way, if there's a job opening at Sakra in Accounts, I'd like to apply,' she said. The thought suddenly occurred to her when she realized that she needed to take care of herself, now on.

'That's my girl,' Mohan said. 'You're going to be fine. Email your resume to me and I'll forward it to the hospital tomorrow.' He put all the dirty dishes in the sink and began to tidy up the kitchen.

After setting the dining table, Shweta headed to the bedroom to check on Neha.

The curtains in the bedroom were drawn and the room was dark. Neha lay on the bed, her arm resting on her forehead.

'Hi!' Shweta said, softly.

Neha stirred and said a muffled 'Hey' not lifting her hand. 'So sorry, dear. This headache is killing me.'

Shweta went to sit by her bed and touched her shoulder. 'I would've come another day, if you'd told me.'

'Oh no, that's okay. Ria was looking forward to it, and Mohan offered to take over the kitchen. So...' Neha removed her hand and gently sat up. 'Come on, let's have lunch.'

'You know, you're so lucky, Neha.'

'Sure,' Neha said, with a forced smirk.

Mohan called out to them just then and they all gathered at the dining table. Shweta observed how Mohan doted on Neha. He was a wonderful man, kind and caring. The feeling overwhelmed her so much that she stopped eating and just stared at her plate.

'What's the matter?' Mohan asked.

Shweta shook her head even as she felt her eyes burn.

Ria saved her from a reply by butting in with news about school. Finally Neha had to ask her to hush and then Ria started whispering in Shweta's ear. It was a sumptuous meal and Shweta realized, too late, that she had overeaten again.

After lunch, Neha went back to her room and Mohan excused himself too. Shweta and Ria headed to the living room where Shweta sprawled on the couch in after-meal drowsiness and Ria knelt beside her, sketching the flowers on the porch.

'Look,' Ria said, showing Shweta what she had drawn.

Shweta looked at her drawing—a red hibiscus with a tall, stately stamen, waving outward. 'Pretty neat.' She ran her fingers through Ria's hair. 'You're really talented, Ria.'

Ria continued to draw. 'If you don't want to go back, Aunt S, you shouldn't. If I don't want to go to my friend's house for her birthday party, Ma can't force me.'

Shweta drew in a sharp breath. She had no idea Ria had heard her entire conversation with Mohan.

'And Ma can't force Papa to stay here if he doesn't like it,' Ria continued.

Shweta stared at her. 'Why would he not like it here?' She cupped

Ria's cheeks. 'Tell me, Ria.'

'Will you promise not to tell anyone if I tell you something?'

Suddenly, Shweta felt like she was intruding into their family matters. 'Look, Ria. If this is something between your parents—'

'But what if they will not be my parents together? What if Papa leaves and never comes back?'

'What do you mean?' Shweta stared at her.

Ria looked her straight in the eye. 'Papa came home very late last night, and Ma and he had a big fight this morning. Then Ma had a headache and she went to her room. What if Papa left us forever?' She threw her book to the side and buried her head in her knees. 'Do you think it'll happen, Aunt S?'

Neha deserved a sound scolding for scaring the poor child. What did she expect of doctors? That they should sit at home and cook lunch for their sisters-in-law? 'Have you told anybody else?'

'No,' Ria said, staring at the floor. 'I was going to send you an email secretly but Ma has my email password. I don't want her to find out. And Grandma will be very sad if I tell her.'

'Don't worry. I'll talk to your mother.' The drama queen! She was taking everything to such extremes! In fact, Shweta decided that both Mohan and Neha needed a talking-to.

But she never got to speak to Neha about it because Neha's headache didn't get better. She stayed in her room, and Mohan went out too. Eventually, Shweta left without bringing it up with either of them.

When she got home, Shweta went up to her room, switched on her computer and emailed her resume to Mohan. While all that Ria had told her still worried her, she knew that *she* had to get her life back on track as soon as possible, and she didn't want to delay it any further.

20

Simbu landed in Bangalore early on December 16. Keertana, Prabhu, Max, and Shweta were all at the airport to receive him.

Lekha had flown directly to Chennai, where things seemed to have stabilized a little, by then.

On 17th morning, Shweta's family also left for Chennai. When they arrived at the airport, they found that some sense of disaster still remained, but things were more or less back on track. Lekha's father had sent an Innova taxi to pick them up. But they were five of them with three large suitcases. It was a tight fit.

Forty-five minutes later they pulled into the driveway of The Grand Hotel that, unlike its name, was a medium-sized one. But as the driver pointed out to them, it was close to the wedding hall.

All of them checked into their rooms. Shweta, her parents, and the Prasads had three rooms on the third floor while Neha's family, Simbu, and Max had three on the second.

More rooms had been booked for the rest of the wedding guests who'd be arriving later.

Shweta dropped her suitcase on the bed and went for a lazy, long bath in the tub. They still had time to go for lunch with Lekha's family. After a relaxing bath, Shweta changed into a comfortable kurta and switched on the TV to while away some time before the get-together in the banquet hall downstairs.

She was interrupted by a call on the intercom. It was Neha.

'Did you hear that Niru is arranging the dinner party tonight?'

Shweta was surprised. 'No!'

'Simbu got in touch with him and asked him to take care of the food and drinks because he was worried about the situation here, since the floods.'

So, she'd meet Niru earlier than expected. She'd assumed that she'd catch a glimpse of him only on the day of the wedding. 'Will his girlfriend be with him?'

'Don't know,' Neha said, laughing.

Shweta could tell from the laugh that Neha was dying to find out who she was too. Just as Shweta was.

The girls were soon called downstairs to the banquet hall for lunch. By the time they reached, Lekha's family had already arrived.

Lekha's father, an affable-looking man with a pock-marked face, stood near the entrance with his brother and two sisters. He made the introductions to his siblings and Lekha's mother's siblings. Lekha's mother, a friendly woman with a dimpled smile, welcomed the guests warmly. She had three brothers and a sister.

Big family, Shweta thought.

Shweta and Neha moved towards the dining area where the buffet awaited them.

'Do you think the food is okay?' Shweta leaned in towards Neha and spoke in an undertone.

'Everything is being cooked hygienically. This part of Chennai is one of the few unaffected areas. I had to ask, especially for Ria's sake.'

'Where is Ria?' Shweta asked.

Neha pointed to the far end of the reception outside the dining area where Ria was hanging out with Max and Simbu. Max and Simbu had hit it off soon after they'd met. Ria was talking animatedly to both of them, pointing to the large mural of elephants on the wall. The trio seemed to be having a good time.

A line formed for the buffet. Shweta's stomach growled at the aroma of hot puris and potato gravy. The big, Indian wedding lunch spread looked inviting. Shweta filled her plate, found an empty seat at an unoccupied table and began to dig in. Neha joined her a few moments later.

Lekha and Simbu suddenly made a grand entry into the dining hall, leading to a hush in the room, followed by audible sighs, and cheering for the handsome couple. Lekha's pictures belied her gorgeous looks. Tall and lean like a model, thought Shweta; she was a stunner.

Lekha bowed and touched Prabhu's feet. Prabhu beamed. Shweta could see he'd been bowled over.

Lekha and Simbu stopped by at all the tables, greeting their guests.

As she ate, conversed with Neha, and watched the people around her, Shweta's eyes caught sight of a fluttering pink stole. The owner was a young woman, standing with her back to them. Her shiny mid-length black hair, cut in stylish layers, fell in smooth waves down her back.

Her long-distance examination of this vision was cut short when Simbu and Lekha stopped by their table. During their brief conversation with Neha and Shweta, Lekha suddenly exclaimed, 'I have to introduce you to my first cousin, Trisha,' as she gestured to the girl with the pink stole to come over. She tugged at Trisha's sleeve, drawing her to their table.

'Trisha, these are my lovely sisters-in-law, Neha and Shweta.'

Trisha had a charming smile.

Neha, who was easily the most curious person at any party, jumped in with a question, right off the bat. 'So, what do you do, Trisha?'

Trisha fluttered her eyelids and flashed another dazzling smile at her audience before replying. 'I'm studying graphic design in Pune.'

'And, she's a wonderful singer too,' Lekha piped in. 'And the next most eligible young woman after me.' She winked and continued,

'And we hope she meets a special someone at this wedding, right?' Lekha gave her cousin a naughty smile.

It was obvious Lekha was very fond of her young cousin.

Trisha smiled coyly. 'Oh come on, Lekha. The right man at the right time, as they say.' Everyone, including Simbu, laughed. Trisha preened at her clever wisecrack.

The group moved away from their table after a few more pleasantries and Shweta went back to eating and people watching.

The line at the buffet counter had grown. She saw Trisha join it and a portly older woman stand right behind her. Trisha fidgeted and made faces when the woman behind moved too close.

The line moved incredibly slowly and then a moment later, something odd at the buffet caught Shweta's attention.

Trisha dropped a spoon as she was walking by the buffet table. She bent down and picked it up, then looked to her right, then left, and satisfied that no one was watching, sneaked it back into the pile of clean spoons.

Shweta's mouth fell agape.

Then, moving forward a couple of steps in the line, Trisha ladled a dahi vada into her bowl. Unfortunately, it missed and plopped on to the floor.

Instead of warning the woman behind her to watch out for the food spill, Trisha quickly ladled another vada into her bowl, this time more carefully, and moved on to the next dish on the counter.

Sure enough, the woman behind her stepped into the gooey vada, didn't realise it, and continued to toddle along, leaving a messy food trail along the floor.

Ugh!

Shweta turned away and focused on finishing her food. She later joined the post-lunch patter with the rest of her aunts and cousins. Something told her there would be lots to keep her entertained the next few days until the wedding.

21

Shweta and Neha were looking forward to the party later that evening. As they descended the stairs to the dance hall, the blaring music told them that the party was already in full swing.

Neha, in a red khadi silk saree, her face glowing and her wavy, luxuriant, chestnut brown hair falling to her waist, and Shweta, in an exquisite green Anarkali suit with silver thread-work, three-inch heels and straightened hair, made their way through the banquet hall to reach the dimly lit, disco-light blazing dance hall.

The hall was beautifully decorated. Several round tables draped with satin white cloth and red trim stood all around, with four or five high-backed satin-covered chairs around each table. The bar counter at the far end of the hall buzzed with guests waiting for their drinks. The DJ took up another corner to the right of the bar, leaving enough space for a spacious dance floor in the front, where a few couples grooved to catchy Bollywood tunes.

Shweta did a quick scan of the room and her eyes fell on a familiar face at the bar counter. She did a double-take when she realized it was Niru. He sported a formal shirt, blazer, and trousers. A silver stud glimmered in his right ear. In ten years he had changed beyond recognition. Gone was the gangly boy she'd known since childhood.

He was handing out drinks from behind the bar counter, and laughing at something a few women at the counter were saying. His smile was open and warm, his laughter dazzling. All of it brought a strange flutter to Shweta's chest. She turned her gaze away and headed towards the table that Neha had picked.

A thud to the right stopped her in her tracks. She whipped around and saw a woman in a pale yellow saree slumped on the dance floor.

As Shweta made her way to help her, a small crowd had gathered at the spot. The heavyset woman remained on the floor, in a pool of her glittering yellow, partly undone saree. The music was still on and it took a while for everybody to realize what had happened. The woman was escorted to a nearby table, where she plonked herself on a chair to catch her breath. Looks of concern and murmurs of shock rippled through the room. The music wound to a stop. Helped by two guests, the limping woman was finally led out of the dance hall. Luckily, she wasn't badly hurt. The situation was forgotten soon after she left; people went back to their laughter and babble, and the music came on again.

It took a few moments for Shweta to regain her composure and realize that she was stranded near the dance floor and feeling a little dizzy. She hadn't eaten anything since lunch, she realized, and hoped to find at least a small snack before dinner was served at the buffet out in the banquet hall. Thoughts of a cool drink to go with it preoccupied her as she made her way to the bar.

Niru was at the counter, flirting with abandon with a lady wearing a backless blouse. Shweta waited for him to turn to her but the backless blouse had his undivided attention. She cleared her throat loudly but the music drowned the sound. She tried again. 'Excuse me,' she said, standing on her toes and shouting. 'A mojito and a plate of spicy potato wedges, please.'

He still hadn't noticed her. 'Excuse me,' she said, finally tapping the backless blouse on the shoulder. 'If you're done, I'd like to place an order, please.'

Backless blouse turned around. She had to be at least fifty. 'Sorry, dear,' she said. 'I was just catching up with my nephew here.'

Shweta bit her lip, guilty that she had literally pushed her aside. The lady moved on with a quick bye to Niru.

Niru turned to Shweta, looking amused. 'Yes, ma'am!' He started to say something else and then as if he'd realized something, he stopped abruptly. 'Right-O!' he said, and pulled out a tall glass.

'There's something vaguely familiar about you,' he said, his brandy brown eyes twinkling as he shouted over the music. He peered at her for a moment. 'But no, you don't exactly remind me of her.' Then he went about making the drink, squeezing a large wedge of lemon into the glass.

Shweta set her clutch on the counter and cocked her head. 'Remind you of whom?' She had to shout back over the blaring music.

'Ah!' he said, as he crushed the mint leaves. 'I haven't seen this person in a while but she's not easy to forget.' He mixed in the sugar syrup vigorously, shouting at the top of his voice the whole time. 'You'll know what I mean if you see her. She had curly hair that stood up like bristles on her crown.' He lifted his hands inches over his head to demonstrate the sort of bouffant he was describing by wriggling his fingers above his head, and chuckled.

Idiot! Shweta pursed her lips but he wasn't done.

'It looked completely silly, if you ask me,' he continued, shouting again, and so totally embarrassing her. She was glad she was the only one standing at the counter right then. 'And she's...well, to put it nicely, on the healthier side...She wore big, black-rimmed glasses that made her look like a grandma. She was also slightly cock-eyed and...Ouch!' Shweta had picked up her clutch from the counter and whacked him. He ducked when he saw another one coming. 'Ouch, Shweta, that hurts.' He came up, rubbing the side of his shoulder, and looked at her accusingly.

'Serves you right!' she said, glaring. 'Let me tell you, you got off lightly because you were behind the counter or I'd have kicked your smart ass too.'

'Sass!' Niru laughed, eyes crinkling at the corners. 'Someone has changed a lot.'

'And you haven't changed at all,' Shweta snapped back.

'Where did the goldilocks go? They looked kind of cute,' he said, smirking, his hands doing a wriggle-dance on top of his head, again. 'I see you got it straightened and all. And, you've gotten rid of your glasses too. My, my, you look different. I wouldn't have recognized you if I hadn't heard your squeaky voice.' He chuckled shamelessly.

'You!' Shweta aimed her clutch at him again.

He caught her arm in mid-air and gave her a teasing smile. 'I see you still have that sizzling temper.'

When I'm not a bag of nerves around you! 'Let go,' she shouted, twisting to free her arm. He pulled her close and flicked her nose before he let go of her.

She glared at him as she rubbed her arm to ease the pain of his rough hold.

Her order of potato wedges came up just then. Handing over her drink, Niru waved a goodbye in her direction.

Shweta hmphed, picked up the wedges, and turned to go. Glancing back just as she was leaving, she shouted so he wouldn't miss her words. 'You haven't changed one bit, Niraj Karthik. Not one teeny-weeny bit.'

Behind her she heard him laugh as she made her way to the table where Max and Neha were sitting.

22

'We're waiting for our drinks,' Neha said, thumping her hands on the table eagerly as Shweta joined her and Max.

Shweta sat down and tapped her feet to the music. She took a sip of her mojito, picked up a potato wedge, and passed the rest around the table. Lekha and a couple of her cousins, including Ms Pink Stole, aka Trisha, were headed their way. Lekha wore a red off-shoulder gown, her hair curled into waves.

'I've ordered a pitcher of the best cocktail there is,' Trisha announced as soon as she reached their table. 'My uncle is a star cocktail mixer.' Everyone cheered as she flipped her hair and sat down with a smug look. Then seeing Max, the only man in their midst, she giggled. 'You look like a Krishna at this table.'

Max laughed just because everybody else did. He had obviously never heard of the mythological hero who the women at the table were laughing about.

The crowds cheered as the DJ played some zesty, new, Bollywood numbers. The cocktail pitcher soon arrived at the table. Glasses filled up quickly. Shweta accepted one as well, despite being wary of drinking alcohol. It tasted like spiked cola. Waiters brought finger foods to the table. Some of the guests chose to sit at the tables while some danced for a while and took a break every now and then to sip their drinks.

Suddenly the DJ put on Tamil songs and there was a loud cheer. Most people jumped at the chance to show off some funky moves on the floor. Neha grabbed Max and led him to the dance floor. Lekha and Simbu were also dancing. Trisha and Shweta were the only ones at their table without partners. Suddenly Trisha rose and headed to the bar counter. There she talked to her uncle and made arrangements for him to man the bar so that she could dance with Niru. Niru and Trisha moved to the dance floor. Shweta was the only one left behind at the table.

She took a long sip of her drink and felt herself loosen up. Niru was at her table almost immediately, and she looked up at him surprised. 'Back for me?' she snorted and then bit her tongue when she saw that he'd just come to leave Trisha's drink at the table. As he turned to go back, he leaned close to her and whispered, 'Come and dance with me on the next song. I dare you, you wimp!'

She blinked and caught his naughty grin. She sniffed, glaring at him as he headed back to Trisha.

Just the sort of idiot who would make use of every stupid opportunity to get on her nerves! Shweta eyed Niru from her vantage spot. He was facing Trisha and dancing really close to her. They were swaying their bodies in tune with the music. He knelt in front of Trisha, while she leaned in really close, saying something in his ear, her long drop earrings touching his cheeks. Something stirred inside Shweta. The idiot was having fun with a girl he hardly knew.

He laughed at something she said and Trisha pulled him closer and closer.

Shweta gulped down the rest of her drink and rose. She wanted to dance too, even if she didn't particularly care for what Niru had said. She went up to Ria, sitting at the very next table with another cousin. 'Come, let's dance. You and me.'

'Me?' Ria asked, surprised.

Come on, dear. Your Ma and Papa are having fun. You and me

can have some fun too, right?' Shweta pointed to Neha and Mohan on the dance floor and the bar respectively, to prove her point.

Ria rose reluctantly and followed Shweta to the dance floor. Pretty soon they were close to where Niru and Trisha were caught up in their cosy gyrations.

Niru was letting Trisha take a spin and they were into some really intricate steps when he turned to Shweta and said, 'You're supposed to dance, not shuffle.'

'Mind your own business,' she snapped, and he laughed.

The songs progressed from Tamil to disco to a bit of Bharatanatyam to Bhangra. Niru and Trisha showed off some cool Bhangra moves, lifting one leg, touching their toes and pumping their hands up, while dancing to the *Balle Balle*. Ria seemed to be having a great time too. Come to think of it, Shweta herself hadn't had such fun in a long while, even if she was mostly only looking around and enjoying the dance moves of people around her.

The DJ changed the sound track to a pop song. Trisha began to dirty dance, rocking her pelvis in a circle as her hips swung from side to side like she was moving a hula hoop with her hips. She seemed to be having the time of her life grinding her hips into Niru's and—

Shweta turned her eyes away. Niru was laughing at her. She scowled and moved away, but not before she had caught him mouthing 'wimp' at her. It was just too much to take. She came around, hoping to step on his foot to teach him a lesson, when the heel of her shoe gave in. She stumbled and almost fell. To top it all, the strap of her shoe snapped and she could no longer move without dragging her shoes beneath her feet.

Frustrated, she gave up and tottered off the dance floor, bristling that nobody even noticed her leave. She took off her shoes and held them in her hand as she headed back towards her room in a huff. If it weren't for Niru rankling her, she'd be still enjoying herself, she thought in frustration.

The door to her parents' room was open. She had just crossed it on her way to her own, when she heard her father call her.

She backtracked and peeked into the room. Prabhu was seated on the lounge chair, puffing at his pipe. He beckoned her in.

Keertana was on the bed, looking at her anxiously when she stepped inside gingerly.

'I just spoke to Raj and he'll be here as soon as he can,' Prabhu said, pinning her with an ominous stare. 'If you had an iota of respect for your family, you wouldn't have put us through this shame. No one, no one in our family has had to bear what I'm going through today. We didn't know we had raised such a wimp.'

That was the third time tonight. Did everyone think she was a wimp? Well, it was time to show them otherwise. 'You know what?' she said. 'I don't care if Raj comes and I don't care if he begs me to go with him because I've had enough of people telling me what to do. I'm going to do whatever I like.'

Prabhu's mouth fell open. Shweta spun around and strode out of the room before he had a chance to react.

She reached her room, unlocked the door, changed into a different pair of heels and headed back to the dance hall. She took the stairs that were closer to her room, so that she didn't have to pass by her parents' room again.

Once in the dance hall, Shweta sought Niru who was still dancing with Trisha, and strode up to him. Trisha's arms were moving all over Niru's body. She looked surprised when Shweta tapped Niru on the shoulder. Shweta grabbed Niru by the arm and led him to the other side of the dance floor. He turned to her and she shouted in his ears, 'Okay, I'm no wimp now, am I? Now show me what you got.'

It was fun to watch the confusion on his face. Just when she thought she had him cornered, the DJ put on a slow dance number. Suddenly Ed Sheeran was crooning *Thinking Out Loud*. Shweta's hands flew to her mouth in surprise. It was her favourite song and to think that she was standing staring like a jellyfish into the face of this idiot. She glanced around, inwardly hoping she could palm him off back to Trisha. But Trisha had already latched on to Max.

'*Take me into your loving arms,*' Sheeran crooned. Niru met her gaze and held out his hand. She had to take it. Then with one hand at her waist and the other in hers, he held her close and they began to sway to the soft, sensuous voice. All the while, Shweta's heart thudded so loud she thought she could actually hear it.

Niru led her into a twirl and pulled her slowly back in. She collided against his chest and he smiled. '*Place your head on my beating heart…*' Her cheeks grew hot and she hid her face by his ear. He leaned in and whispered close to her ear. 'I was wrong. You haven't changed.'

She pulled apart and squinted at him. 'What do you mean?'

He laughed and grazed her cheek playfully. 'First,' he said, 'I think, we should get a nice cool beer or something. You look like you could use a drink.'

Holding her hand, Niru led Shweta to the bar counter, where they perched themselves on bar stools as he ordered two beers.

'I don't drink beer,' she said.

'Okay, a mojito for the lady, please,' he called to Trisha's uncle who was still manning the counter.

Trisha's uncle winked at him and got busy with the order.

Niru swivelled to face her. 'So tell me, how have you been?'

'I've been called a wimp three times tonight. So, obviously not too good.' She was muttering but he caught it.

'Three times?' He laughed.

Uncle brought the drinks to the counter. Niru raised his bottle in cheers to her. She only smirked in reply. 'Hey,' he said, tipping her chin, 'I was only kidding.'

Bloody hell! When had he become so nice?

He took a swig from the bottle and swallowed. His eyes gleamed under the overhead lights. 'You remember the time?' he said.

'Which time?' She cupped her ear. The DJ had put on deafening music again.

'The time you stood guard for us?' he said louder.

'At the drinks party?' she shouted over the music.

He nodded. 'And your father busted us?'

'And I got into trouble too.' Shweta turned to stare at the floor.

'Like I have now.'

'Trouble still following you around?'

She pretended not to hear that.

He took another swig from the bottle. 'Sorry,' he said. 'I heard about Raj.'

Was he teasing her again? All the closeness she'd felt moments before disappeared. Maybe she'd had one too many drinks but the words were out of her mouth, just dying to be said. 'Aren't you happy you were right all along?'

'Me?' It was Niru's turn to be surprised. 'Hey, nobody knows if they're right,' he said.

But Shweta was already off the bar stool by then.

'Hey, wait!' he called after her.

She'd heard enough of Raj for one night. Nobody could understand where she was coming from. Not her father, and now, not even her childhood friend. Before Niru could say another word, Shweta was off, striding across the room, her eyes lowered so she wouldn't have to talk to anyone else tonight.

23

In her room after lunch the next day, Shweta was lounging on her bed and surfing TV channels when a knock sounded at the door. It was Ria.

'Hi, Aunt S,' she said, bounding in and flopping on the bed. 'Did you hear Trisha and Max went out for coffee today?'

'What?' Shweta rolled her eyes. 'So, he's not coming here?'

'He's coming now. He said he's bringing brownies for us.'

The words were just out of Ria's mouth, when there was another knock on the door. Ria ran to open it and Max entered, beaming, the brownies in one hand and a coffee cup that he'd brought from his room in the other.

Shweta scowled, mad at him for going off with Trisha, but when he apologised, it made her laugh.

'I couldn't help it. Trisha said she wanted to show me the first Starbucks in Chennai. She insisted!' he said, sheepishly. 'But I got us some brownies.' He placed them on the table and switched on the coffee maker to make coffee for them.

'Coffee for me too?' Ria shook her head with excitement.

'As long as you don't tell your mum,' Max said. Shweta glared at him but he shrugged it off with a smile. It was true; it was difficult to get anything past Neha where Ria was concerned. Even Max got the feeling that Ria was being over-protected and smothered 'for her own good'.

With the steaming coffee and the brownies, Max and Ria curled up on the bed to watch a movie.

Shweta plugged her hard disk into the hotel's TV and scrolled down the list of movies, most of which were Hindi.

'Does he understand Hindi?' Ria asked, surprised.

Max and Shweta laughed. 'I like the beautiful women and the songs,' Max said.

'He doesn't mind,' Shweta told Ria. 'Besides we only watch those that have English subtitles so Max should be okay.'

'Ah, there's *Pretty Woman*. I just saw it on the list. Can we watch it?' Ria said, screaming with delight.

'That's an adult movie,' Shweta said.

'Please.' Ria pouted. 'Ma never lets me watch adult movies.'

'What do you watch?' Max asked her.

'*Nemo, Ice Age.*'

Shweta shook her head. 'I'm sorry I don't have any of those,' she said and continued to scroll down the list. Then she caught another name on the screen. 'Ok, *Ramona and Beezus* is probably the closest children's fantasy adventure movie I have.' She caught Max's curious stare. 'Don't know why I saved it,' she said. 'Guess I like Ginnifer Goodwin!' She shrugged by way of explaining her eclectic collection.

Ria jumped with excitement. 'Yay, Ramona it is.'

They were all in splits when Ramona yelled the bad word 'Guts!' at the dining table. Shweta had loved that part every time she watched it and the rest of the movie too. It had probably something to do with the chemistry between Aunt Beatrice and that no-good boyfriend of hers.

They were in the middle of the movie when another knock sounded at the door. Shweta realized they hadn't locked the door when Max had come in.

'Shweta!' Neha yelled, as she pushed open the door and entered. 'I thought you had more sense than this.'

Shweta started and immediately hit the pause button.

'Why is Ria watching an adult movie with you?' Neha hollered.

Aunt Beatrice and her boyfriend were in the jeep, talking. Shweta couldn't understand the fuss. It seemed like a harmless scene but obviously not to Neha.

Neha then turned to Ria, glaring. 'I've been looking for you everywhere. Shouldn't you tell me before you go? Let's go now.'

Ria threw a tantrum, saying she didn't want to miss this part, but Neha wasn't having it. She dragged a wailing Ria off with a warning and slammed the door behind her.

Phew!

Shweta and Max exchanged helpless glances. Shweta sighed and restarted the movie. There was nothing else to do except return to it anyway. Nobody felt like doing much sightseeing because there was so much else to do before the wedding, and only two more days to go. The mehendi party was scheduled for late evening that day so they had plenty of time to kill until then.

Max rose to leave after the movie ended. 'Will we get our hands painted too?' he asked Shweta on his way out, one hand still on the door knob.

'I will. It's only for the women.' She laughed. 'But you can have fun with the music and the food.'

'Mmm...more food. There's just so much food every day.'

'That's an Indian wedding for you,' Shweta said, waving a goodbye so he could leave to get ready for the evening party.

He stopped at the door and turned around, grinning. 'By the way, don't you want to know why I went out with Trisha?'

Shweta's antennae went up immediately. She made a face at him. 'I thought she wanted you to.'

'I was helping you.' He flashed her a smile.

She cocked her head. 'Helping me? For what? I didn't say I

needed any help.'

'Oh, I'd say you needed a lot of help last night, especially in getting Trisha off someone.' Max winked at her.

'I don't know what you're talking about.' Shweta threw a pillow at him in mock frustration. He ducked and slipped outside, shutting the door behind him.

Shweta lay back on the bed and hugged a pillow. *Was it so obvious that she had wanted to dance with him?*

* * *

Shweta's father hadn't spoken to her since the night before and now Neha was upset with her over the movie. So when Lekha called her on the intercom, asking her to come to the mehendi early, she'd already lost the excitement to go.

'You can finish with your mehendi early and save yourself from waiting in the lines later,' Lekha said.

What Lekha said made sense. Who liked lines anyway?

But when she burned a hole while ironing the dress she was about to wear for the mehendi that evening, it was the last straw. She gave up and slumped on the bed, her head buried in her hands.

Someone knocked at her door, and she hoped it was Neha, but it was her mother. 'Aren't you ready yet?'

She burst into tears.

'What happened?'

'Why does everything have to go wrong with me?' Shweta cried.

Her mother came in and saw the dress laid out on the bed. Right on the beautifully patterned yoke in soft crepe was a gaping hole. 'Oh!' she exclaimed. 'What have you done now?'

'How could I not have been careful?' Shweta cried. 'Now what am I going to wear to the party?'

Her mother shook her head and sighed. 'Why don't you go out and buy a new one? Anyway, what else can you do?'

Shweta pouted. 'How can I go now and who will go with me?'

She doubted that Neha would agree to come. And Lekha had told her that Simbu had taken Max along for some shopping for the wedding.

Keertana checked her watch. 'It's only five. Call Neha. She'll go with you.'

'You know Neha, Ma. She won't be free now and she also has to get Ria ready. Why don't you come with me? Please?' She tugged at her hand and swinging the door open, said, 'Go quickly, tell Papa, and let's leave.'

Her mother shook her head firmly. 'Not me, Shweta. I have to stay with Papa. I'll take you downstairs and call a cab to take you. Just be quick. You'll have to do this alone.'

Shweta let her mother accompany her downstairs. Maybe she'd change her mind at the last minute if the cab driver looked 'dangerous' (her mother's words for a shady looking driver).

But just as they were passing the reception, they spotted Niru exit from the banquet hall.

'What are you doing here?' Keertana asked him.

'I just came by to drop some things for the party.' He eyed Shweta with a confused look. 'And where are you off to?' he said, as though he knew she was headed outside.

'She needs a new dress for the party. The one we brought along is ruined,' Keertana explained.

'That's pretty last minute,' he said, stuffing his hands into his pockets. 'Need help?'

Why was he being all nice and helpful suddenly? 'No, I don't think so. I'm sure you're very busy with the party this evening.'

'It's no problem at all,' Niru said. 'I'd be happy to help.'

Shweta almost refused him again but Keertana spoke before she could say anything. 'So kind of you, Niru. Can you accompany her to the store and get her back quickly? I can't leave now and I'm not so sure she'll do well on her own.'

Shweta glared at her mother. That's not what she'd said to her just a few minutes ago.

Keertana wasted no time in herding them out. There was not a single cab in sight. 'Oh, now what do we do?' Keertana said. Niru fished out his phone from his pocket and booked an Ola cab, much to her delight.

A few minutes later Keertana had seen them into a cab and watched them go, waving them off with a big smile.

24

Shweta and Niru headed off to the nearest clothing store. As she didn't know the city at all, having Niru with her was a big relief, though Shweta wasn't going to say that out loud. He gave the driver the name of the mall, and she finally relaxed in the air-conditioned cab.

Just as she'd started enjoying the quiet ride with the sights rolling past her window, Niru cleared his throat and said to her, 'I hope you're not angry with me?'

Shweta continued to look out of the window. 'What should I be angry for?'

'Look!' He took a deep breath. 'Consider this an apology. I didn't mean to say whatever it was that I said, though for the millionth time, I can't remember what it was, and believe me, I've tried to think of what exactly I was saying, but like I said, I don't know what it was, and I really don't know what upset you. If something has upset you, I apologize, and let's forget—'

'Shut up!'

'What?'

She scoffed. 'You sound like a quacking duck. Just forget it.'

He grinned. 'Ok, so now we're even. I hope you're happy that you hurt my feelings too. Just now.'

'Really?' She smirked.

'Really.' He touched his chest in a sign of mock pain.

Shweta turned back to watch the cityscape on her side as Niru fell silent again.

Then, remembering something all of a sudden, she turned around to him. 'What happened with you and Ms Italian?'

A shadow crossed his face. She couldn't understand his expression. Was he offended?

'Let's just say that it doesn't matter,' he said curtly.

She knit her eyebrows.

'Some things are better left unexplained rather than analysed and killed to death.' Niru shrugged. 'It didn't work out and there was not a single thing I could do.'

She hadn't known. 'I'm sorry,' she said.

'Love and girlfriend wait for no man.' He chuckled and she felt the tension between them dissolve.

By then, they'd reached their stop. They paid the cab driver and got out.

'Let me show you the latest Anarkali kurtas,' the salesgirl told her when they headed to the counter in a shop. She showed Shweta a beautiful, long, flowy pink dress-like kurta that almost touched her toes.

Shweta eyed it appreciatively and then looked towards Niru for his reaction.

Her glance was met with a frown.

'Not this one,' she said to the salesgirl. 'Can you show me something else, please?'

While the salesgirl was selecting a few more pieces to show her, she asked Niru, 'So I'd heard you were in Dubai. When did you get back?'

'Some time after your wedding.'

She blushed. 'Yes, I had no idea where you were.'

'After quitting my job in Dubai, I finally decided to move back to India and join a restaurant in Chennai run by a friend and alumnus of the institute I graduated from. Now I have the opportunity to open a new restaurant in Bangalore. In the meantime, Simbu needed me here, so here I am.'

'So has life turned out the way you planned?' she asked.

'Pretty much. What about you?'

Before she could reply, the salesgirl spread an array of new Anarkali kurtas for her to choose from.

They rifled through the pile, and Shweta picked a few to try out. Niru plonked himself on the sofa outside the trial room and waited for her. He watched as she tried out one dress after another. Mostly, he frowned at everything she tried on. If he nodded at something, she thought it was too expensive. Doing the trial rounds, she was reminded of her shopping with Shipra in the US, and she felt a sudden pang. She wished Shipra were here now.

Finally Shweta came out of the trial room and plopped on the sofa next to Niru.

'Liked nothing?' he asked.

She shook her head.

'Let's get the first one and get out of here. We're already very late.'

She looked back at the counter in dismay. What was she going to wear tonight?

'This one will suit you,' the salesgirl said, pulling out a teal blue Anarkali that looked gorgeous. She held it up for Shweta.

'Come on,' Niru urged, 'Make up your mind.'

The teal blue felt right. It was soft and when she held it against herself, it complemented her skin tone beautifully. 'I'll take this,' she told the salesgirl, excited at last.

They headed back in an auto because one was standing right outside the mall; they decided it was best not to waste time waiting for a cab.

Shweta picked up the thread from their earlier conversation. 'Is this what you always wanted since the time you announced you wanted to be a chef?'

'An announcement that was met with a giggle and scorn from you.' He stuck his tongue out at her.

'That was so long ago. I had no sense then.'

He laughed. 'That was all the more reason for me to prove myself to the girl with the pigtails.' He held his hands up to the side of his ears.

Shweta slapped his hand and grinned. 'For whatever it is worth, I'm sorry *now*.'

'What about you?' he asked. 'Are you going back to the US after the wedding?' He raised his hands when her eyebrows shot up. 'Hey! It's a friendly question. You don't have to tell me anything if you don't want to.'

Should she tell him about Raj? 'It's not going to get sorted out, and I know it won't,' she blurted out instead.

He stared at her. 'Not sorted out, like the time when you thought your dad would never forgive you when you were the only girl among us at the alcohol party?'

'Papa won't rest until I've packed myself back to the marriage I left.'

If he realized she'd told him too much, he ignored it. 'Don't all fathers want their daughters happily settled?' he asked.

'And mothers want their sons happily settled too.' Shweta narrowed her eyes at him.

Niru chuckled. 'I see! Now you've turned the tables on me.' Suddenly he became serious. 'My ex-girlfriend, Lisa, and I parted ways in Dubai. She didn't want to come back to India with me.'

Shweta gave him a puzzled look. 'Oh!'

'I knew you were just dying to find out,' he said, flicking her nose. 'Yes, we're officially broken up.'

As Shweta relaxed beside him, it somehow felt like old times again.

The wind blew her hair and sent it across his face. He brushed it aside, laughing. A light drizzle had started outside and the air had turned cooler. Water sprayed on her hands through the open side of the auto. She was jostled against him as the auto rattled on the bumpy road, the hair on his arm brushing against her, and giving her goose bumps. It was getting dark outside, but the enjoyable ride and the promise of a wonderful time afterwards kept her in good spirits.

They parted ways when they reached the hotel. Shweta went to her room, hugging the huge bag that held her dress, and Niru said he was going back to the dance hall to continue with the arrangements for the mehendi party.

* * *

When Shweta came down to the dance hall, it looked transformed. Red and yellow roses adorned the walls and the makeshift stage. There were bouquets everywhere and urns filled with flowers. The room smelt of rose attar, generously sprayed.

Lekha was already seated in the middle of the stage decorated with muslin drapes. She looked like a princess, wearing a band of flowers on her head and dressed in an orange sleeveless kurti and a rich pink lehenga. Two mehendi artists worked on her simultaneously, creating thick, green, intricate mehendi designs on her hands and feet.

Many girls and women sat on thick pillow seats surrounding the stage, where more mehendi artistes pored over their hands, creating beautiful patterns on their palms. Shweta gazed at the beauty of their work and waited for her turn. She'd decided to get just one of her hands done so she could still use the other.

Stalls of chaat and paani puri had been put up at one end of the room and Bollywood music played from the stereo placed at the other end. The centre of the room was left empty for those who felt like dancing. Many women with mehendi-covered hands took to the dance floor, and moved with awkward steps as they tried keeping their hands out of the way.

Shweta felt like she had been transported to some college festival. Everyone dressed in their finery mingled with everyone else, laughter bounced off the walls, and the DJ addressed the crowd from time to time as he brought in frequent transitions in his playlist.

She spotted Niru's mother in one corner. Savitri walked over when she caught Shweta's eye.

'How are you, my dear? It's so good to see that you're having a good time.'

'Same to you, Auntie,' Shweta said.

Savitri pulled her into a nearby seat and sat next to her. 'Don't think I'm intruding,' she said, coming straight to the point. 'But boys from good families don't come every day. You should reconsider your decision and reconcile as fast as you can. Things can certainly go out of hand if you wait too long.'

Shweta looked long and deep into her eyes, and then held her hands in hers. 'Auntie, I think you should find Niru a suitable girl.'

Auntie looked flummoxed at the change of subject. She took a while to answer. Moving her hand over Shweta's, she looked warmly into her eyes and said, 'There was a time when I thought another girl was more suitable for him, but then he didn't have the courage to ask her. I think it's too late now to reconsider our choices. But sometimes, first loves are...'

She didn't know Niru loved someone else. Whatever became of her then? Shweta waited for Savitri to continue, mulling over what she meant.

Savitri shrugged and went on, 'What do you think about Trisha? Do you think she'll make a good match for Niru?'

Shweta felt uncomfortable at the question.

Savitri squeezed her hand and continued, 'You should talk to Niru. Make him see sense about settling down. How long is he going to travel and think only about work?'

Shweta turned her gaze away. 'I don't think Trisha will make a good match for him,' she said softly.

'Really? Why? Is she not good for him?'

Just then her turn for applying the mehendi was announced and Shweta was saved from a reply. She took her leave and headed to claim one of the plush pillow seats.

25

While the mehendi artiste, a girl who was around Shweta's age, was drawing intricate patterns on Shweta's palms, the lights in the hall flickered.

'I wonder what's happening today?' the girl said. 'Hope there won't be an electricity cut. The lights have been flickering all evening.'

Shweta looked at the design on her hand. The girl had drawn dots, lines, dashes, loops, paisleys, and spirals, by gently squeezing out the cool, green paste through a cone on to her palm.

People milled around them in the hall. Shweta spotted Neha and Max standing by the chaat counter, Neha showing him how to put the entire paani puri into his mouth in one go. She turned to Shweta and waved. It appeared as if Max had brought her around to a good mood. Thank God for that! Ria was with her grandmother, showing her what the mehendi artiste had drawn on her hand. Lekha was still getting her hands and legs done. For the amount of skin she had to get covered, Shweta knew it would easily take her about two to three hours.

A group of girls crowded around the DJ, requesting a number. When he started playing their song, they were joined by an equal number of boys and they took centre stage on the dance floor, gyrating to rehearsed steps for the Bollywood item number they were presenting.

Shweta was quite surprised to see the pains that Lekha and her cousins had taken to make the mehendi party a success. Although Shweta had told Max not to expect what he'd seen in *Queen*, here was Lekha's family, integrating the best of North Indian practices into their South Indian wedding routine. It was certainly a lot more fun than a traditional Malayali wedding ceremony that usually lasted only a few minutes.

The crowds inside the hall increased as time went by. Entering late appeared to be so cool. In fact, people were just warming up. A drinks counter opened up at one corner and uncles from both sides of the family gravitated towards it. Niru and a help were manning it.

The girl's and the boy's families mingled freely. Shweta hadn't spotted her father yet, though her mother had arrived and was busy chatting with some women.

Suddenly a singing programme was announced and Trisha, the acclaimed singer of the family, was requested to be the first to take the microphone. She tried to wriggle her way out but finally succumbed to the cheering and nudging. She cleared her voice and asked the DJ if he had the Karaoke track for the song that she wanted to sing. Luckily for her, he nodded and she began, with *Kaisi Paheli* from the movie *Parineeta*.

It was Shweta's favourite song too, and Trisha, true to her reputation, turned out to be quite a good singer. After the applause at the end of her song and requests for a few more, which she happily obliged, she stepped away. The show continued for a while with a few more enthusiastic people joining in.

Shweta laughed when they managed to push even Simbu into singing although he swore that he was only a bathroom singer. But she had to say, he sang *Yaaron Dosti*—an anthem of sorts that celebrated friendship—pretty well. She beamed when her brother ended his rendition to whistles and table-banging applause.

The party went on. With her mehendi on one hand, Shweta decided she needed to get something to eat. She was glad she'd got only one hand done because she could always use her other hand unlike a few women who had to be fed as both their hands were out of commission. She giggled at the funny sight—grown-ups opening their mouths to be stuffed with paani puri or chaat. Lekha was being fed right where she sat because her mehendi would take some more time.

Shweta went to the paani puri counter and ordered a bowl for herself. She took the first paani puri she was served, brought it up to her mouth, and stuffed it in entirely. But that first crunchy puri was so spicy, her tongue was on fire. She had forgotten to ask for less of the spicy chutney. Looking around for water, she made her way to the bar counter to check if they could help her.

'Water! Water!' She fanned her mouth, looking desperately at Niru.

'Hold on,' he said, taking out a bottle from one of the racks. Opening it in a jiffy, he offered it to her.

The lights flickered again and she looked up wondering what was wrong.

Trisha made it to the counter just then. 'Hey,' she said to Niru. 'Can I also get a glass of water, please?' She continued to flash her smile at him while he pulled out a bottle and a glass.

Shweta felt better after she'd downed almost half the bottle.

'Why don't you ladies have a drink?' Niru said as he offered Trisha the water. 'Can I make you a special cocktail?'

Trisha fluttered her eyelashes and Shweta noticed how she planted her hands on the counter next to Niru's. She had long nails painted in red and a large blue flower ring adorning her middle finger. Compared to hers, Shweta's hands were embarrassingly plain and unpainted.

Suddenly, as she was thinking of how ugly her hands looked, the lights flickered again and went out.

'Oh no!' Trisha wailed.

Niru tried to calm her down. 'The generator will be on in a minute. Just stay where you are.'

Shweta placed her hands on the bar counter for something to hold. Nobody was going to judge her not-so-pretty hands now. Unless, of course, the lights came on and Trisha noticed them. Before she knew it, though, a hand clamped on one of hers. Shweta shrugged it away, but it came back, the hold stronger this time.

As she was wondering about this mysterious hand, the lights came back, suddenly. Shweta was surprised when she saw the hand was Trisha's.

Apparently shocked at what she'd done, Trisha pulled her hand away. Shweta stared at her but before she had a chance to say something, Trisha murmured, 'Uh…Sorry! I'm scared of the dark.' She excused herself and was gone in a jiffy.

Shweta was still thinking about it when Niru broke into a grin. 'So, are you scared of the dark too?'

'Surely, she thought she was holding on to you,' Shweta teased Niru. 'I'm wondering how she couldn't tell the difference.'

Niru extended his hand and motioned for her to hold it. 'Let's see if you can.'

Shweta rolled her eyes. 'I don't need to.'

Niru leaned closer, his eyes daring her. 'I'm not going to eat you.'

Slowly, Shweta pulled her hand out and held his. Niru covered it with his other hand and chafed it gently. 'What do you think?'

'What's going on here?'

Shweta spun around at her father's voice. Neither of them had seen him come up.

'Nothing, Uncle,' Niru cut in. 'I was just checking to see if she had a fever. She looked kind of sick when she came asking for water.'

'Fever?' Shweta's dad roared. He glared at Shweta. 'Do you have a fever?'

'N...no,' she stuttered. 'I'm just a little feverish.'

'You need to take some rest in that case.'

She nodded and escaped while her father got busy ordering a drink for himself.

26

Shweta tasted a few of the items from the spread laid out in the banquet hall, wandering around by herself because she was hungry, though nobody inside the dance hall seemed to be. Suddenly she spotted someone standing at the entrance.

Raj!

A wave of shock shot up her spine. She froze and held her breath. Even though her father had invited Raj, she'd never expected him to actually show up.

Her mouth turned dry as she watched him deep in conversation with someone, his bulky frame turned sideways. He was unshaven and in terrible need of a haircut. Any moment now, he'd turn around and see her.

She panicked, not knowing what to do. The banquet hall suddenly became so stifling that she needed to get away. She saw a door to her right leading outside to the terrace and hurried towards it. The terrace was dimly lit and the ground wet. She stepped out anyway, holding on to her dupatta and clutch in one hand, watching out for puddles. She closed the door behind her and exhaled. It felt so good to have escaped Raj's notice. She hoped he'd never find her here.

Sidestepping the puddles, she walked up to the railing and inhaled the cool, fresh, night air. Up in the pitch black sky, not a single star was in sight. A line of yellow street lamps lit the road that stretched between the hotel and the building across, which was probably an office because there was only a small lamp at the entrance by the gate.

A noise behind her made her turn. She hadn't heard the door open. Her breath caught as a figure moved towards her in the dark.

Her voice shook. 'Who…who is it?'

When the figure came closer, she made out his face in the dim light. 'You?'

Niru laughed. 'Why, were you expecting somebody else?'

'Why did you come out here?'

Niru snorted. 'I didn't expect anyone to be here.'

Shweta turned back to the view outside. 'Why have you left the bar?'

He joined her by the railing. 'I had to take a very important phone call, and I just needed some fresh air.'

'Is everything all right?'

'It's my uncle, Nambishan. He's run into a problem and he wants to meet me. I thought I'd go to meet him right after the party.'

Shweta nodded and a peaceful silence fell between them. She felt safe from Raj now that Niru was with her.

'Wouldn't it be nice,' Niru said, at length, 'if you and I were out here for a fag or a drink, like the old times.' He turned to her, smiling.

'There is something about the dark, isn't it?' she said, remembering the long nights out with her siblings and Niru, back in the days. She stuck her head out, resting her elbows on the railings. 'It makes you want to bare your heart, let all your secrets out.' Though, it was usually Simbu or Neha who rambled on the most, after their drinks.

Niru nodded. 'Is there something you want to share with me in the dark?' He was grinning. 'Where nobody would know your secret?'

'I have no secrets.'

'You didn't tell me a word about what happened back there in the US.'

It felt odd to hear Niru ask her about it, especially when Raj was just outside. As they stood there under the dim lights, only the two of them, she finally decided it was okay to tell him about it.

Niru grew silent as she told him about running away from Raj's house and ending up at Julie's.

When she had finally finished, however, he burst out, his voice sounding thick, 'That bastard! If he ever sets a hand on you again, I'll kill him, I swear.'

Shweta held Niru's hand and gave it a squeeze. 'I'm back now, aren't I? Everything's going to be fine.'

Niru's shoulders loosened. She slowly let go of his hand. 'I'm sorry,' he said, tipping her chin up.

What for? She wanted to ask him, feeling a tightness in her chest. *She had made the wrong choice, hadn't she? She'd made the mistake.*

Their gazes held. There was that overwhelming protective look in his eyes that made her heart flip. Tears pricked the back of her eyes and she tore her gaze away from him.

'Shweta!' he said, forcing her to look up at him again. 'I think you should have filed a police case and had him arrested.' A gentle admonishment.

Shweta frowned, blinking back the tears, and pushed his hand away. 'This is what I get for being open? You think I was thinking straight then? You think I should have stayed and kicked his ass?'

To her surprise, he nodded, a tiny smile sneaking up on his lips. 'Retaliation?' His eyes crinkled at the corners, sending a tingle of warmth through her. Raking his hands through his hair, he grinned at her. 'Yes, I like the idea.'

Shweta chuckled, feeling the tension drain away. 'It was more running like a rabbit down a hole. That was me.'

'That's not the real you, the one I know.'

'Oh yeah?' she teased. 'What do you know about me?'

Niru scratched his head, feigning a struggle in coming up with an answer. 'I know you're sensitive.'

Shweta nodded slowly. 'Go on.'

'Definitely impulsive.'

She nodded again, smiling now.

'And a little foolish, if you ask me.' He grinned and flicked at her nose. He ducked as she hit his shoulder. 'Ow! What was that for?' he yelped, his eyes dancing with mirth.

'You tell me,' she said, all her present troubles forgotten as he threw his head back and laughed heartily.

They were interrupted by the bang of the terrace door. 'There you are,' called out a voice in the dark.

Shweta and Niru turned around to see Neha step in, followed by Max. 'What are you guys doing in this damp and dark place? I've been looking for you all over. Because if you haven't had a drink, I just happened to bring along a bottle.' She walked towards them, swinging the bottle, and laughing that high-pitched laugh that was so her when she was drunk.

As she made her way towards them, Neha almost tripped on her saree, and Max lunged to steady her. Niru took away her bottle and holding up four fingers in front of her face, he asked, 'How many fingers are these?' He smiled, waiting for her answer. The moment she said 'four' he switched his fingers to three. 'No! It's three!' He chuckled.

'Oh, shut up, Niru!' Neha said. 'Don't bullshit me. I'm not drunk. I'm just enjoying myself.'

'Neha, you've had too much to drink,' Shweta said, feeling her cheeks grow hot. 'We should take you back to your room.' This was so embarrassing.

'Give me a break,' Neha said and touched Niru's shoulder. 'This is our Niru, for God's sake. He's a sweetheart.' She pulled his cheeks and laughed at him. 'You may have forgotten,' she said to him, 'but you cried on my shoulder when the first girl you tried to kiss laughed in your face.'

Shweta's mouth fell open. Had he told Neha the story?

Obviously, he hadn't told her who the recipient of that awkward kiss was. Shweta felt her face flush at the memory. She glanced at Niru who looked equally anguished at this disclosure. He prised Neha's hands off his cheeks and said to her. 'Enough! We're not discussing me tonight.'

'Why not?' Neha seemed belligerent. 'I know I'm drunk and I know it's not fair, but if you liked someone, and you'd been the littlest'—and she pinched her forefingers together—'bit brave, you would have told her.'

Wait a minute! Was Neha hinting that Niru liked her, Shweta, back then?

Niru slapped his forehead and then immediately grabbed Neha to close her mouth. 'Hey! Stop talking.' He looked towards Max for help. 'I think we should take her to her room. She's talking too much.'

The terrace door flew open just then and Simbu and Lekha tumbled in, tipsy, laughing and hugging each other. They both stopped short of kissing each other when they realized they had a wide-eyed audience standing right in front of them.

'What's going on here?' he said, peering, so that he could make out the people standing in the darkness. 'Looks like the whole family needed some fresh air.' He laughed and pulled Lekha closer to his side, winding his arm tight around her waist, his other hand clamped around the neck of a bottle. Lekha's hands, Shweta noticed, were gloved with plastic bags, and she was barefoot, the henna pattern snaking up till her calf where her three-fourth tights ended. Her lehenga was missing. Smart move!

Simbu's bottle was passed around. After a round of swigs from it, Neha began to tell a story about Simbu's childhood. 'So, one day, Ma was so tired of Simbu's sugar addiction that she put the sugar jar away beyond his reach. But when she returned from the market, believe it or not, he had with him a jar of Boost.'

Even Shweta hadn't heard this one. It was probably from the time when she was too little to remember. Lekha egged her on.

Neha continued. 'So, when mother came home, she saw him sitting in the middle of the kitchen floor, and he was so startled to see her, that he presented the jar to her quite proudly. And dear Ma thought she'd see the universe in the jar that her son—mini Krishna in her eyes—cradled in his arms. Surprise, surprise! The jar was totally empty, only sticky brown bits stuck at the bottom. And that night, she sent her Krishna to bed with only a glass of milk without Boost, as punishment. Simbu hated his milk without Boost, but Ma would have none of it. After that day, he never entered the kitchen again.'

Lekha reached up to touch Simbu's cheek and looked at his face, bursting with love. 'Is there a reason you'll continue that tradition today, my love?'

'Of course not, love. You know I like to help out in the kitchen.'

Their gazes remained locked until Neha groaned. 'Enough, love birds!'

They were all still talking and teasing one other when the door was flung open again and another figure stood at its threshold.

Shweta froze when she realized who it was.

Raj had finally managed to find her.

27

Raj's body language spoke of rage. His hands were fisted by his sides and his jaw clenched, as he strode towards the group and stood menacingly in front of Shweta. 'Where the hell have you been? I've looked for you everywhere.'

Shweta found the words stuck in her throat. Niru, who was standing closest to her, said, 'We were all here. There's no reason to sound as if she was lost.'

Raj turned his glare on Niru, his face now clearly furious. 'And who are you to tell me what to do? I'm talking to my wife.'

Niru made a move to take on Raj, physically if need be, but Max held him back.

Neha cut in. 'Hey, Raj, we don't want a fight. We were just hanging out and having some fun. We didn't know you had arrived. Don't worry about Shweta. She'll be fine with us.'

Raj ignored her and went for Shweta's arm, grabbing and shaking her. 'Come on. It's too cold out here, and I'd like to get some dinner and sleep. We have a lot to discuss tomorrow.'

Shweta wriggled out of his hold. 'I'm staying out here with them for a while,' she said, 'and I'm not going anywhere with you.'

'You!' Raj said, wagging his finger at her. 'I'm at the end of my patience. Come now.'

Lekha's face had paled. Neha looked uncomfortable. Finally Simbu took matters in his hands. 'Now, now, Raj. This is a pre-wedding party. We all want to have fun. If you're tired and hungry, please get some dinner and sleep. We'll see you in the morning.' Niru and Max moved in closer to Raj.

Raj's stance fumbled. His only option seemed to be to leave without further ado. He turned to Shweta one last time, muttering ominously, 'We'll talk soon.' Then he turned around and stalked off the way he had come, leaving the terrace door wide open behind him.

Shweta let out a breath and glanced awkwardly at the group around her. Suddenly Neha hitched up her saree and widening her eyes into saucers, mimicked Raj. 'Where the hell have you been?' She followed it with a hooting laugh.

Simbu put his arm around Shweta protectively. 'Don't worry, little sis. We got you.'

Shweta snuggled closer to his chest, glad for his support. Neha came around and group hugged them. 'I told him everything,' she told Shweta. Everyone relaxed after that, and in minutes, the conversation went back to the joking and laughing; all the bad vibes were dispelled.

By the time they had finished Neha and Simbu's bottles of whiskey and a new bottle that Max had got from the bar, they wished they had some chairs they could plonk themselves on. Neha could barely stand and Lekha's legs were hurting too. Finally, they decided to call it a night.

'How will I go home?' Neha said, swaying as she stood, holding on to the railing. Her hair was askew, her saree coming off at one end.

Oh God! Shweta looked at Neha in horror. Neha's saree was going to come undone any minute.

'You don't have to go home, only to your room,' Niru teased Neha.

Finally Max offered to take her. Shweta offered to help, allowing Neha to rest one arm on her shoulder. Together, Max and Shweta held her up from both sides, as she hobbled out of the terrace and into the nearest elevator.

After letting them off on the second floor, Shweta took the elevator up to the third. She felt tipsy too, and as she crossed her parents' room, she was glad it was so late that their door would be shut. Hopefully they were fast asleep.

Even so, she tiptoed to her door. When she reached the door to her room, she looked at her clutch in despair, wondering how to get to her key, knowing that her mehendi would ruin the clutch if she wasn't careful.

Looking both ways across the hallway and satisfied that there was nobody watching her make a fool of herself, she dropped on to the floor beside the door to make things easier. Squeezing the clutch in her lap for a tight hold, she managed to unclasp it with her clean hand. She then got out her room key and closed the clutch; it made such a loud click that she started. She struggled to get back on her feet, slipping on her dupatta twice. She finally managed to stand up by dragging her back upwards with the support of the wall. If there was a camera in this corridor, Shweta knew she would've made a great comic sight.

Struggle finally over, she tucked the clutch under her armpit and put the key into the lock. This wasn't a hi-fi hotel with electronic keys that buzzed. So after the quiet struggle of turning the key with her clean hand, and trying to get its handle to go down so she could push the door open, she finally entered.

And froze at the sight that met her eyes.

Her clutch fell from her underarm.

Sitting up on the bed, propped against the pillow with a laptop cradled in his lap, and looking quite intently at her, was her husband.

Raj.

On her bed.

Her soft white bed, where she'd slept peacefully last night.

'Wh…what are you doing here?' she said, stammering as she desperately tried to gather her wits.

'In our room?' Raj replied as he eyed her coolly.

'Our room?' Shweta said, rooted to her spot, one hand still on the door handle.

'Yes, yours and mine.'

'How did you get in?'

'I asked Papa and he got me the spare key.'

'Papa?' Shweta was aghast, imagining Papa sitting smug on his seeming victory. 'I c… can't be in the same room as you!'

'Why not?' He looked at her incredulously as he began to get up from the bed.

'Don't bother.' She blurted out with the utmost courage that she could muster. 'I'm off to sleep in my parents' room tonight. We can discuss this in the morning when I'm sober. Good night!'

Shweta grabbed her clutch and slammed the door closed, not bothering what mehendi stains she was causing in her wake.

Pausing only for a moment to decide where she was going to go, to her parents' room across the hallway or to Neha's, down on the second floor, she bolted towards the staircase on the opposite end, away from her parents' room and the elevator.

Shweta was already past the half-landing when she heard the door to her room open. She crouched and stayed still, hoping Raj wouldn't see her.

He waited, and hearing no sound, probably assumed that she had gone into her parents' room. Without further investigation, Raj went back into the room and closed the door. Shweta breathed easy again and headed down the staircase and across the hallway on the second floor towards Neha's room.

She paused right before Neha's door and shook her head. *No.* She'd have to wake Neha, Ria, and Mohan in the middle of the night. She'd rather not!

She backed up and knocked on the door before Neha's room.

Max opened the door and rubbed his eyes. 'You? What happened?'

'No time to explain,' Shweta said, pushing her way in.

She went straight to the bathroom and washed the mehendi off her hand. It left a deep orange stain of the most beautiful motifs across her palm. Her eyes glazed at the pretty sight, even if only for a moment, before she collected her thoughts and prepared to explain the cause for her intrusion to Max.

Instead, she noticed a figure sprawled on his bed.

'Wait!' Max tried to stop her as she sprang towards the sleeping person.

But she'd already pushed aside the blanket and was shocked to see Neha!

'What is she doing here?'

Max was still scratching his head. 'She didn't want to go to her room like that, so she suggested we go to yours. But in the condition that she was, I could only manage to bring her in here.'

'I can't go to my room either,' she said, slumping on his bed. 'Raj has taken up residence there.'

'You too can sleep here,' Max suggested. 'I'll take the floor.'

Shweta nodded thankfully, too tired to think of anything else. All she wanted to do was collapse on the bed.

Before Max could find an extra pillow and blanket, Shweta snuggled under his covers and went out like a light.

28

As Shweta dragged herself to the restaurant for breakfast in the morning, all her thoughts were centred on slipping into her room and getting her things without running into Raj.

But events took a different turn when she walked in through the restaurant door. Across the large tables around the room, she felt all eyes on her. She scanned the restaurant and found Keertana. Her face looked washed out. Right next to her, Prabhu looked like he could barely control his anger: there stood their daughter from America, in her crumpled Anarkali from last night, her dupatta lost, she didn't know where.

Shweta looked a fright with black kohl smudges around her eyes and her hair, messy, and uncombed. She had washed her face but the makeup refused to come off despite all the scrubbing.

As Shweta shuffled across the room, all eyes following her, and sidled into the seat next to Keertana, her mother turned around to her, hyperventilating. 'What have you done with yourself? Where were you last night? Raj was here just a while ago. He said you weren't in your room.' She could barely contain her whisper.

'Relax, Ma. Can you get me a cup of coffee before we talk about this?' Shweta tried to slouch inconspicuously in her seat, partially hidden by a pillar.

Keertana rose with a huff and brought her a cup of coffee.

Shweta sipped it gratefully and felt her head clear up a little. Keertana continued to stare at her. Finally, pursing her lips, Shweta said, 'Please, can you also fix a plate for me?'

Keertana did that too, albeit with a big scowl on her face. She set the plate down for Shweta.

'I need my things from my room,' Shweta told her mother, her head bent over her breakfast.

'Why?' Prabhu roared from across the table. Keertana's hand flew to her lips, gesturing Prabhu to hush. 'Where were you last night?!' he roared again.

'Please, Prabhu,' she pleaded with him as softly as she could. 'Must everyone know? It's all *your* fault that you called him to the wedding.'

'There was a reason for that. I made myself very clear.'

Shweta's eyes were still fixed on her plate. Keertana began to sniffle into her saree as Prabhu continued to huff.

Shweta realized she had nowhere to go after breakfast. No room to return to. Her own room was out of the question. She couldn't join her parents or Neha. That left only Max or Simbu. She picked the least complicated option.

At least she'd be left in peace in Simbu's room.

Shweta finished her breakfast and rose. Averting her eyes from Prabhu's glare, she addressed Keertana. 'Ma, please bring my things to Simbu's room. I'll be there until the wedding is over. And please don't tell Raj where I am. You can't possibly put me in the same room as him, and I've made up my mind about that.'

Prabhu opened his mouth to speak, but she was gone before he could.

* * *

Simbu was helping out at Lekha's house, doing last-minute things for the wedding, and had left his room to Shweta since morning. After a heavy lunch, Neha, Mohan, and Ria ventured out to the mall while Shweta decided to stay back and take a nap in the room. She was woken up some time later when somebody called her on the room's intercom.

'Hello?'

'Oh, hello, Shweta, glad I could reach you. I called your room and Raj picked up the phone. Is everything ok?'

Her head still felt fuzzy. 'Who's this?' she asked, groggily.

'Can you hear me?'

'Niru?' Shweta was surprised that it was him. 'How did you know I was here?'

'Simbu told me. Listen, I need a favour,' Niru said. 'You remember my uncle, Nambishan?'

'The one who had a problem last night?' The fuzziness seemed to have cleared up a little.

'The same, yes.'

'Yes, I remember him.' They'd all heard that the wedding lunch was contracted to Niru's uncle, Nambishan, who was the best cook in Chennai when it came to weddings.

Niru blurted out the problem, his sentences tumbling out pretty fast. Nambishan had suddenly taken ill last night and had called Niru to manage the lunch sadya preparation in his place.

Shweta's eyes shot open in surprise. 'But will you be able to handle it? It seems like an awfully big responsibility.'

'It is a big responsibility but at least I don't have to take care of all the cooking. His cooks are well trained. All I have to do is check that things run smoothly, and everything is organized and ready on time.' He paused to breathe. 'And I'm going to need help.'

'Help? But it's a wedding sadya for God's sake. How will you manage without Nambishan?'

'Don't worry about that. If he didn't have the confidence that I could take care of it, he wouldn't have asked me.'

'But…' She still didn't get why he was telling her all this.

'The flood situation has caused some scarcity in supplies. I need someone to man the kitchen while I run around sorting things out and getting the provisions organized. That's why I'm calling you. Will you help me?'

'Me?' She pinched her arm to ensure this wasn't a dream.

'You've worked in a kitchen before. You know how stressful things can be, right? I just need someone to stand by and make sure things run smoothly until I get back.'

'But…but Julie's kitchen was nothing compared to this. It's…it's not exactly the same thing,' she spluttered.

'Please?'

'Niru, you've got to be kidding me. Besides, I have no idea what to do.'

'All you have to do is keep an eye on things and be in touch with me until I get there. There were some provisions and supplies that our source has delayed. I have to make sure they reach on time. Meanwhile, some vegetables and rice are already on their way. Can you be there until I sort this out and reach back?'

'But where are you now?'

'I had to make a trip to another town to take care of a few delays and cancellations. And it may be late tonight when I return. If there's nobody to take care of the kitchen, it'll be a disaster.'

Shweta hesitated.

Niru's voice crackled through the intercom, pleading. 'Can I count on you?'

She absolutely couldn't refuse. Niru was her childhood buddy. She'd do anything he asked, in a blink. She couldn't let him down, especially when he needed her. She only hoped Niru knew what he was doing.

Niru hung up the phone and Shweta buried her head in her hands. Her brother's wedding was in some serious trouble. First, her husband was here. And now, the head cook was out of action. But at least in the kitchen, she would be far away from Raj, least likely to bump into him. It was just the escape she needed until the wedding was over.

29

The family was so rattled by the news of Nambishan's sudden illness that they held a big conference in her parents' room. Shweta slunk in unnoticed and pulled Keertana aside. 'Niru has asked me to help in the kitchen and I'll be late.'

Keertana gasped. 'Is everything going to be okay?'

Shweta nodded. 'Of course!'

Keertana looked very worried but also kind of happy that she was helping Niru. Shweta made Keertana promise that she wouldn't tell Raj where Shweta was. Then she went to find Max and ask him to come along too. He agreed immediately, only too delighted to see the workings of a wedding kitchen, up close.

It was barely three in the afternoon when Max and she left for the kitchen. That's how early the work for next day's lunch needed to start.

The so-called kitchen was really an anteroom behind the wedding hall. Shweta stood at the doorway, awed. Never before had she seen so many wide-mouthed, enormous uralis—king-sized cooking vessels—mounted on stands and packed neatly against the walls. Everything, in fact, in that room was king-sized.

The room, with plain cemented flooring, was as big as two of her kitchens combined. The cooking facilities were arranged against the walls, allowing a large open space in the centre of the room that made movement easy for the cooks. Long fluorescent tubes on the ceiling made the already huge room look larger because of their brightness. Long handled ladles, strainers and large woven, basket trays, all organized in one huge basket, sat in a corner. Several serving buckets, glasses, bowls, and serving spoons, all in steel, were stocked in a side room, barely large enough for two men, at the far end of the larger room.

The room bustled with activity with men already at work. Some were setting up the firewood and igniter material beneath the uralis, a couple were checking the packets of spices, oil, salt, jaggery, and other stock that had already arrived; a few were sitting on a small bench outside the exit door. She headed towards the exit and noticed the bare-chested men puffing away at their beedis. They were attired in white, cotton mundus tied around their waists and cloth turbans around their heads. Mundus hitched up, the men were laughing, chatting and gearing up to start the activity that earned them their livelihood.

Shweta went up and introduced herself to one of the oldest men there, sitting on the bench with a beedi, bald with wisps of white hair on his chest, clad in a thread-bare mundu that was already half soaked in sweat.

The old man, his eyes gleaming with surprise, looked up at her with kindly interest. 'What do you want?' he asked.

He reminded Shweta of her grandfather. 'I'm just here until Niru comes. He said he needed someone to help you with the supplies.'

He nodded. 'Come. Let me show you where things are.'

She followed him back into the kitchen.

He stopped short of the side room and gestured to the kitchen. 'Have you seen a kitchen like this before?'

She smiled and shook her head.

'This is a place where we create magic. This is our kingdom,' he said, waving his hand around. 'Is this your friend?' He gestured to Max.

'Yes, he wanted to help too. He's good at chopping vegetables.'

'We could always use a few extra hands,' said the old man, beaming.

He brought Shweta up to speed with where everything was, and what was left to come.

Shortly, one of the vans bearing a ton of vegetables showed up.

Shweta called Niru to let him know that the remaining vegetables had arrived; then she made sure that they were placed in one corner of the room, and the coconuts heaped in another. Bunches of plantain bananas, small bananas, sacks of beans, green chilies, large gourds, pumpkins, and drumsticks strung together were unloaded. Bigger sacks of onions, potatoes, tomatoes, and curry leaves were next. It took an hour for everything to be unloaded, and pretty soon the room resembled a market place.

At last, a water tanker arrived. The water was filled up in drums, sufficient, for now, to wash the vegetables and for other basic requirements. More water was to arrive later.

A large table was brought into the middle of the kitchen. The men soon gathered around it to start the chopping. There was a whole process of knifing through the big melons and skinning of the rest. There must have been at least ten helpers working as a team in that room, for the preparations.

After accounting for all the things that were supposed to arrive, Shweta took pleasure in being of help to the men busy at work, passing on the washed vegetables for chopping.

Max joined them in the chopping exercise. It was fun to watch him seated on a low stool, slicing beans, peeling potatoes, and producing mounds of chopped vegetables like a pro.

Presently, the fires were started and the frying began. Shweta was struck by how organised everything was, how some men had taken over the marinating and preparation of pickles, while some fried the banana chips and prepared the jaggery coating for the sweet banana fritters. Some grated the coconuts and pressed it for milk to be used in the morning for the payasam, while a couple were engaged in the preparation of the flat rice squares called ada, by spreading the thick rice batter into long strings on a banana leaf, rolling it, tying it up and cooking it in boiling hot water.

And to think, this was only the prep phase! Shweta had never seen such preparations on such a grand scale and she was excited to be a part of what felt like a Herculean adventure.

As the number of fires lit went on increasing, the room began to get hotter. Some of the men used their mundus as a towel to wipe the sweat pouring down their faces and backs. Shweta was sweating too and wished she had a cotton dupatta to wipe her sweaty forehead and brow. To hell with formalities, she thought. Unable to take the sweat rolling down her face anymore, she just lifted one end of her long kurta and wiped her hot face.

Luckily her kurta had a pocket to keep her phone in. Niru called regularly to check the status of the arriving goods and the progress in the kitchen. Of course, he didn't need to. These guys were veterans and knew exactly what to do. In any case, this being the prep day, a lot of things were automatically handled by the men without being supervised.

During the day, her mother and Simbu called her several times. They were both very worried, but Shweta managed to assure them that everything was progressing as it should.

When Niru returned it was already close to 8 p.m. He looked tired yet happy. There was a cheer from the workers as he entered and greeted them.

Shweta was surprised. 'Do they know you?' she said, when he'd finished going around the room and talking to the men, patting some on the back, and inquiring about the families of some.

'I've spent some of my childhood summer vacations with Uncle Nambishan,' he said. 'I've been inside the kitchen, helped during the sadya preparations, and eaten some meals with these men. I've known some of them for a long time now.'

That explained the good vibes between the workers and him. She was glad to see that no one resented Niru in the place of their chief,

Nambishan.

'How is Uncle Nambishan?' Shweta asked Niru. 'Will he be able to come tomorrow?'

'He said he'll try, but I think it'd be better if he didn't. He was hit by a sudden bout of diarrhoea. Something about the water in his area, it seems.'

That was bad news.

Niru unloaded the banana leaves that he had brought along in his tempo. At the end of a very long day, Shweta who had never before seen this degree of activity even in Julie's kitchen, sat down to a simple meal prepared by the men, with Max, Niru, and all the workers. It was delicious, Shweta thought. Much better, in fact, than so many sadya feasts she'd eaten before. It was wonderful how food brought men of different classes and kinds together, from the old to the young, from workers to their superiors.

When she saw the laughter and the cheer within the group, the camaraderie among the men, and the lightness of their hearts despite the physical hardship of the day, it lifted her spirits. Niru laughed at someone's joke and her heart skipped a beat. She had never seen him look so happy and content. The kitchen was truly where he belonged.

As Shweta watched him, sitting crossed-legged on the floor and eating the simple fare spread on a banana leaf, she felt a tug that surprised her. Niru was so engrossed in eating that he hadn't bothered about his hair falling over his eyes. She reached out and pushed back the strands, and laughed at him when he glanced up at her, surprised. He smiled back. It was the smile of satisfaction, the smile of a day's job done well and the anticipation of a fruitful morning the next day. She wished him well from the bottom of her heart and hoped he'd carry through what his uncle had so proudly entrusted to him.

Everyone had been working for so many hours and there was still so much more to do. It was almost 11 p.m. when they all wound up for a couple of hours of sleep. The main course and the dessert payasam would be started only later, and the men decided to grab some rest before another gruelling stint began. They'd have to wake up at 2 a.m. to start the preparation of the main course and the payasam.

'I'll drop you to the hotel,' Niru offered.

He'd booked a tempo for a couple of days. Max and Shweta got in beside him and Niru drove them to the hotel.

'Why was Raj in your room?' Niru asked, as they drove silently through the empty streets.

'Because Papa gave him the keys to my room.'

'So where are you put up tonight?'

'I've moved to Simbu's room for now.'

'Are you going to go his room now, in the middle of the night?' Niru asked, sounding aghast. 'He's the groom, Shweta. He needs good sleep tonight or he's going to have baggy eyes in the morning.'

Shweta hadn't thought of that.

'You are welcome to mine,' Max said.

'Oh, thanks,' Shweta said. 'I'd forgotten I had that option.' She flicked Max's arm gratefully.

When they reached the hotel, Niru locked his tempo and came in with them.

'Where are you put up?' she asked him.

'This place, only for tonight. In fact, my mother's room.' Then, suddenly as an after-thought, he said. 'In fact, why don't I go to Max's room and you stay with my mother for tonight? Anyway, all of us have to be up pretty early tomorrow. In fact, I have to be back in the kitchen in a few hours.' He turned to Max. 'I hope I won't be disturbing you, buddy.'

Max, the ever-helpful, kind sort, gave an emphatic shake of his head. 'Of course not! You're most welcome.'

With that settled, Niru and Shweta switched places for the night.

Niru's and Max's rooms were right next to each other.

As they parted, Niru held her gaze just before she turned in. 'Thanks for everything today.'

There was a gentleness in his eyes that had replaced the naughty, wicked grin he'd always given her. 'Thank you too,' she said, thinking of how Niru had come to her family's rescue.

'I wasn't getting any sleep anyway,' Savitri said, most pleased to see Shweta when she answered her door. She'd stayed up for Niru.

Shweta changed into a nightie that Savitri offered to lend her. She got under the covers, the events of the day playing in her mind. She thought of what Niru had told her, just before they had parted for the day. More than the *what*, it was how Niru had said it, which had struck a chord with her. Something seemed to have changed between them, Shweta felt.

Oh, well! Anyway, she thought, it was high time that she got credit for being herself and not just Simbu's little sister.

30

The morning of the wedding brought along a bit of a chaos. Shweta woke up late and then realized to her horror, when she went to Simbu's room for her clothes, that his door was locked.

Damn!

She banged at Max's door. He opened, clutching his stomach. He looked ghastly, his hair mussed and clothes crumpled.

'Max, what's wrong?'

'I think I have a bad stomach,' he said, doubling over in pain.

'Oh, no, we'll have to call Mohan and get you some medical aid. I hope you won't miss the wedding.'

He nodded grimly.

With Max tagging along, she headed to Neha's room and knocked on her door.

Ria, partially dressed in her petticoat and long silk skirt, answered the door, with Neha right behind her.

'Is Mohan here?' Shweta asked, her fingers crossed.

'What happened to him?' Neha asked, looking at Max, her face creased with worry as she opened the door wider to let them in. Max, who could hardly stand, tottered towards Neha's bed.

'He has stomach cramps.' Shweta followed Max inside while

Neha knocked on the bathroom door to tell Mohan that Shweta and Max were waiting for him outside. While they waited, Shweta took a chair beside the bed and sat, twiddling her thumbs. Ria finished putting on her top and Neha helped her quickly with her earrings and hair before coming over to check on Max.

'What do we do now?' she said, pulling up a sheet to cover him and touching his forehead. He opened his eyes and gave her a weak smile.

Ria came up to Shweta. 'Aren't you getting dressed, Aunt S?'

'Oh dear!' Shweta remembered suddenly that she still didn't have her room keys. What was she to do about Simbu's room key now?

Mohan came out of the shower, wrapped in a bath towel. Max had begun to moan in pain. Mohan went straight to his bag to get his stethoscope.

He examined Max and asked him a few questions. 'It looks like a bad case of indigestion.

Max winced, his hands clutching his stomach as it cramped again. 'Will I be able to go to the wedding?' he croaked.

Mohan pursed his lips. 'Let me give you an injection first,' he said, going to check in his bag if he had it. 'Good, I have it here. Lie down for a bit now, and in about an hour, you should be feeling better. Try not to exert yourself in the meantime.'

There was nothing else to do except hope the injection would provide relief. Shweta looked on as Mohan gave him the shot.

Mohan and Ria left for breakfast while the sisters waited with Max. Once Max had settled down a bit, Shweta and Neha headed down the hallway towards the breakfast hall. They left Max sleeping in Neha's room. It was already 8 a.m. by then.

To Shweta's relief, Simbu was there. He and their parents were just finishing up in the breakfast hall.

Keertana glared at her. 'Where were you? It's quite late and you...'

'Ma, give me Simbu's room keys,' Shweta said, cutting her off.

'We'll all be in my room,' Keertana said, handing over the keys. 'The mini bus leaves by eight-thirty. We have to be at the hall by nine.'

Simbu smiled at them as he passed by. 'Sisters, don't be late now,' he teased. 'You are the most important women who need to be by my side at the wedding.'

It was a mad blur after that. Shweta and Neha hurried with their breakfast and rushed back upstairs to dress, first to Neha's room to get her saree and then to Simbu's, so both could change in there.

Neha was an expert at saree draping but even so, given that they were under such time pressure, she fumbled and had to redo the criss-crossing of the pleats a couple of times.

Shweta, in the meantime, finished putting on her makeup, quickly dabbing a little concealer on the dark circles under her eyes, applying a dash of lipstick, lining her eyes with kohl, and pinning up a couple of strings of jasmine in her hair.

Neha finished with her own saree, and helped Shweta with hers.

Next, they put on their gold jewellery: bangles, earrings, and a couple of necklaces. Shweta made sure the thaali on her neck showed. It was important she have it on so that folks at the wedding wouldn't know that anything was amiss.

Slipping into her three-inch heels, Shweta checked herself one last time in the mirror. Satisfied with her bright eyes and flushed cheeks, she was ready to leave.

The sisters hurried back to Neha's room to get Max. But he still had to get dressed. They'd forgotten all about that. And he was fast asleep. Neha's phone rang just then. It was Keertana telling them the mini bus was ready to go.

Shweta ran back to Max's room to look for the kurta they had bought for him. There was no time to change his jeans, so she rummaged in his bag, grabbed the kurta and the colourful matching stole and rushed back to Neha's room.

Between them, they managed to take off his shirt and slip on the kurta.

'You girls are pretty quick at undressing a man,' Max quipped.

The sisters exchanged naughty giggles.

'You are so lucky we're letting your jeans stay,' Neha said, laughing as she wrapped the stole around his neck, suspending it from his shoulders. Then, she sprayed Mohan's cologne on him. The poor guy could barely sit straight on the bed.

They raised him to his feet, pulled his arms around their shoulders, and walked him to the elevator, holding him tightly on both sides. Max's steps were very slow and deliberate, but at last they managed to reach the mini bus. Seeing Max flanked by the sisters and struggling, Mohan and Simbu jumped down to help. They managed to get him on the bus and they were off, at last.

* * *

The marriage hall looked gorgeous, decked with marigold garlands and bright brass mini lamps at the entrance. Shweta and her family had reached just in time for the muhurtham.

The sounds of the nadaswaram and beating drums welcomed the groom and his family, and they were all ushered into the wedding hall by the bride's parents and uncles.

Simbu was led to his seat on top of a specially decorated stage where the ceremonial wedding fire was ablaze. Her parents and all of their family went up the stage next and gathered behind him as he took his place in front of the fire.

The bride's procession arrived soon after. From up on the stage, Shweta watched the procession in wonder. Lekha was being brought to the stage by beautiful bridesmaids carrying brass lamps and trays of flowers and vermillion. Trisha led the procession, gliding towards them in a gorgeously rich, purple saree, crusted with semi-precious stones, her face radiant.

Niru certainly deserved someone beautiful like her, Shweta ruminated, a lump forming in her throat. An unmarried, pretty, accomplished girl like Trisha. Even though Trisha did have her faults, that did not excuse being mean to her, Shweta thought.

She spotted Niru, standing in the crowd, waiting for the ceremony to start. His best friend's wedding. Niru's eyes were glistening with happiness as he watched Simbu.

Shweta's heart lurched. She suddenly felt a strong urge to tell Niru about the little secret she'd kept from him all these years.

Her cheeks burned. Why had she not told him? And why did the secret still bother her all these years later?

No, she decided. It wouldn't do to NOT put things straight before Simbu's wedding was over. Right old wrongs, she resolved. She'd probably never see him, after. It was now or never.

The renewed sounds of the nadaswaram and the ululation by the women brought Shweta back to the present. Lekha was seated next to Simbu now. He was tying the sacred thread with the thaali pendant around her neck, helped by Neha who was lifting Lekha's heavy braid out of its way.

A sob rose in Shweta's chest. She felt a ton of happiness for Lekha, but the picture of her own moment six months ago, rose unbidden in her thoughts.

The unfortunate day when she had been the bride.

Her eyes unconsciously sought Niru again, and her chest tightened.

A thought flitted into her mind, catching her unawares. *Had it been Niru tying the thaali around her neck that day, would her life have turned out differently?*

She shrugged away the now seemingly frivolous thought and quickly dried her eyes.

Finally, the thaali was tied. Simbu and Lekha rose, and took the three circumambulations around the sacred fire to consecrate the marriage.

After the ceremony, the couple readied themselves for the photo shoot with the guests, who were already forming a line to congratulate the newlyweds. Shweta looked around for Niru but he was not to be seen.

Max wasn't feeling too well and wanted to leave. Neha arranged for a packet of rice and curd from the kitchen for him, and had Mohan drop him back to the hotel.

Shweta made a quick exit towards kitchen. She needed to see how the kitchen staff was getting along, and most of all, she needed to catch Niru alone for a few moments before the rush for lunch began or she lost her nerve.

31

The kitchen was bursting with aromas as Shweta neared it.

Peeking from the door, she spotted Niru at the far corner, wearing an azure shirt and a mundu folded up to his thighs. She'd never seen him in a mundu before. His calves gleamed below it. Although he'd been up here since the crack of dawn, he looked fresh and bathed, as if he'd changed just now, before the lunch was to begin.

Hands akimbo, he was laughing at something, with the helper standing beside him, pointing intermittently to the large urali containing a dish that the helper stirred with a huge, long ladle.

Shweta hitched her saree higher, afraid to ruin it in the busy and messy kitchen, and entered, watching her step.

She passed a pot of cooked rice, another of boiling sambar, and some finished dishes covered with large banana leaves. Several men recognized her as she passed by, and smiled or nodded to her.

She reached the spot where Niru stood, by the gurgling pot of ada pradhaman payasam, a dessert that let out a heavenly aroma of rich coconut milk and jaggery. His back to her, Niru was still engaged in talking to the young helper, asking him to check the dish to see if it was done, and didn't see her until she was right beside him.

He turned around in surprise when she tapped his shoulder.

'You? What are you doing here?'

Shweta couldn't smile at him, her heart beating faster by the moment.

He noticed her grim look. 'What's wrong?'

'Nothing. Can we talk?'

'What? Now?'

She nodded.

Niru said something to the helper and led her outside, to the bench near the exit. He gestured to a lone man sitting on the bench, puffing at his beedi. The man rose and went inside.

Niru took a seat on the bench. 'Oh, my legs are killing me. Do you want to sit?'

Shweta shook her head and just stood there, watching him.

'The cat got your tongue?' He patted the place next to him. 'Come, have a seat. Is everything okay?'

Shweta hesitated. She didn't know what she was going to say but it was better if she didn't chicken out now.

'I tore up the letter,' she blurted out, not knowing where to start.

'What letter?'

'The one Dolly wrote to you. She gave it to me to give you the night we all met at your house.'

There! She'd finally said it. Dolly had a crush on Niru back when they were in school, and she was sure Niru had felt the same way about her too.

Niru looked up at her in surprise.

'I knew she liked you so I tore up her love letter.' And now that she'd begun she couldn't stop. 'I guess I was plain jealous, because I didn't like her. She was smart, good looking, and intelligent. But I just couldn't stand her. I don't know how she managed to look so pretty even in her school uniform with her hair tied up high in a sleek pony tail and her socks rolled down to her ankles. She looked like some model, walking down the school corridor like she was walking the ramp.'

A small grin began to play on his lips. She didn't care.

'I just couldn't stand her and I don't know why you'd invited her to our party when it was supposed to be only our gang. When she gave me the letter to give you, I was shocked. I wondered why a girl like her needed me as a messenger. But I took it anyway, promising her I'd pass it on to you. Only, I never did.' She paused just to see his reaction but he continued to look at her more incredulously with every word she spoke. 'I just wanted to tell you,' she began again, 'I'm probably responsible for the fact that you never got married. Maybe Dolly and you would have gotten together that night. Maybe you'd have been a couple. Maybe you'd have been married today. It was all my fault.'

Niru crossed his arms; it egged Shweta on.

'And now…now, I see Trisha, and I know she likes you. I think you like her too. I mean, I could be wrong, but still. But you see, when your mum asked me about her, I hinted to her I didn't think she'd make a good match for you. I don't know if I'm still being jealous. I just wanted you to know that I don't mean to be. I mean, you can have any girl you want. I mean, you're smart, good looking and intelligent. I'm sure a lot of girls like you. I'm sure that Italian girlfriend of yours didn't want to leave, either. You know, it could have been a mistake. Maybe you still love her. Maybe you won't get over her.'

His heart was racing. *Are you saying you like me…liked me too?* 'Why tell me this now?' he asked her.

'Because…because…I don't know. Perhaps, I'll never get a chance later. Maybe we'll never meet again after this. Maybe you'll stay in Chennai and I'll be in Bangalore, and our paths will never cross, although I wish they would. I wish we could stay in touch. I wish we could be friends, and I wish that even if we never meet again, we remember this time fondly. I will. I know I'll never forget this wedding and all the fun I've had with you. And I think I have to go now. They must be looking for me. Goodbye, Niru.'

Niru tried to call her back but she'd turned around and fled already. He buried his head in his hands and let out a deep sigh. How had he been such a stupid fool?

Shweta sighed as she made her way back to the hall. Oh, how would she face him again? Although relieved that she'd finally told him about the letter, she'd never felt this embarrassed before. What exactly had happened there? She had wanted to tell him about Dolly. How did she end up talking about Trisha, his mom, and his wedding? Oh blast! She might just as well have made a bigger fool of herself by telling him that she liked him herself—something she'd never admitted to, even when he'd hinted he liked her years ago. But then, she hadn't been certain it wasn't just because she was his best friend's sister. She'd been peeved when he hadn't pursued her and proved her wrong. But none of the past mattered anymore.

She was back just in time for the bride's saree-changing ritual, before lunch. It was the groom's sisters who had to help the bride change her attire after the wedding.

As Neha and Shweta and a few of their close cousins led Lekha to the changing room, the words she'd exchanged with Niru ran over and over in Shweta's head.

Lekha was to change into the traditional Kerala cream saree with gold border. The sisters fussed over her, helping their new sister-in-law become the most beautiful bride ever, going to her first lunch with her husband.

When they were done, Shweta beamed at the final result. Lekha looked resplendent. Neha seemed pleased with their effort, and together they headed towards Simbu, waiting for them in the lunch hall.

As was Niru!

32

Niru was not in the lunch hall, Shweta noted with relief. She guessed he was probably still busy in the kitchen.

Simbu and Lekha sat at the lunch table, with Shweta and Neha by Lekha's side. The photographers came to click pictures of the bride and the groom at their lunch. The newlyweds posed as they fed each other, the bride feeding the groom first and vice versa. It was fun, for laughs.

The traditional meal was laid out on big banana leaves. The fries, pickles, pappadoms, appetizers, and the sides were served first. Then came the first course of rice, ghee, and dal. Everything smelled fresh. Shweta swelled with pride, knowing she had been a part of this great effort.

After three more courses, the desserts were served and she remembered the helper boy who'd stood stirring the pot of ada prathaman. He had got it absolutely right. The aroma was heavenly and it tasted just perfect, the right mix of coconut, cardamom and jaggery. She couldn't have asked for a more delicious dessert.

Finally Niru came around to congratulate the couple and inquired if they liked the meal. Simbu was beyond ecstatic that Niru had pulled this off so brilliantly.

Shweta saw Niru steal a glance at her. She looked away, her cheeks hot. It felt as if something had changed between them.

Niru then came around to stand where Neha was seated. 'How's the lunch?' he asked her.

'Splendid!' Neha said, her beaming face saying it all.

He smiled and gestured towards Shweta as if to acknowledge her part in it. But she couldn't take any credit for all the hard work that had gone into it. All she'd done was help.

After they finished lunch, Neha went to check on Ria. Shweta was just coming out of the dining hall, when she heard a familiar, grainy voice. 'Hello.'

She stopped in her tracks, a bolt of shock shooting through her body. Her palms turned cold as she whirled around and looked up, trying to put on a show of nonchalance that belied her distress. She'd forgotten all about Raj. In fact she hadn't even seen him at the wedding. Where had he been hiding?

'Weren't you expecting me?' His grey eyes gleamed with amusement.

She crossed her arms.

He grabbed her and forced her into a corner against a wall.

'What are you doing?' she shouted, trying to free her arm.

'I needed to talk to you alone.' He released her hesitantly, his eyes never leaving hers. 'I told you that already, but you didn't care.'

Her eyes darted here and there, looking for an escape. But Raj loomed over her, making her feel like a trapped mouse.

He took a moment to give her the once-over. 'You look great, by the way. Just like you did when you were the bride.'

Shweta rubbed her arm. 'What do you want?'

'I'm happy to see you. I had really wondered where you'd gone.'

She scoffed. 'Enough that you never bothered to find out?'

'I looked everywhere for you,' he growled. 'I did everything I could, short of putting your face up in the missing column. Your number was switched off. I didn't want to alarm your father. I thought you'd have the good sense to come back soon since I had your passport. Then I lost my phone. But I knew you'd come back. Believe me, I was alarmed to see you in custody.'

'Of course!' Her words spewed venom. 'You were so alarmed that you didn't want to give me my passport! You'd rather I spent time in jail for illegal stay in the country?'

'I didn't know if I was going to get into trouble too,' he blurted out. 'It was a shock to see you that evening.'

It felt great to see you squirm and believe our little charade, you scumbag!

'After the cop brought you along, I didn't want to take any risks. I moved to a new apartment and got a new phone number.' He touched her arm but she jerked his hand away.

She cast about for help but there was no one around.

'But, we'll forget the past,' he continued. 'I've come back for you, Shweta. I want you to come back with me.'

She fixed him with a stare. 'You must be joking, Raj. Why would I want to come back with you? You almost tried to kill me.'

He threw up his arms. 'Look, I'm sorry if I scared you.' In a mellow voice, he continued, 'I'm on medication now. Don't you see I'm better already? I'm migrating to Canada next year, to be near mum and sis. It will be good for us too, you and me. We can have a good life.'

She couldn't believe her ears. Was this man out of his mind?

He smiled awkwardly and scratched his stubble. 'Sis says the process would be a lot easier for a married man.'

Now she got it. 'Is that why you need *me* back?'

'Of course not!' he snapped. His eyes were hard and shifty. 'That's not the only reason. Although technically since we're married, it'd be easier to go to Canada. Start a new life. Wouldn't you like that?'

'What if I don't want to go anywhere with you?' she said, glaring back with all the boldness she could muster.

He thrust her against the wall and grabbed her arm. 'You better not make this worse for me or…'

'Let go,' she yelled.

His laugh, deep and hollow, sent a shiver through her spine. 'You fuck up my immigration and your old man will pay.'

'Let go of me. My father owes you nothing,' she cried. 'I want a divorce.'

He tightened his grip on her arm. 'Ask him why he had to sell his daughter to save his stocks. Huh? He owes me my money or *you*.' He laughed, mocking her.

'Let go of my hand. I'm not going with you.' Shweta wriggled but he wouldn't let go.

His eyes glinted with cheap joy. 'I'll make him and you pay for this, you bitch!'

The smirk on his face pushed all her buttons. She raised her hand, surprising herself, and—

Thwack!!!

She struck his face so hard that her own hand stung.

Raj's face swerved to one side. Teetering, he released her as his other hand flew up instinctively to touch his cheek.

Her body trembled with rage. 'You deserve that, you pig!'

Before he could recover, she pushed him away and escaped, leaving him standing alone, his hand still nursing his shamefully reddened face.

It was a good thing that it was a large wedding hall and there were lots of people milling around. There was no way he could run after her or hurt her without drawing the attention of so many people who knew her.

She bolted across the hall in search of her father. She had to sort this out that very minute.

Prabhu and Keertana were in an anteroom, stacking the gifts received at the wedding. Prabhu was asking Keertana to check if all the boxes had been accounted for, when Shweta barged in.

'How much money did Raj offer you?' She threw the question at her father, daring him to reply.

Keertana intervened. 'What are you talking about, Shweta? What money?'

Shweta stepped up to Prabhu. 'How much money?' she repeated.

Prabhu stared, too shell-shocked to respond.

'Tell me, for how much did you sell your daughter?' she screamed. 'Is that why you wanted me to go back to him? Is that why you wanted to save your face? Is it because money is more important to you than your child?'

Prabhu looked away.

Shweta couldn't stop. She wouldn't even if she could. 'I'm ashamed to say that I'm your daughter,' she lashed out.

Keertana tried to stop her but tears rolled down Shweta's cheeks and she choked on her next words. 'The *divorced* label would have been far more bearable than the *sold* label.'

Prabhu grimaced, his hand rising to his heart.

Shweta wiped away the tears that were gushing down her face. 'Are you asking me to go back to Raj because you owe him money?' she wailed.

Just then Raj appeared at the door, his arms crossed, his face bearing a menacing glare. Looking around the room, he saw all the gift boxes and pounced on them. One by one he grabbed each one, tore the packaging, and threw it on the floor. 'You think you can ruin my marriage and conduct this wedding in peace?' he roared.

Shweta watched in horror as the ruined boxes littered the room.

'Stop it!' Prabhu rushed at Raj but he was no match for him.

'Move!' Raj yelled at Prabhu, shoving him aside. Prabhu staggered backwards and toppled over a table.

Raj glared at Prabhu. 'You give me back my money or I'm going to tell everyone what a scoundrel you are.'

Prabhu's eyes were bloodshot. 'You cheap bastard!'

Raj lunged at Prabhu while Shweta rushed towards Raj to pull him back, pounding on his back to make him stop.

'You bitch!' he screamed at Shweta, and pushing Prabhu aside, he went for Shweta's neck, strangling her so hard that it brought tears to her eyes. Choking and spluttering, she struggled to free herself from his grip. He pushed her to the wall, pulled out a Swiss knife, and held it to her neck. 'Now tell me, you won't come with me, huh?'

Keertana let out a sharp cry as Prabhu rushed to intervene. Raj lashed out at Prabhu and the knife swung inches from Prabhu's face.

Shweta screamed and pushed Raj away. Keertana ran out of the room, hollering for help.

Raj's knife was back at Shweta's neck with Prabhu trying to distract him, when Niru, Simbu, and some others rushed into the room. In moments, Shweta and Raj were pulled apart. A tussle ensued. It took all the men to tackle Raj and pin him to the ground.

Niru seized the knife that had fallen on the floor and pouncing on Raj, thrust it against his throat. 'Don't you ever touch her again!' he thundered. 'Or I will kill you myself!' Simbu pulled Niru away and wrenched the knife from his hand. Meanwhile, the others hauled Raj up to his feet and pushed him out of the room.

'I'll show you, you cheats!' Raj yelled, kicking and shouting as he was dragged away.

Things happened so quickly, the room began to spin around Shweta. Everything became a blur and she collapsed in a heap on the floor.

* * *

When Shweta came to, Keertana was hovering over her with a jug of water. Prabhu was standing by, shaken and speechless. Neha was by her side, trying to get her back on her feet. Finally, Keertana and Neha managed to get Shweta into a cab.

At the hotel, Neha checked with the reception and learned that Raj had checked out of Shweta's old room in the morning. Neha ordered them not to give the spare key to anyone. Shweta still had her key.

Neha took Shweta to her room and settled her on the bed, propping her up with pillows. She gave her a long tight hug, asked her to rest, and left, locking the door behind her.

Shweta lay back against the soft pillows and closed her eyes, relieved to be back in the privacy of her room.

She'd talk to her father in the morning, she decided, and apologize for her rudeness. But she had to find out exactly what Raj was insinuating about him. There had to be some mistake.

33

Shweta stayed in her room and ordered room service for dinner. Her mother had called up twice to check on her. 'Are you okay? Don't worry. Everything will be fine.'

Shweta told her she was fine and wanted to go to bed early.

When Shweta felt a little relaxed, she called Max's room to check on him.

Max was overjoyed to hear her voice. He couldn't stop oohing and aahing at all the wedding arrangements and the actual wedding itself. 'I'm so glad I could make it. I loved every bit of it. A girl was actually eyeing me and smiling at me. How cool is that?'

Shweta laughed for the first time that day. 'I'm sure if you were up for it, you'd have picked a bride for yourself too,' she teased, and could imagine Max's wide-mouthed grin at the other end.

'Did I miss anything else?'

Shweta let out a sigh. 'Not much,' she said. 'Only some crazy things that could wait to be told another day.'

'Something about Niru?' Max quizzed her for more.

'That too.'

They laughed a little about some more juicy titbits from the wedding, and then she let Max hang up and got back to rest.

Finally, after a quiet meal of soup and bread rolls, she settled down to watch TV when she heard a knock on her door. She didn't answer. Moments later, Niru's voice sailed through. 'Open the door, Shweta.'

She slapped her hand to her forehead and stayed put.

The knocks turned louder.

'Go away, please,' she yelled.

The knocks stopped. She let out a sigh of relief. A few minutes later, the sharp ring of the intercom startled her. She looked at it suspiciously even as the shrill ringing continued.

After the umpteenth ring, she picked it up warily. 'Hello?'

'This is not fair,' Niru barked, and suddenly Shweta realized how happy she was to hear his voice just before a pang of regret set in. 'It's my last night here,' Niru said, 'and you won't even say bye?' No mention of how sorry he felt for her, she noted thankfully.

'Bye,' she said, instantly relieved because she didn't want to face him after what he'd seen with Raj earlier, and was about to disconnect the line when she heard him say something.

'Wait,' he said. 'That's it? We meet after so many years and all you have to say to me is BYE?'

'Look, Niru, I'm exhausted. Please, let's keep in touch. I'll call you.'

'Hold on!' Niru was persistent. 'If you're staying away because of Dolly's letter, I must tell you there's no need. She'd told me about it.'

Shweta winced. 'Really?' She wouldn't have made a fool of herself if only she'd known.

'Yes. But why did you hold on to that for all these years?'

'No reason. I tend to carry guilt around. Strange but true.'

'Then why did you tell me about Trisha? You should have let that be too.'

'Why are you annoying me, Niru?' She flicked her errant hair off her face. 'What do you want?'

'Only a small get-together at the club next door. Think you can make it for old times' sake?'

Tsk! 'I don't feel like it. Seriously!'

'I'm sure a drink will do you good.' Niru's voice was smooth. 'Besides it's just close family. I'll see you there in fifteen minutes.'

'I think I'll pass.'

'I swear I'll come up there and drag you down myself even if I have to break down the door.'

She sighed.

'There! I knew you'd be a sport.'

'Whatever.' She hung up.

Shweta clambered off the bed reluctantly, washed her face, and ran a brush through her hair. Then she put on her jeans and an indigo spaghetti top that she really liked. She dabbed on some lip gloss for good measure. She needed to shake off the despondent feeling that had been suffocating her since lunch. Also, Niru was right. She'd probably never see him again and she owed him this last goodbye. All he wanted was a decent farewell. For old times' sake.

She trudged down the stairs and out of the hotel. The club he was talking about was to the right, in the unit adjacent to the hotel. The bouncer at the entrance gave her a nod as she opened the glossy wooden door.

Shweta entered a dark room with heavy woodwork that resembled a den. Dim lights swept the room, and smoke and trance music filled the air. A heavy oak counter stood to her right. One of the two men at the bar counter flashed her a smile. She hoped she didn't cut a sleazy look.

Her eyes spotted her group to the far left. Simbu looked dashing in a midnight blue shirt and tan corduroy pants. Lekha dazzled in a sleeveless black gown, her hair up in a chignon. Not to be outdone, Neha wore a cream shimmery dress and matching pumps. Niru's purple formal shirt and black jeans looked effortlessly classy. His hair was gelled and spiked. He was facing the door and broke into a wide smile when he saw her walk towards them.

'Hey, you're not too late.' He gestured to the seat beside him. 'We just ordered the drinks.'

The rest of the gang smiled and hugged her. They were seated on two large comfortable semi-circular sofas facing each other. Simbu and Lekha were seated across while Neha sat on Niru's other side.

Shweta sat down. The others had been in the middle of a conversation.

'Simbu was just telling us an old story,' Neha said.

Shweta nodded, glad the group was carrying on as if nothing had happened earlier that afternoon.

'I think you should start again, Simbu.'

Simbu smiled eagerly. 'Okay, I was just talking about the time we only had landline phones. You remember the time, Shweta?'

She nodded. Yes, she vaguely remembered.

'So, one day the phone rang and Neha picked it up. Ma and I were sitting in the dining room right beside the phone and we were both ears, of course. So when we heard Neha say *Yes, Yes,* our eyes were all trained on her.'

This was where he had stopped before Shweta joined them so Lekha kicked his foot playfully and egged him on. 'And then?'

'We were just wondering who it was when at the end of all the yes-es Neha suddenly said *Wrong number* and hung up.'

Lekha's mouth fell open. 'So, you were having a *Yes* conversation with a wrong number?'

Everyone cracked up, for those who knew Neha, knew how much she loved to talk, even to a wrong number.

'Oh, I was just having a bit of fun with a telemarketer,' Neha explained.

Shweta laughed hard at the anecdote and felt herself loosening up. 'Where's Mohan?' she asked Neha.

'He's keeping Max and Ria company. He said he'd join us later.'

The drinks arrived, and while Shweta waited for her order, she related an incident from Simbu's childhood that she remembered.

'Simbu's girlfriend would call the house when Ma was out.'

Lekha narrowed her eyes at Simbu, who returned her glance with a shrug. 'It was just a crush,' he said, laughing. 'The girl on the phone had a crush on me and not the other way round.' Lekha mock-pouted.

Neha put an end to the couple's little spat with a flourish of her arms. 'Shush, you two! Let Shweta continue.'

'And Simbu was finally caught one day when Ma happened to be home. She was so furious when he argued that he wasn't the reason for the sudden spike in the phone bill that she sent him to bed without dinner.'

Everyone cracked up again. Eager for a break from the silly tales about him, Simbu egged her on. 'Tell them about the boy who called Neha.'

'Oh yes, I forgot about this boy who wouldn't stop calling our house,' Shweta said, giggling. 'One day Neha picked up the phone and he just started talking to her. Then he called practically every day. One time, Ma happened to pick up the phone and this boy, in his sweet drawling voice, said, "Hello, what were you doing?" Ma was so scandalized that she almost dropped the receiver. "Who is this?" she asked in her meanest voice and the boy cut the call in a hurry and never called again.'

Simbu hooted. 'Oh, yes,' he teased Neha. 'Ma ordered you girls to stay away from the phone after that. Only the men were allowed to pick up calls.'

Neha frowned. She'd had a very tough time talking to her boyfriend after that.

'What about you, Shweta? Niru gave Shweta a teasing glance. 'No boyfriend tales for you?'

'No,' Shweta said curtly and looked away.

'Oh, she was lost in the world of books and movies,' Neha said. Suddenly turning to the group, her eyes glittering, she said, 'We should have a family WhatsApp group, no? It would be awesome if we could all stay in touch. Gosh, why didn't I think of it before?'

Everyone nodded. Neha immediately took it upon herself to create a group and add everyone, including Niru, who she said was like family too.

Niru waved his hand, dismissing the idea to include him. 'Me?'

'Come on,' Simbu said, 'she's right. You're like family too. We should all keep in touch. Right, Shweta?'

'Of course!' Shweta didn't want to lose touch again after all these years.

Neha high-fived Niru. 'Welcome to the family.'

Shweta's drink arrived along with the seconds for everyone. After the loud cheers and hearty sips, the conversation flowed more easily. Shweta felt her troubles melt away. They pulled each other's legs, especially rejoicing in teasing the newlyweds.

34

As time went on, the gang grew boisterous. Everyone was laughing, now that childhood skeletons were tumbling out of all their closets.

Shweta watched Niru. His eyes glistened with a dreamy glaze as he chuckled, his body shaking with laughter. She found herself staring at him too often, but was unable to pull her eyes off him.

'Helloooo,' a voice travelled towards their seat.

It was Trisha, wearing a black cocktail dress. She went up to Lekha and hugged her. 'Well, here you are and I've been looking all over for you. Mum asked me to check if you could arrange a car to drop me home.'

Shweta was surprised to hear that. There were cabs and there were other folks who could arrange the cab. Why come to find Lekha?

'Hi, Niru.' Trisha waved at him, greeting the others at the table too.

'Why don't you join us for a bit, Trisha?' Lekha said. 'I've sent a message to Papa. He'll call me back soon.'

Trisha was only too happy to oblige and took the seat beside Lekha. She crossed her legs and put her hands daintily on her knees. 'What's this party about?'

Nobody said anything.

'I thought you guys would be long gone home. And then I saw Niru through the glass.'

Simbu snorted, quickly improvising to make it sound like a sneeze. Neha caught on. 'Are you cold, Simbu?'

'I think so. I think Trisha brought in a sheet of cool air with her.'

Trisha pouted. 'Oops, so sorry! I hope I didn't interrupt?'

Neha rolled her eyes surreptitiously. 'Why did you stay back so late?' she asked Trisha. 'Didn't you need to get back home?'

Everyone's attention turned to Trisha. She began to squirm.

She uncrossed her legs and crossed them again, adjusting her dress. 'My friend Charu and I went out shopping and I just dropped her back. She's staying at the hotel tonight. Then I saw you guys and thought I could probably join you.' She turned to Lekha, squeezing her arm. 'I heard there was a commotion at the wedding. Is everything alright?' She noted the silence around the table and added quickly, 'But I must say I had such a great time today. This was the best wedding ever.'

Lekha smiled but none of the others did. Neha had her head bowed over her phone. Simbu went to check about that special drink he'd ordered. An awkward silence fell upon the group, thankfully disrupted by the ring of a phone—Trisha's.

'Oh, it's my mom,' she said, swiping her screen to answer the call.

'Hi, Ma...Yes...Yes...Yes.'

Shweta couldn't help smiling at the yes-es, remembering Neha's story. She caught Niru smiling too and they exchanged amused glances.

Trisha disconnected and looked distressed. Her eyes wobbled as she turned to Lekha. 'Mum's mad that I hadn't told her I was going to be late. She asked Uncle Shakti to arrange a cab. It's waiting outside. I'd better go.'

She waved goodbye to everyone. 'Bye, Niru,' she said to him specially. 'The food was amazing. I'll get in touch with you if I have a party in the future. I'll get your number from Lekha.'

'Sure.' Niru waved back with a smile.

Everyone turned their eyes to Niru and exploded into laughter the moment she left.

'What?' Niru gave a nonchalant shrug.

'I think she likes you,' Lekha teased.

'Ooh, she wants your number,' Simbu followed.

Niru was enjoying the attention, much to Simbu's amusement.

Shweta shifted in her seat uncomfortably. Why did she care who liked Niru? Their eyes met briefly and she looked away. Another round of drinks arrived at the table and Shweta focused her attention on the pink cocktail in her glass rather than on the annoying man sitting beside her and grinning like a Cheshire cat. A few, quick, large sips made her feel much better.

Neha dove right back into the party spirit. 'Ok, let's play this game called Lovers. Let's start with Lekha.'

They were all so sloshed that nobody bothered to ask what it was. Shweta, for one, had never heard of such a game.

Lekha giggled. 'Why me first? Let's start with Simbu. A woman should never reveal her age or her lovers.' She looked at Simbu coyly and cozied up to him.

Ah! So she probably knew what the game was. Simbu and she locked into an embrace. It certainly looked as though, instead of playing group games all night, the couple needed some privacy. After all, it was their wedding night.

Oblivious to the change in mood, Neha carried on. 'It's okay, I'll start. There was this guy—'

'No-no!' Shweta cried, and shook Neha by the arm. 'I think you should keep it for another day. Look at the lovebirds. They need some rest too.'

Simbu jumped at the suggestion. 'We'll drop her to her room.' He pulled a very reluctant Neha to her feet.

'I don't need you to haul me up,' Neha complained and just then, one of her pumps tottered under her uneven footing. 'Shit!' Neha cursed.

'Oh, come on now. Be a good girl!' Simbu said, and held on to her tight. Finally, flanked by Simbu and Lekha, Neha was led away.

Shweta continued to sit, while Niru settled the bill.

'Let me drop you to your room.' His voice startled her. She didn't realize Niru was done and was standing next to her, offering her his hand. She stood up cautiously, tottering a little. She was almost not okay. She put her hand into his and let him lead her outside.

A breeze whipped her hair as they exited from the back into the parking area. Shweta wrapped her arms around herself. It was quiet outside. They stepped out onto the path, lined with trees. The pathway snaked along the edge of the lawn, all the way over to the front of the hotel.

Shweta looked up at the pitch-black sky and took a clumsy step forward. She fumbled as her heels wobbled and before she could grab Niru's arm for support, her ankle gave way and twisted. 'Ouch!' Her ankle stung.

Niru made a grab for her waist before she could trip over. 'You okay?'

She straightened and laughed, wiping away the tears that had sprung up in her eyes. He saw that and held on. He looked so angelic, gazing down at her with concerned eyes that she almost felt like laughing despite her pain. A few strands of his hair tumbled over his forehead. She reached out to sweep them back but they fell again. Shweta grinned.

'Thanks!' Niru said, touching his hair self-consciously. 'Do you want to sit down?' He pointed to the nearby ledge.

She didn't mind sitting down for a bit. 'Sure.'

Shweta limped, making her way to the ledge, supported by Niru. She settled down and he sat down next to her.

He smelled of eau de cologne. The hair on his arm tickled her bare hand. He sat with his hands planted firmly on the ledge, his legs swinging a little off the ground. She hadn't realized how chiselled his features were—a sharp nose and high cheekbones. Her gaze travelled further down to his mouth.

Stop it! Shweta scolded herself, sure it was the alcohol. This wasn't supposed to turn into some romantic fantasy.

But this was Niru, for God's sake, she thought. She needn't feel awkward. Perfectly smug over that theory, she leaned over and rested her head on his shoulders.

He shifted, then pulled her in closer, a hand lightly touching her shoulder. Suddenly this didn't feel like a good idea. She rose. 'Ouch!' She shouldn't have jumped up like that, given that her ankle was still bad.

He held her hands so she had to turn towards him. 'I wanted to thank you for everything.'

'You've already thanked me.'

His eyes crinkled at the corners. 'Again then?'

She snorted and sat down. 'Gosh, are you so nice when you're drunk?'

'I'm honest too.' He tucked a long strand of hair behind her ear. 'Besides, I'm not drunk.'

'Then tell me honestly, why did you and Lisa break up?' Shweta had no idea what was it with her that she kept bringing up Niru's Italian girlfriend. And that she remembered her name. But the enigmatic Italian girlfriend begged to be in every conversation.

Niru looked surprised. 'I told you already.'

Shweta dug in her heels. 'You said you were officially off because she didn't want to come to India.'

Niru let out a breath. 'Okay, here's the simple reason. She wanted me to go back with her to Italy and I didn't want to.'

Shweta nodded, urging him to go on.

He paused, eyebrows drawn in. 'Tell me, why are you so interested in me all of a sudden?'

She ignored that question and crossed her arms over her chest. 'You don't believe in making compromises for love?'

'I believe in compromises, sure. But she gave me an ultimatum, which I thought was very unfair.' He ran his fingers through his hair. 'So I refused.'

'Good.'

'What's so good about that?' he said, turning to look at her, and laughed.

'That you didn't get married.'

Again the eyebrows drew in. He had that teasing look. 'That makes you happy?'

'If you'd married…'

'If I had married?' He leaned in and cupped her chin before she could finish.

She looked away, flustered. 'If you'd married the wrong girl, I'd have been…sad.' That sounded surprising, even to her ears.

'Sadder than you feel for yourself?' His voice rasped.

All of a sudden a wave of despair washed over her. She hopped off the ledge and stumbled as she tried to get away from him.

His hand locked on her wrist and pulled her back. 'Sorry, I'm an idiot!'

Tears pricked the back of her eyes. She tried to free herself of his hold but he wouldn't let go.

He pulled her close and tipping her chin, kissed her.

It took her completely by surprise. She stiffened, her heart lurching into a frenzy at the brush of his lips, his kiss, hard at first, then slower.

As his kiss went deeper, crushing her lips with an intensity that was demanding, she moaned and felt her knees tremble and give away. In an instant, his hands grabbed her waist and held her steady.

He smelled like a heady mix of aftershave and wine.

So good!

She felt herself relaxing and responding with a need of her own. Her hands buried deep in his hair, she clung to him, her skin tingling as his hands travelled the length of her back and pulled her in.

Only the sounds of their kissing and the loud unsteady thrum of their heartbeats ruffled the tranquil silence of the night.

They came up for air momentarily and he asked, his voice a sexy whisper, 'Do I kiss better now?'

She nodded, grinning like a silly young girl of sixteen.

He stroked her hair gently and his gaze roamed indulgently over her face, taking in her forehead, eyes, nose, lips, and finally, the chain around her neck. Her thaali. He froze. A flicker of emotion crossed his eyes.

A shrill whistle sounded suddenly. Sweeping down the path, the headlights of a car shone.

They started and pulled apart.

The car came into view. It was headed to the parking lot at the back.

Their eyes met again briefly before the car passed them and the path was engulfed in darkness again. Niru spoke softly. 'Sorry, I didn't mean for that to happen.'

Shweta's cheeks burned. Who was she kidding? She was still married.

He walked her back to the hotel elevator in silence. 'Ma left after the wedding,' he said. 'I have to return the tempo and leave soon.'

Nothing about seeing her again or keeping in touch.

The elevator pinged when it arrived on the ground floor. They said goodbye. Shweta stepped in and the door closed, with Niru standing outside wearing an unfathomable expression.

When the elevator reached her floor, Shweta was bursting with agitation. In her room, she changed into her pyjamas, brushed her teeth, and got into bed, but couldn't get any sleep. She got up and began pacing the floor, hoping to crash out of sheer exhaustion. But sleep eluded her despite her working herself into a tizzy all night.

Over a kiss! A stupid, idiotic kiss!

35

The next morning Shweta woke up to an incessant banging at her door. She squinted at the clock. It was nine in the morning. The banging continued. She dragged herself out of bed and, making sure her nightshirt was pulled down appropriately, made for the door.

'Ria?'

Ria barged in, in tears.

Alarmed, Shweta pulled her in and shut the door. 'What happened?'

Ria burst into wails and took a full minute to calm down. 'Max came to our room and made Ma cry,' she said, and burst into tears again.

'Why? What happened?'

'I don't know! She was crying when I came out of the bathroom.'

Shweta wondered what had happened overnight. 'Go to Grandma's room,' she told Ria. 'And stay there. It's the second room to the right. I'll go down and check if everything is okay and come right back.'

Ria nodded and was about to leave, when Shweta said, 'Don't tell Grandma anything.' Ria nodded again and wiped her wet cheeks.

Shweta rushed downstairs to Neha's room.

Neha opened at the first knock. Her eyes were puffy, her kohl was smudged, and her face was blotched with tears.

Shweta stepped in and did a double take when she saw Max sitting on the bed. 'Max, what are you doing here?'

'I was just going to go back to my room. Wasn't feeling well this morning and wanted to see Mohan.' He looked crestfallen. 'Sorry, I can't help but think this was all my fault.'

Shweta didn't get it. 'Your fault?'

'Yeah, Neha said Mohan hadn't come back to his room last night. I told her he'd left last night to meet Sita.'

Neha looked at her anxiously. 'And he hasn't come back all night.'

'Who's Sita?' Shweta asked.

'He was chatting with me last night when Sita called,' Max said. 'After that, he sent Ria back to her room and told me he had to meet someone. When I told this to Neha, she began to cry.'

'See, I told you something was wrong,' Neha cried.

'Now that you're here,' Max said, getting up and opening the door, 'I'm going to head back to sleep.'

Shweta turned to Neha after Max had left, closing the door behind him. 'Have you heard of Sita before?'

'No!'

'Must be one of his patients.'

Neha flung her arms in despair. 'Then why didn't he come back all night?'

Shweta was trying to console her when she was interrupted by a knock at the door. Shweta rushed to open it.

Ria stood outside, looking terrified. 'Grandpa is very sick. Grandma is calling you, quickly!'

Neha jumped out of bed and the three of them rushed upstairs to their mother's room.

The door was open and Prabhu was sprawled on the bed, clutching his chest in pain.

Keertana stood next to him, rubbing his chest. She whirled around when she heard them. 'He was sitting here with his newspaper and he'd just finished his coffee. Suddenly he started feeling a pain in the chest. Luckily Ria came in just then. Call help soon. Quick!' she said.

Neha ran to Prabhu's bedside and punched the number for the reception on the intercom. 'Please can you call for an ambulance soon? It's an emergency.'

Next, she punched Mohan's number on her cell phone and waited anxiously as it rang. Words tumbled out of her mouth when Mohan answered. Quickly she told him what had happened. He told her he'd meet her directly at the hospital.

The four of them huddled together, and waited until the ambulance reached. Within minutes, Prasad and Simbu also arrived in Prabhu's room.

Things moved pretty fast, thereafter. The front desk called to inform them that the ambulance and doctor had reached. The doctor started CPR and ordered the attendant to bring the stretcher in. Within ten minutes, the ambulance screeched away from the hotel, Prabhu and Simbu in it.

While Neha was calling for a cab, Shweta rushed to her room to get her purse. Her heart thumped in her chest as she unlocked her door. All sorts of worrisome thoughts crossed her mind. Did Papa's heart attack have anything to do with the incident with Raj yesterday? Did he threaten Papa? Did it mean she'd have to go back to Raj?

Whatever had happened and would happen, Shweta hoped her father would recover. That's what mattered the most to her right now. She said a little prayer as she locked the door behind her and got into the cab that took the three of them to the hospital.

36

Prabhu lay on the hospital bed, his eyes closed and tubes hanging over his arm.

The doctors had finished the angiography and discovered a couple more blocks. They recommended inserting new stents.

Keertana stood by Prabhu's bed, clinging to his hand, an anxious look on her face. Neha, Shweta, and Simbu waited in the room for the doctor's call into the OT.

Mohan arrived just then and all eyes swivelled to him. 'I've just spoken to the doctors. Nothing to worry about.'

The moment she saw him, Neha's eyes began to well up. She started sniffing aloud.

Mohan went over and put his arm around her. 'He'll be fine. Don't worry.'

Neha looked up at him and hissed, 'Where were you last night?'

Shweta, who was the closest to Neha, ushered them out into the hallway. When she was sure they were out of earshot, she said to Neha. 'Have some common sense. Papa's unwell. Can't you wait until that is over?'

Mohan looked surprised. 'What's the problem here?'

Neha turned to him, her eyes flashing with anger. 'First tell me where you were last night.'

'What has that got to do with Papa's condition?' Neha glared.

'Okay. I was meeting up an old classmate.'

Neha huddled over and sobbed.

Mohan threw his hands up in the air. 'What?!'

Shweta patted Neha's back and shushed her. 'Look, you can't be loud in the hospital.'

'Listen.' Mohan put his hand around Neha but she jerked it away. 'Okay,' he said. 'Whatever it is, let's go over to the canteen or somewhere outside so we can talk. I really don't get what's to cry about.'

The three of them took the elevator to the ground floor.

The moment they were outside the building, Neha lashed out at him. 'Max told me a Sita called you last night. Where were you the whole night?'

'I was with Sita.'

'What?'

'Wait, let me explain. How about we sit down and you let me tell you everything over a cup of coffee? Honestly, I really need a shower but that can wait.'

They settled down in the hospital canteen. None of them had had their breakfast, so they ordered masala dosas with coffee.

Neha fidgeted, impatient for Mohan to start talking.

'Ok, ok.' Mohan nodded.

Neha squinted at him. 'I want the whole story.'

'Like I said, I went to meet Sita,' Mohan began.

Neha pounced on him. 'Who is Sita?'

'Sita is Sita, short for Sitaraman. He's an old classmate from school.'

Neha continued glaring at him but said nothing, so he continued. 'So, Sita called me late last night because he needed my help. A woman had fallen in his bathroom and fainted, and so he wanted me to come over to his house.'

'Why did he have to call you?' Neha blurted.

'He called me because the woman needed medical attention.'

She shot him a curious look. 'Why couldn't he take her to the hospital?'

'He wanted to keep it confidential.'

'Why?' she cried.

'Neighbours and all, you know. Now, will you stop being so nosy and let me finish the story?'

Neha let out an impatient sigh.

'Sita got nervous when she didn't move so he called me. He knew I was in Chennai and called me as soon as it happened. When I went over, this woman's nose was bleeding and she had fainted in the bathroom. Sita and I lifted her up and got her in bed. I gave her a cold compress and checked her pulse. I waited till she regained consciousness, which took some time. She had a sprained ankle so I put on a temporary bandage. Sita offered to drop her back, except she could barely move. So I helped him take her to his car and we dropped her off at her place. By that time it was so late that I decided to go back to Sita's place for the night.'

He paused to catch his breath. Right on time, the waiter arrived with their coffee and dosas. There was silence as they dug in.

After he'd polished off his breakfast, Mohan wiped his mouth, and looked around the table brightly. 'Then,' he continued, 'since we were meeting after so long, we decided to have an early morning coffee and breakfast at Adyar and catch up on our lives. But I had just finished ordering my coffee when I got your call.'

'Didn't you think I'd worry?' Neha said, sounding like she was going to cry. 'Why didn't you call me?'

'I did try to call you. Have you checked your phone?'

Neha fished out her phone from her bag. Sure enough, there were three missed calls.

'I figured the party last night must have been too loud.'

Neha and Shweta exchanged guilty looks.

'By the time I'd decided to stay at Sita's, it was too late to call. By morning, I'd completely forgotten I hadn't told you.'

Neha looked up at him, her eyes welling up again.

He patted her cheek. 'Look, you have to believe me. Sita made me promise I wouldn't talk about his lady friend to anybody but you.'

Neha lowered her eyes to the table. 'I have to tell you something too.' Her voice was so soft, Mohan had to lean forward to hear. She shifted uncomfortably in her seat, before finally blurting out, 'I kissed Max this morning.'

'You what?' Mohan glared at her in shock. 'What for?'

Still staring at the table, she said, 'Because I was angry with you.'

'Wait!' Shweta cut in before Mohan and Neha could start an argument over Max. 'Max didn't tell you he was gay?'

Mohan stared at Shweta. 'What?'

Neha covered her face with her hands. 'No wonder...' She smarted and then turned to Shweta. 'Why didn't you tell me?'

Mohan broke into hoots of laughter. 'Poor chap! He mustn't have known what hit him.'

'How did I not know about it?' Neha cried.

'Your sister is crazy,' Mohan said to Shweta, as he laughed, his head thrown back.

Neha looked at Mohan, pouting. 'Is that why you're not upset?'

Mohan brushed it away. '*Uffo*, my upset wife! What a fabulous way to take revenge! I'm not as upset as you were with me. Are you okay now?'

'Well, it wasn't really a kiss,' Neha admitted slowly, after a few moments of silence. Shweta and Mohan stared at her in astonishment. 'I think I shocked him but he was quick enough to stop me. Poor guy! I feel so sorry for him now.'

Shweta and Mohan cracked up, and there were tears in their eyes. Neha permitted herself a guilty half-smile.

'I guess, now that the mystery is solved, we have to go,' Mohan said. 'Ria's alone. We'll come in and check on Papa later.' They left and Shweta headed upstairs, back to her father's room.

At the door, she heard voices from inside, and paused.

'The doctor has asked you not to take on any more stress.' It was Prasad's voice.

She heard her father saying, 'I need another week to make arrangements for the money.'

'Or what?' Prasad's voice rose. 'He'll make life hell for you and Shweta?'

Shweta hesitated for a few moments, wondering if she should enter the room. Stifling her fears, she decided she had to. She had to find out what had happened between her father and Raj.

Shweta slid the door open and stepped in as four pairs of eyes turned to her.

37

Her mother, Simbu, and Prasad were gathered around her father.

Shweta walked up to her father's bedside.

He turned his head to look at her, his eyes moist and sad.

'Papa, about Raj…' she began softly.

Keertana cut in. 'Not now, Shweta. Your father is not allowed to take on any stress.'

Prabhu held up his hand. 'No, I want to explain this. I want to tell her everything.' He stared at the ceiling and let out a deep breath. 'It's true,' he admitted. 'I needed the money and I'm going to tell you everything before I go into the OT.'

'Not now, Prabhu,' Keertana pleaded. 'Please don't talk too much.'

Prabhu shook his head. 'I must.' He stretched his hand reaching out to hold Shweta's.

Shweta clasped his hand and waited.

'A week or two after you were married,' he began, 'I wanted some money for trading. It was a good investment in the market, something that was sure to make a profit if I sold it at the right time. It would have helped clear the marriage debts. So I borrowed some money from Raj and promised to return it within a month.'

He paused and sighed. 'But, it was not to be.' Hurt swirled in his eyes. 'Due to the troubles in the market, I started making losses and I couldn't return the money. But now Raj insists on having his money back immediately if Shweta wants a divorce.' Prabhu shut his eyes and tried to breathe normally.

Shweta squeezed his hand. 'Papa!' she cried out in anguish.

He opened his eyes and gazed at her. 'As much as I'd like to save this family, I cannot sacrifice my daughter to that bastard.'

Shweta looked at him, surprised. She hadn't expected her father to get on her side.

Prabhu's voice was soft. 'Simbu told me everything, and after what I witnessed yesterday…' His eyes welled up. 'I was wrong. I should have listened to you.'

Shweta broke down. Her mother drew her close and hugged her in an embrace. Was her father really on her side? Shweta shivered in disbelief.

Prasad intervened. 'Now we have to handle the whole issue rationally and judiciously. To get back to what we were discussing earlier, I can break my mutual funds and arrange for some money.'

Simbu agreed to pitch in too. 'But before I let that bastard go,' he said, 'we have to make sure he signs the divorce papers.'

Prabhu's eyes widened in surprise.

'Mohan has already got the papers ready,' Simbu explained. 'All we need are Raj's signatures.'

'I'll go with you,' Prasad said to Simbu.

Shweta turned to her father. 'Papa, we still have the gold you bought for my marriage. We can always sell that. Of what use is it, if not for such emergencies?'

Papa shook his head. 'Not the gold,' he said. 'But we'll manage by selling some stocks, and with Prasad's and Simbu's help.'

The nurse and attendant entered to wheel Prabhu away. Keertana said she'd wait until the operation was over. Simbu and Prasad left together to decide on the arrangements before going to meet Raj.

Shweta herself was too tired to stay back. The morning's events had left her rattled and exhausted.

She returned to her hotel room and headed straight to the shower. The warm spray of water over her shoulders and back felt exceedingly good. Eyes closed, she thought of how the day had unfolded, and relief swept over her.

She pushed away thoughts of Raj. The fact that her father had been convinced was what mattered.

Slowly, as she relaxed, her thoughts went back to the events of the night before.

She thought of Niru. And…

She felt a dull ache in her chest. Had it meant anything, Shweta wondered, mournfully.

She bit her lip and sighed as she turned off the shower. She faced the mirror and wiped off the cloudy haze. Her gaze fell on the thaali still around her neck. What did she need it for, now?

She took it off and cupped the chain in her palm. Still wrapped in her towel, she went to her suitcase and put it along with the rest of her jewellery. She didn't need her thaali—the root of all her unhappiness and misery—any more. As far as she was concerned, this marriage was over. Only the legal formalities remained.

Which would soon be over too, she hoped.

38

Prasad's lawyer friend had suggested an annulment instead of a divorce for Shweta, since it was within a year of her marriage. Prasad and Simbu managed to settle all the payments with Raj in exchange for his signatures on the annulment papers. Raj signed the papers willingly when they threatened him with harassment charges, which would delay his immigration to Canada.

Bindu and Prasad left a few days after the wedding. Simbu and Lekha left for Bali on their honeymoon. From there, they were to fly back to Singapore.

Prabhu, Keertana, Shweta, and Max returned to Bangalore by car instead of catching a flight because of what the doctor had advised for Prabhu.

* * *

Prabhu looked forward to his rummy evening with his neighbour and friend, Prasad, the following Sunday. Despite Keertana's worry about his exertion, he insisted on going. It had been so long since Prasad and he had got together.

Keertana and he reached Prasad's house by 5 p.m.

Bindu had made a heart-friendly, light snack - bruschetta - instead of the usual pakodas with tea.

The men sat on the porch and began the game in earnest while the women sat on nearby seats and caught up on community gossip.

By 7 p.m., after they had wound up the game, they moved indoors to continue with their customary karaoke session followed by dinner.

Mic swinging and head swaying, the men belted out old Rafi and Kishore numbers, while the women picked songs by Lata Mangeshkar and Asha Bhosle.

As the evening wore on, the songs turned raunchier. Prabhu frowned at Prasad's offer of lemonade in place of the customary glass of whisky but accepted it graciously nevertheless. He was just happy for the company again. It was a joyous evening, just like the old times. Prabhu's recent heart attack was forgotten and the conversation flowed as they sat down at the table for dinner afterwards.

Prabhu was touched by Bindu's light version of the special biryani that she had made especially for him.

As he inhaled the aroma of biryani and cast a look around the table of happy friends, a wave of nostalgia swept through him. Overwhelmed by the trouble the Prasads had gone through to take care of him after his attack, his eyes misted and he couldn't control his emotions.

Prabhu felt a sob escape his lips and before he could stop himself, he was bent over with tears rolling down his cheeks. He covered his face with his hands and wept like a child. Keertana rushed to his side and touched his shoulder. 'Prabhu, are you okay?'

Shortly, Prabhu wiped his tears and addressed Prasad and Bindu. 'I've been very ungrateful lately. I hope you'll forgive my arrogance and pride these last few months.'

Then he turned to Keertana and squeezed her hand. 'I have wronged Shweta too. I hope she'll forgive me.'

Keertana nodded quietly.

Prasad came over to Prabhu's side and patted his shoulder. 'Prabhu,' he said, 'it's better late than never. Let the children choose their life and be happy. That is what we can do for them. Shweta is a smart and capable girl. I'm sure she'll find somebody who deserves her. The Gods will take care of her, just as they helped her escape from Raj's clutches.'

Prabhu clasped his hands gratefully.

'Cheers!' Bindu said from across the table, lifting her glass of water. 'Now, let's eat before we let my efforts go to waste.'

They all laughed and began eating. The mood in the dining room went back to joyous as they shared more anecdotes about the wedding.

Finally, at 10.30 p.m., Prabhu and Keertana left for home.

A cool breeze blew against Prabhu's cheeks as he stepped outside. It was dark but peaceful, the path lit by street lamps that rendered a soft glow of light.

Prabhu reached out to hold Keertana's hand as they walked back home.

All would be well in his world again soon, he hoped.

* * *

One evening, a few days later, Shweta was alone on the porch when her father came up to her, his pipe in his hand.

'You know,' her father said, 'I've been thinking ever since we came back from Chennai. Max is a good boy. Although I don't approve of him a hundred per cent, I think he'd make a good son-in-law. If you like him, I will give you my blessing.'

Shweta's jaw dropped. What had come over her father's sentiments for Max? She eyed him curiously.

He took a deep puff before pulling out his pipe. 'I mean it,' he said. 'I mean, there's no point forcing you to do what we want. It's your life.'

She hugged him tight. 'Thanks, Papa,' she said, tears welling up in her eyes.

Her father looked at her, eyebrows raised. 'Well?'

She decided to put him out of his agony. 'No thanks, Papa,' she said, grinning. 'Max is not my type.'

'Thank God!' her father exclaimed, his hand to his chest. 'Now, let's go in for dinner.'

She giggled and followed him to the dining room. Her father had become a changed man since his attack, more humorous and entertaining. Even Max was surprised to see Prabhu's change towards him. 'Is he the same person I met when we came to India?' he asked Shweta one day, conspiratorially.

'That's my Papa,' Shweta said, beaming.

Max was to leave for Delhi for his Himalayan expedition early the next morning, and Neha came home to bid him farewell.

She hugged him, the earlier awkwardness between them now a laughing matter, an episode they knew would be fodder for entertainment at all future gatherings. 'I'm going to miss you.'

The sisters drove him to the airport. After the Himalayan trip, Max had a flight straight back to the US from Delhi. So this would be the last time they were going to see him. They bid him goodbye. Shweta sent her love to Julie and Sarah. Max promised to email her as soon as he reached home.

Neha stayed over that night, without Ria this time.

'How did you manage to leave Ria at home?' Shweta asked, surprised.

Neha smiled. 'I guess I don't need to hover around her all the time,' she said. 'She'll be fine.'

Shweta fidgeted with her kurta.

'What?'

Should she tell Neha? 'Nothing.'

Neha's eyes were still on her. 'Tell me, what's wrong?'

Shweta confessed about the night Niru had kissed her.

'What!' Neha was shocked. A moment later, however, she chuckled.

'I think I love him,' Shweta said, and bit her lip.

'High time you acknowledged your feelings for him,' Neha said, smiling.

Shweta frowned. 'What do you mean?'

'Did you tell him?' Neha asked, eagerly. 'Does he love you too?'

Shweta shrugged. 'Not sure. He apologised for kissing me though.'

'Typical Niru,' Neha said, and chuckled again.

'How do I know if this isn't just one-sided?'

Neha looked around for her phone. 'Well, find out! Call him up and ask him. Or I will.'

'No!' Shweta jumped to stop Neha, who was in full search mode already. 'I don't want anyone to say a word.'

Neha frowned at her.

'If he likes me, he'll let me know,' Shweta said, her chin up.

Neha tsk-tsked. 'Stay that way. But don't cry on my shoulders later when he gets married to someone else.'

'Let me remind you that I was the one who got married first.'

'Yeah, and he never attended it.'

'He couldn't come. He was busy.'

'You can believe that, if you like. I don't,' Neha said and turned her head away in a huff.

What exactly was Neha getting at?

But no matter how hard Shweta tried to talk to her, Neha wouldn't say another word.

39

It was the week of departures. Neha, Mohan, and Ria left for Sri Lanka at the end of the week.

Keertana was, surprisingly, in tears to see her oldest daughter go away from her for the first time in all these years. Ria's excitement couldn't be contained and she jumped up and down at the airport, not standing still even for a moment.

Shweta came back to an almost empty house, with just her parents and her. Time passed very slowly while she waited for the interview call from Sakra Hospital where Mohan had forwarded her resume before the wedding.

At breakfast one morning, Keertana said that Trisha's mother had asked her advice about a proposal to Niru for Trisha.

Shweta paused while bringing the sambar-dunked idli to her mouth. 'What did you say?'

'I said he's a good boy. Decent and hard-working,' her mother replied. 'Trisha's mother was very keen that the two should get engaged when Trisha graduates by mid-year.'

Shweta nodded and put the uneaten idli back in the bowl of sambar.

'What happened to you?' Keertana asked. 'You haven't touched your idlis.'

'Nothing, Ma. I guess I'm just nervous about finding a job.'

But Shweta could do nothing more that day than think about Niru. In the quiet of her room, she took out her phone to check out his display picture on WhatsApp. He looked dashing in a long maroon-coloured kurta and a black Nehru vest. His smiling eyes crinkled at the corners.

Have you forgotten me, she asked the picture.

He didn't reply, obviously, and kept smiling at her, much to her chagrin.

Shweta was beginning to grow listless as the days passed.

She rarely came down from her room except for meals, which were brief, uncomfortable moments spent with her parents at the same table where her dad tried to make her smile, and her mum tried to fill all the silences. But she didn't feel like talking to them.

She forgot to brush her hair. Sometimes she didn't feel like a shower. As she was coming down the stairs one day, her mother said, 'Shweta, you look terrible. Are you okay, my dear?'

She wanted to shake her head and go bawling to hug her mother but instead she said, 'I'm fine, Ma,' and ran back upstairs to straighten herself up.

It was a relief when, after a few more weeks of utter despair and sadness, Shweta was finally called for an interview at Sakra Hospital. It went well and she was offered a job in the insurance department. Her joining date was set for the following month.

'We should go shopping for your purse materials,' Shweta said to her mother one day, now that she had so much time on her hands. It was also what she needed to keep her idle thoughts off Niru.

Keertana looked excited and eager to start on the new project. A lot of women had admired her purses and one of her cousins had placed an order for a good number to be given away at a marriage in her family.

Shweta and Keertana took off to Commercial Street right after breakfast, and shopped until they dropped, returning home with bags filled with an assortment of brocades, lace trimmings, fancy buttons, and everything that caught their fancy.

Her mother soon got started on the purses.

* * *

Almost a month had passed with no news from Niru. Shweta was quietly beginning to lose hope.

Her joining date at Sakra neared. She was to start on Monday and realized she had nothing to wear to work. So she forced herself to step out with her mother and buy a few salwar suits and a pair of heels. Her mother also said she'd lend her some of her sarees so she'd have enough to start with. The arrangement suited Shweta just fine.

Surprisingly, two good things happened during this period.

The annulment of her marriage by an ex-parte decree came through, because Raj was not in the country to make his appearance in court.

Secondly, Max emailed to say that he was moving to Florida, and had found a new job at housekeeping, and a new friend. That had brightened up her morning and she replied immediately to congratulate him.

Soon after, her new job started. Going to work again was a relief; it kept her busy. Life acquired a routine again and she was spared the boredom of idleness. In the evenings after work, she liked to gaze out of the window of her room until it grew dark outside. On weekends, she stayed at home and avoided going out with her parents. Sometimes they called her to the Prasads' house for their rummy evenings on Sundays, but she preferred to stay at home, watch TV, make a bowl of Maggi, and call it an early night.

She knew her new life didn't hold much charm. She had thoughts about moving to a place of her own. She couldn't have her parents take care of her their whole life and she certainly didn't want to treat their home like a guest house. She was waiting for the right time to bring it up. In the meantime, she started talking to her colleagues to check about rental apartments near the hospital.

She still gazed at Niru's picture on WhatsApp sometimes, but had given up hope that he'd get in touch ever again. He hadn't called or texted. Even Neha hadn't heard from him in a long while. She wished she knew where he was.

Sometimes, when she watched a movie she couldn't help thinking of what Niru might have said had he been there...sitting next to her. Wouldn't he have laughed about how Mili looked completely fake when she cried, or how Sanjeev Kumar spoke like he had a lozenge stuck in his throat? She remembered all the good times they'd had when they were younger. It all seemed like such a long time ago.

She longed to see the crinkles around his eyes and hear his laugh. But most of all, her heartbeat still accelerated every time she thought about their kiss. Try as she did, that memory just wouldn't go away. She touched her lips and felt their smoothness. Her breath caught as she imagined Niru's lips on hers. How heady that kiss had felt! Oh, how she longed to be held and remain in his embrace for as long as she wanted to! Had he felt the same way that night about her? Had something changed for him too, and not just her? Or had she been imagining the urgency and the hunger of that kiss? Shweta squeezed her eyes shut and let that feeling wash over her.

Before she knew it, fat tears were falling on her lap. She'd been staring out of the window of her room, crying like a fool.

40

It had been weeks since Neha's return from the family vacation to Sri Lanka, but Shweta had gotten around to visiting her home only now.

She was met by an exuberant Ria at the door, who hugged her and ushered her in.

'We had such a good time in Sri Lanka, Aunt S,' Ria bubbled over with excitement.

Shweta ruffled her hair and smiled. 'Where are your mum and dad?'

Ria tugged at her hand instead. 'First, let me show you my drawings.'

Shweta allowed herself to be led to the balcony where Ria had been busy with her drawing sheets and colour pencils. Spread on the floor were A4 sheets full of drawings, some coloured, some shaded, and some simple sketches. A rose bush, a bunch of hibiscus flowers, and trees that she could see out of her balcony. Ria had used her surroundings as her muse and created paintings that were worth marvelling at. There was a half-done sketch of the tulsi plant that Shweta had seen the last time, and a water colour of the pretty bamboo shoots that had now grown taller. Ria beamed proudly as Shweta oohed and aahed at every one of her drawings.

'You draw nature so well,' Shweta said, as she gave Ria back her drawings. 'And you have such a lovely theme.'

'Niru said the same,' Ria said, putting her sheets in order.

Niru? Why hadn't Neha mentioned that to her? 'Niru was here?'

'He came to congratulate me on my prize,' Ria said, looking up proudly.

'Congratulations? What prize?'

'Remember the omelette that he taught me to flip? My teachers liked it very much. Everybody's eyes grew so wide when I did the flip not once, but three times.'

Shweta laughed. 'Really? Well, that must have been quite a sight. I must talk to Neha now. And we'll talk more after lunch, okay?'

Ria nodded, satisfied. Shweta headed towards the sounds coming from the kitchen, itching to settle her curiosity about Niru's visit.

And what a sight met her eyes! A curry gurgled on the burner as Neha held a spoon to Mohan's lips. 'Mmm,' he said, tasting it.

Shweta cleared her throat and the couple turned around, surprised to see her.

'Oh!' Mohan said, smiling. 'When did you come?'

Shweta laughed. 'I suppose you guys are busy. Didn't you even hear the bell?'

Neha came over and gave Shweta a hug then pulled apart to give her a close inspection. 'You look awful! You've lost a ton of weight. What have you been doing to yourself?'

Mohan, now peering into the refrigerator, looked over his shoulder at her. 'You look fine, Shweta.'

Shweta smiled. 'Said like a kind, older brother.'

'So, how's your new job?' His eyes twinkled.

'First, thank you so much for the recommendation.'

'Hey, I just passed on your resume,' he said, holding up a juicy red apple. 'I had nothing to do with your selection.'

Shweta pulled out the envelope she had brought with her and handed it to Mohan.

'Oh, no, no,' Mohan said when he opened it and realized what it was. 'I don't want you to return your flight money.'

'Please, I insist. It's the least I can do.'

Neha touched Mohan's shoulder. 'Take it, *na*!'

Mohan put the envelope into his pocket with a shrug. 'I guess I am so very proud of you, Shweta!'

'Thank you!' Shweta said. 'And I like my job. It's a great place, and the timings and co-workers are good. It keeps me occupied.'

'Oh good!' he said. 'See, that's why I enjoy going to work.' He winked at Neha. 'Now you see why I spend so much time there.'

Neha sniffed. 'Ya, if it were possible, you'd never come back home.'

It was good to see the light-hearted sparring between the couple. The vacation had done them good and both seemed to be in great spirits. This was the first time since she'd returned to India that Shweta had seen Neha smile and talk so much in Mohan's company.

But she couldn't wait to catch Neha alone to ask her about Niru's visit. It was quite surprising that Neha had not called her up to tell her the news.

The light banter between the three continued through lunch, and as soon as the table was cleared, and Mohan took his leave for a snooze, Shweta dragged Neha into another room.

'What?' Neha said, as Shweta pushed her towards the sofa and stood over her.

'Why didn't you tell me Niru had come?'

Neha face-palmed. 'Who told you?' Then it clicked. 'Of course, Ria did.'

'Why didn't you tell me?'

'Because he didn't want you to know?'

'How crazy! Why not?'

'He said he was busy setting up his new restaurant in Koramangala.' Neha slapped her head. 'Now I've told you that as well.'

'Serves him right for making you keep secrets from me!' But Shweta couldn't help thinking about why he hadn't even called her. 'Did he stay long? Did you ask him about his plans? Is he moving to

Bangalore?'

'*Uffo*! So many questions, Shweta!' Neha tsk-tsked. 'He wouldn't say anything else except what I've told you, but he said he'd keep me posted.'

Shweta looked at the floor.

Neha brushed her hand sympathetically. 'He did ask many questions about you.'

Shweta's eyes shot up. 'What did he ask?'

'Well he asked if Max was well, and what had happened with you and Raj.' She paused. 'You told me not to poke my nose into this, so I told him very subtly that Raj and you were officially divorced now.'

Shweta twiddled with the end of her kurti. 'Well, did he say anything else?'

'He seemed surprised that he hadn't heard about it from his mother. Then he said he was going to be very busy for a few weeks for his restaurant launch. And he wanted it to be a secret.'

That's it? Shweta's heart sank.

Neha rose from the sofa and held out her hand. 'Come on, let's go out,' she said, enthusiastically. 'Let's have some fun instead of crying over men.'

Shweta clasped her hand, feeling a tiny bit better. At least she had Neha to pour out her heart to.

Together, they decided to hit the mall. They left Ria with Mohan, who seemed to have finally learnt how to relax at home over the weekend instead of rushing off to the next emergency.

They headed out to Central Mall and caught a movie before spending the rest of the evening shopping.

By the time Shweta returned home, she'd forgotten about the thoughts that had troubled her. She'd eaten so much at the mall that she skipped dinner and went straight up to her room.

She switched on her computer and was surprised to see an email from Shipra. It brought tears of joy to her eyes.

Shipra was going to have a baby. The couple had moved to Pleasanton, California, and had bought a new town house. Shipra had sent her many pictures. One of her with her new baby bump, another of her and Virat standing outside their new home, and another cute one of the grapevines they'd planted in their backyard. Shweta gazed at the pictures, never happier for her friend.

'Raj has moved to Canada with his sister and isn't going to return to the States. He has started a company of his own there,' Shipra's email said. Shweta was relieved to read that Raj had moved far from her life. Shipra also mentioned Julie's café and how Virat and she had gone there to eat their usual burritos and fish cakes, and to say goodbye.

Shweta replied to Shipra's email immediately, sending her heartiest congratulations for the baby and the new house.

Then she collapsed on the bed and slept like a baby herself.

41

'You look so gaunt!' Neha looked at Shweta, concerned. 'I really meant it the other day when I said you looked awful. Have you been dieting?'

It was a Saturday evening. Neha had dropped in to meet Shweta and the sisters were up in Shweta's room after tea.

'I guess the long hours at work are tiring. And life sort of feels empty.' This was sort of true!

'You should come home. Ria misses you.'

Shweta nodded. 'Yes, I'll come by. I haven't seen her in a month.'

'I'm so happy that you're busy again.' Neha smiled and squeezed her hand. 'Also,' Shweta paused, thinking this was probably the best time to tell her. 'I'm going to have to talk to Papa about moving out.'

'Nonsense,' Neha snapped. 'You'll do nothing of the sort.'

'Neha, I'm twenty-eight, almost twenty-nine. I can't live with Ma and Papa forever. Besides I think seeing me every day makes Papa sad. If I live by myself, he won't have to worry about me constantly and I'll have the freedom to do whatever I want.'

'That's not going to make them forget about you. But it's up to you.' As if to change the subject, Neha pulled out her phone and began scrolling down the screen. Then having found what she was looking for, she showed it to Shweta. 'Have you seen Simbu's new pics on the family WhatsApp group?'

Shweta had seen them. They were pictures of their honeymoon in Bali and their home in Singapore. She'd also seen one small message on the group from Niru, telling them that he was in Bangalore and that his project was going to be inaugurated soon.

'Has Niru called you yet?' Neha asked, as if she'd read Shweta's thoughts.

'If he's interested in me, he'll come over and say it. I'm not going to do anything about it. '

'Let me know if you need my help,' Neha teased.

'And what do you propose to do?' Shweta scowled at her. 'Go tell him I love him so he can think about it?'

'You better make your move, baby, or you'll lose him forever.'

'I don't think I need to worry about that. Trisha's mother has probably snagged him for her daughter even as we speak.'

'You leave that to me.'

Shweta rolled her eyes. 'Don't do anything that will make me look like an idiot,' she warned her.

A knock sounded at their door and their father entered the room. He rarely came to Shweta's room. This had to be something important.

'I'm glad both of you are here,' he said, beaming. 'You remember Prasad's nephew, Captain Unni?'

Both nodded.

'He's now been promoted to Ship Captain and he's here on a visit. We should all go to meet him on Sunday.' He looked at them expectantly.

'Tomorrow?' Shweta asked, surprised. She did remember Unni. He was a tall boy with big brown eyes and he used to come over to spend the summers with the Prasads several years go. But why was this so important that her dad had to come up to her room to tell her? Unless, of course…

'Didn't his wife die of some illness just two years after their wedding?' Neha let in casually.

Alarm bells sounded in Shweta's head. She'd forgotten that he'd been married once before. 'Papa,' she said, slowing down to gauge her father's expressions as she spoke. 'Is this another matchmaking scheme?'

Prabhu waved his hand, shrugging her off. 'We're just being good neighbours. I don't see what's wrong with that. Aren't you curious to see Unni now?'

Shweta groaned and Neha began to chuckle.

'Neha, you can come too,' her father offered. 'Shweta won't feel self-conscious about this meeting if you're there.'

'No thanks, Papa. I don't think I can make it tomorrow.' She turned to Shweta. 'But you guys should carry on.' Neha gave her a knowing wink.

Before Shweta could say anything else, Prabhu came to her and ruffled her hair. 'It's been ages since you went anywhere except to work. I think meeting friends will do you good.'

The gentleness in his tone caught her by surprise. What was her dad up to now?

He left the room, whistling a happy tune, leaving Shweta and Neha to exchange puzzled glances.

'I know what you're thinking,' Shweta said, frowning at Neha.

Neha giggled. 'Exactly what you're thinking! But I got to go now, babe. The traffic on Outer Ring Road will be a killer if I don't leave soon.'

The sisters hugged and Neha left.

Shweta lay back in bed and ruminated on the latest situation.

A ping on her phone interrupted her thoughts.

It was a message from Niru on the family WhatsApp group.

Hey guys, hope to see you all for my new restaurant's inauguration next week. I'll come personally to give the invites.

Shweta opened and enlarged Niru's new display picture. It was rather cute. He had a chef's hat on and was smiling, like he did when he was thinking of something naughty to say.

She looked at the screen ruefully until it went blank. Maybe Niru was not interested in her. After all, he hadn't even come to see her or call her since he had come to Bangalore. Weren't they friends? Maybe Trisha had beaten her to it.

Ugh! She had never felt so helpless and insecure. Shweta let out a heavy sigh and just as she put the phone down, there was another message, this time from Neha.

Congrats, Niru! We'll be there.

Followed by another from Neha again.

Congrats, Shweta! Is the boy coming to see you tomorrow evening? <wink emoticon>

What?!

She stared at the message again. What was wrong with Neha?

Shweta wished she could strangle Neha. How irritating of her to have sent this to the family group!

No more messages. Everyone had gone quiet, most likely the effect of the bombshell Neha had just dropped on them.

Shweta cringed as she switched off her phone.

42

It was Sunday evening. At her mother's insistence, Shweta wore a pink crepe saree with a simple gold border, a matching gold blouse, heels, and accompanied her parents to the Prasads' house.

Bindu answered the doorbell. From her gushing smile and profuse welcome, Shweta could tell that their special guest had already arrived. Prasad came to the door behind his wife and ushered them in.

Unni rose when they entered and greeted Shweta's parents, then her.

He looked dapper in a suit and tie, his black shoes polished and shiny, his hair gelled and combed back. Even without his uniform, Unni resembled a young and fit officer.

Prasad immediately took it upon himself to introduce Unni and tell them about his latest promotion to captaincy. Bindu excused herself to make tea after a few more pleasantries were exchanged. Shweta took the opportunity and followed her into the kitchen. A few minutes later, Keertana followed them into the kitchen too.

'What is this?' Keertana hissed. 'Why didn't you sit outside and talk to Unni? What are you doing in the kitchen?'

Shweta scowled. 'What's the harm if I stay here until the tea is ready? We've got the whole evening to catch up with Unni.'

Keertana made a face. Bindu was so excited she could barely contain herself. 'What a brilliant chance that Unni called us to say he wanted to visit.' Keertana panicked and wildly gestured to her to stop talking about Unni, but Bindu continued nevertheless. 'He hasn't been here in ages. He'll be returning to the ship in a few days. What luck that he's here now, no?'

Keertana tried to steer her away to another topic, but Bindu brought the conversation right back. 'Did you ask astrologer Kini if the time was auspicious?'

Keertana made frantic gestures with her eyes. The two women cut a ridiculous sight, Keertana trying hard to make Bindu change the subject, and Bindu focused on the tea, relentlessly prattling on, oblivious to the hints.

Shweta laughed inwardly at her mother's clumsy attempts, quite enjoying the nonsensical banter between the two.

The tea was ready soon and the women trooped out, led by Bindu holding the tea tray, followed by Keertana, and lastly by Shweta, carrying a tray of laddoos, murukkus and some bread rolls that Bindu had taken the trouble to make at home.

Shweta felt Unni's gaze on her as she set the tray on the centre table and took a seat diagonally across from him.

Prasad, who had been animatedly discussing the price of onions and potatoes, paused at the sight of the tea tray and invited everyone to help themselves to tea.

After everyone got their tea, dipped into the snacks, and had a bite or two, Prasad jumped right back in where he had left off. He and Prabhu continued their argument about hoarders of essential goods hiking their prices and the ration shops who sold everything at a profit.

Bored, Shweta turned to look around. She hadn't visited the Prasads' home in months, and was pleasantly surprised to see a beautifully carved, polished, and gleaming veena in the far corner of the living room. It looked like Bindu had a new hobby.

Just as she was admiring the shiny new instrument, Prasad turned to her. 'Shweta, why are you wasting your time sitting here and listening to us oldies rant about onions and petrol prices? Why don't you and Unni enjoy the breeze, out on the porch?'

Suddenly a silence fell on the room and all eyes were on her. Surely, Prasad had put her in a spot right there. She hesitated and looked at her mother. Keertana gave her an encouraging smile and so did her dad. Unni was already up on his feet.

Shweta shifted in her seat uncomfortably. But then, she thought, what was the harm in a little conversation, and got up.

Shweta walked ahead of Unni into the dimly lit porch. It was cool and a strong breeze blew her saree. She wrapped her arms around herself and settled on the low porch wall. Unni preferred to lean at the doorway. She couldn't quite believe she was already meeting another man. It seemed ridiculous to go through the whole marriage rigmarole all over again.

Unni cleared his throat. 'It seems ridiculous to act like this,' he said.

She looked up at his face with a start and began to laugh. 'Exactly my thoughts!'

'So, now that that's out of the way,' he said, 'let's just not think of this as anything formal.'

Yeah, this sounded a bit more interesting. Shweta nodded.

'Let me tell you a bit about my life,' he said. 'Which is not easy, by the way.' He laughed. 'I have to be out on the ship for days and days with nothing but the blue seas stretching out in all directions in front of my eyes…' and he went on.

Her thoughts wandered to Tom Hanks encountering Somali pirates at sea in *Captain Phillips*. Or, to the movie where Hanks was marooned on a faraway island in *Castaway*. No, that was a bit far-fetched but those stories were so much more interesting than Unni's long-winded yarn.

Unni showed no signs of stopping, describing the locations he'd been to and the things he'd seen. Shweta stifled a yawn. She'd rather be out doing something else instead of waiting for his life story to end. *Don't be so mean!* Shweta scolded herself. But truth be told, she was a little tired. The old-fashioned way of meeting a person she hardly knew, and trying to like him after a few meetings had lost its charm. If only this had been the guy she was really comfortable with and liked. Like that *somebody* she knew, who was missing in action as it seemed.

The sound of the doorbell interrupted Unni's talk. She jumped up at the chance to escape his monologue and returned to the living room. And went still when she saw who it was.

Niru!

Speak of the devil, she thought to herself.

He looked so adorably dashing in a soft grey polo shirt that her heart missed a beat. This was the first time she was seeing him since that night after the wedding, she realized with a pang. Niru's eyes sought her out, resting on her for a moment before he glanced away.

A minute later, his mother walked in right behind him.

Everyone was as surprised to see them as Shweta was.

Niru's mother stopped in her tracks when she saw the gathering. 'Sorry to interrupt,' she said, possibly realizing that she had disturbed an important get-together.

'Oh, no, no,' Prasad said, making her feel comfortable. 'We were just…it's just an informal meeting.'

Niru and his mother took their seats. Niru looked oddly uncomfortable and fidgeted a lot.

Savitri held out a box of sweets she'd brought. 'I have some good news,' she announced. 'Niru's new café will be inaugurated next Saturday evening at Koramangala, and I would like to invite you all to grace the occasion.'

She took out two white envelopes with gold embossing and handed one to Prasad and the other to Prabhu. 'Since we met here, I might as well give yours to you,' she told Prabhu.

Her gaze took in Shweta's saree. 'I'm hope I haven't interrupted something important,' she said. 'You're looking so beautiful, Shweta.'

Shweta smiled awkwardly.

'We came to visit Prasad's nephew, Unni,' Keertana said conspiratorially. 'He captains a ship.'

A round of introductions followed.

'I would have come tomorrow,' Savitri said. 'But this idiot wanted me to come right this evening.'

Niru seemed to have a fit of coughing all of a sudden. He doubled over, emitting a series of spluttering, nerve-racking coughs.

'Do you want some water, son?' Keertana offered.

'Yes,' he croaked. 'And the bathroom, please.'

'Right there,' Bindu pointed to the bathroom.

'I'll get water,' Shweta said quickly.

He followed Shweta to the kitchen as she went to get water, and just as they were out of sight and earshot, he trapped her against the wall and hissed, 'So, is that the guy you're going to marry?'

Why was he angry? If anyone had to be angry, it had to be her.

'Fair of you to want to know now,' she hissed back. Pushing him away, she went to fill some water for him. 'What about you?' she said, handing over the glass. 'Aren't you engaged to Trisha?'

'Trisha!?' Niru snapped, as if he'd never heard that name in his life. 'Trisha never featured in my life.'

'That's not what I heard from my mother. She said Trisha's mom was going to speak to your mom.'

He looked baffled. 'If it's me they were talking about, I haven't heard.' With a smirk he lashed out at her, 'But you've been in a hurry. One marriage barely out of the way, and you've already set your eyes on another.'

That hurt, but she stood her ground. 'Does it bother you Mr Niraj Karthik that other people move on with their lives too? Or do you think only you have the privilege of flitting from one woman to another?'

'That's not fair,' he said. 'I haven't flitted at all. If anything, I've stayed committed in my relationships until it was over. Unlike you.'

Shweta swallowed. 'Me? If you're talking about the night at the bar, I...I was vulnerable and dizzy at that moment, but it wasn't like you think. I don't throw myself at people.' She ran her trembling hands through her hair.

'Blame it on being drunk!' he murmured.

'What exactly do you want me to say?'

'That I'm not too late, dammit!' He thrust the untouched glass back into her hand.

As she stared at him puzzled, he spun around without another word and went back to join the others.

After Niru and his mother left, they played rummy for a while. Unni turned out to be a lousy rummy player. He tried to make more conversation with Shweta during the game, but she excused herself a little while later, saying that she had a headache. They had a subdued dinner and then left.

After reaching home, Shweta went straight up to her room and flung herself on the bed; she lay there thinking about the evening and Niru. She didn't know what had hit her. Was she relieved at having seen Niru or even more confused? Was he implying something or simply making sure she wasn't marrying the wrong man again?

Shweta tossed and turned in bed all night, unable to sleep a wink.

43

Shweta called Neha the first thing next morning. She needed to get the Niru episode from last night off her chest.

Neha took full credit for Niru's gate-crashing, much to Shweta's chagrin. 'None of this would have happened without me,' Neha said, sounding quite proud of what she had done. 'Niru would never have shown up so quickly if it hadn't been for my message.'

'And you know that how?' Shweta said, not willing to give her the credit entirely.

'He called me to say he was up to his neck in work for his launch and inauguration, and wanted to find out what was going on with you. As soon as he heard that you were seeing Unni at the Prasads', he made up an excuse and hung up. The next thing I know, Ma was calling me to say he'd come over to the Prasads' that night.'

'Oh! That explains Niru's mother telling us that Niru insisted on giving out the invites that very evening,' Shweta said, musing.

'Yes, and the fact that he was totally unprepared to talk to you.'

Shweta wasn't buying it, though it all sounded like a well-put-together plan, the way Neha said it was. Something was definitely not adding up.

'If Niru wanted to say something, he very well could have said it without beating around the bush,' Shweta argued. The sisters talked some more but reached no convincing conclusions and the conversation eventually ended with both of them tired of making assumptions.

* * *

It was the second time in two consecutive weeks that Shweta had dressed up for an evening. The prospect of seeing Niru at his café launch caused flutters in her chest.

When she and her parents, accompanied by the Prasads, reached the venue, Niru was standing at the entrance. Looking incredibly handsome in a blue silk kurta, he looked so proud of his new venture. He spotted Shweta, hesitated at first, and then waved. Shweta climbed up the steps to join him and the others waiting just outside the entrance. NIRU'S CAFÉ, the plaque read, the words written in bright, gold embossed letters.

Niru's mother and his uncles, with their families, were present too. Nambishan, the famous wedding cook she'd never met, was also among them. Niru introduced Shweta to Nambishan, a portly old man with a gentle smile and a distinctive long red mark drawn across his forehead. 'So, you're the beautiful young girl my kitchen staff was telling me about.'

Shweta blushed and stole a glance at Niru but he wasn't looking at her. He was too busy to even give her a glance, she noted.

Neha, Mohan, and Ria arrived shortly after.

Niru waited until all his friends and family had gathered, before starting the ceremony. With everyone standing around him, he cut the silk ribbon tied across the entrance and entered the café to the cheers and claps of the spectators.

The space was modestly decorated. Yellow chairs and tables were spread out on the polished, dark wooden dining room floor that gleamed. Sparkling cutlery and plates were laid out at all the tables. In the kitchen section, buffet arrangements were being made in earnest.

There was a separate nook with tables and chairs for reading. Niru mentioned that it was meant for expansion into a small independent bookstore, in the future.

As the family members and guests took their seats at the tables, champagne was brought in. Niru popped the bottle and more claps followed. Soon the buffet was set up and everyone filled their plates and tasted the food.

Shweta thought the food was delicious, as was also evident from the praises that kept pouring in. Niru stood proudly, shaking hands with the guests, and smiling a lot.

Shweta left the group at her table to get some juice. Standing at the juice counter, she was trying to drip the last bit from the tap into her glass, when suddenly the clay pot dispenser tipped. She gasped in horror, unable to do anything but watch it slide down when, midway through its fall, a hand miraculously appeared below it and caught it. Relieved, she looked up and found herself staring into the eyes of her saviour.

Niru smiled at her benevolently and slowly put the dispenser back in its place.

'Thanks,' she breathed, rattled by his closeness.

Niru hadn't been able to take his eyes off Shweta since the moment she'd arrived.

Yes, he'd always been in love with her.

Then, he'd fallen for her all over again at Simbu's wedding. There were so many things he'd wanted to tell her but he'd never had the chance. And now, he wanted to. So badly.

That saree she was wearing drove him insane, and those luscious strands of curls, spilling out of her top knot along her face and neck, made him ache to send them tumbling on to her shoulders. She looked adorably beautiful and radiant this evening. He'd been watching her when she went up to the dispenser, and he was glad for it now. While she continued to stress on the disaster just averted, all he wanted to do was to pull her into his arms, kiss away the creases between her brows, and render a thousand more kisses trailing all the way to her neck.

'My pleasure.' He settled for those words instead of saying what he really wanted to say. Damn the launch and everything that had made him wait so long to talk to her. And damn the dick who had gotten to meet her before him. The urge to find out if that 'ship captain' had cut him out was too much to handle.

'So,' he said, trying to make it sound pretty casual although his heart was going like a fire alarm. 'I guess last week's party went well?'

Shweta's expression changed, from grateful to horrified. Her eyes were fixed on a situation unfolding a few tables away, where a toddler, being fed while seated on top of the table, was inching dangerously closer to its edge. His mother's eyes were off him for a few moments as she rummaged in her bag for something. A second more and the boy would fall backwards. Shweta rushed towards the table and Niru hurried behind her. Before the mother had a chance to look up from her bag, the boy veered closer to the edge. His rear wobbled and he lost balance. He gave out a wail as his body broke into a free fall, toppling backwards and straight into Shweta's outstretched arms. She caught him and pulled him close. The little fellow blinked in surprise and then bared all his teeth, smiling at her with excitement as if it had been a joy ride. The mother jumped from her seat and gathered him into her arms. She looked utterly relieved and thanked Shweta profusely.

As Shweta was about to get back, the boy threw his arms out towards her as if he wanted to go back to her. Shweta laughed and took him from his mother. She took the spoon from the mother's hands and began feeding him herself. The boy happily ate up his food without any fuss.

Niru watched amused, as Shweta managed the toddler, making sure he ate only small portions and didn't spill anything on his clothes. When a bit of the mash fell on her outfit, she wiped it off easily and didn't seem to mind. She loved children, Niru could tell. And they adored her, in return. He'd seen how Ria clung to her every word and now this toddler wouldn't let her go.

'Congratulations!'

Niru turned around to see Mohan, Ria, and Neha waving and making their way towards him. A round of congratulations and handshakes followed.

'Looks like you guys averted a terrible accident,' Neha teased. Shweta was still feeding the toddler, her mouth imitating the open-close of the toddler's mouth as the little boy gobbled up every single spoon of food she fed him.

'It was Shweta's foresight,' Niru said, shrugging off the praise directed at him.

'Oh, look!' Ria squealed. 'The little boy is tugging at her saree for more.' They couldn't help laughing at the funny sight.

'Shweta was always a one-woman rescue squad for all emergencies,' Neha said. 'She would spend all her free Sundays at our house trying to get some food into Ria when she was a baby.' They laughed at that memory. Neha turned to Mohan and Ria and said, 'We should get some food too before they run out.'

Just after they left, some other friends walked up to congratulate Niru. He tore his gaze away from Shweta before turning to his guests. There was no way he could catch her alone tonight.

The party soon drew to a close with no further opportunity to speak to Shweta that evening. Shweta and her family left soon after.

Niru was left wondering where and how he could catch her alone soon.

44

Shweta lay lazily on the couch wondering about fixing a bowl of Maggi for dinner, catching a show on TV, and calling it an early night, when the doorbell rang. She looked up, surprised. She wasn't expecting anyone at this time.

It was Sunday evening, and she was home alone; her parents were at the Prasads, as usual. She rose reluctantly, taking her time to get to the door.

She yanked the door open and her eyes fell on Niru standing there with his hand on the door jamb, and her heart skipped a beat.

She took in his hair, still wet from a recent shower, and his bright eyes. Butterflies fluttered low in her stomach and it took her a few moments to gain composure. 'What are you doing here?' she asked. 'Ma and Papa are out tonight.'

'I came to see you,' he said. 'Am I interrupting anything?'

She hesitated for a moment.

'Are you going to keep me out here or are you going to ask me to come in?'

Shweta moved aside to let him in. His shirt brushed her arms and he smelled like her favourite cologne.

'You can wipe that frown off your face,' Niru turned around and said. 'I'm not going to eat you.' He held up a packet he was carrying, something she hadn't noticed. 'I brought some food. Can you tell me where to put this?'

'What is that?' It smelled like something heavenly, something she could do with, right now. Shweta pointed towards the kitchen and Niru made his way in that direction.

'How are you here at this time?' she said, following him. 'Aren't you supposed to be busy at the café?'

Niru placed the packet on the counter. 'Took some time off,' he said, and began rummaging in the drawers. 'I hope you haven't had dinner. I was hungry. Thought I'd get us some biryani from the café.'

'You came here to eat?'

He found the spoons and the plates. 'Come on,' he said. 'I was working all day. Can't a guy expect a friend to share dinner with him?'

'I was just about to fix myself some dinner,' she lied, dusting an imaginary speck off the kitchen counter.

'Maggi again?' he asked, teasing. 'Well, you don't have to now.' Niru began setting two places right there at the kitchen table, complete with a table runner and place mats that he had found from God knows where.

'I didn't know you served biryani at the café.'

'We don't!' he said. 'It's new on the menu. Thought I'd test it on you.'

So that's what this was all about. 'Why? Because I like biryani?' She crossed her arms. 'And I happen to be free on a bloody Sunday evening?'

'That's not such a bad reason, is it?' He laughed and moved a vase of yellow flowers from the window sill to the table. 'Don't,' he said, holding her hand, when she tried to take the vase away. 'They look pretty.'

'But the table's crowded already. It'll probably get knocked off.'

'Will you just sit down?' he ordered, and then went back to rummaging in the kitchen drawers.

'What are you looking for?' she said, when a full minute had passed and he was still searching.

'Candles.'

'Candles?'

He found one with a candlestick and put that on the table. 'Just in case of an emergency, you know? Current cut or something like that.' And he again went back to the drawers. 'Now, where are the matches?'

'Don't be ridiculous! There's never been a current cut here. We have backup.' Shweta sat down. 'Now, will you please tell me what the hell's going on?'

'I need a rating for this biryani.' He'd still not found the match box.

'A what?' Irritated by his fruitless search, she pointed to the top cabinet. 'It's in there.'

'Aha!' Niru struck a match and lit the candle. 'Now give me a minute.' He disappeared back into the living room. A second later, the lights went off.

'What the hell…'

'Hold on!' he said, coming back with his cell phone flashlight on. He took the chair opposite hers, let out a breath and rubbed his hands together. 'What do you think?'

The candle blazed brightly, the flame flickering a little in the breeze, and casting a long shadow on the opposite wall. The flowers smelled fresh. He was looking at her expectantly. She gestured towards the table. 'About this?'

He caught her waving hands and held her gaze. 'You know?' Niru started, 'The first time I saw you at the wedding I knew I was doomed.'

She was completely taken aback but his gaze held steady. She lowered her eyes. 'Oh, make fun of me all you want.'

Niru let go of her hands. 'It's true,' he said. 'Sorry, telling you all this took so long.'

He was looking at her with doleful eyes.

'I just didn't know if it was the right time even after I came to know about the divorce,' he said. 'I wanted to give it some time.'

She rose. 'I think you forgot the napkins.' She turned her back to him so he wouldn't see her eyes welling up. *Where were you all this bloody time,* she wanted to scream.

Niru buried his head in his hands. I've ruined this, he thought. There was no time to think now. He rose quickly and joined her at the counter. Shweta was bent forward into a cabinet. He grabbed her shoulders and turned her around.

'Please!' he said, tipping her chin and forcing her to look into his eyes. 'It was only when I saw Neha's message that I realized I was already too late.'

She looked miffed. 'Are you telling me I pushed you into this…this…'

'For God's sake, listen to me! I've loved you since the time you were sixteen. I was just stupid and…'

Shweta pulled back, narrowing her eyes and crossing her arms.

It was now or never. 'Sorry for not telling you how I felt…feel about you. I was a coward then and…and I've been a coward… until now!' Niru tried to hold her hands but Shweta jerked him away. He continued nevertheless, fumbling through his words. 'I wanted to be successful first. Worthy of asking for your hand. When I heard your marriage was fixed I wished I'd had more time to prove myself. But I've waited too long. I want to know if you'll still have me. I love you! I always have.'

She looked at him in bewilderment.

He shoved his fingers through his hair and slowed down. 'I'd like to tell you something. Remember that party with Dolly?'

She nodded, remembering Dolly who wanted to use her as a messenger for a love letter. She remembered that hollow moment all too clearly.

'The letter you were guilty about, for all these years?' He paused for a breath. 'It was me who gave it to Dolly. I asked her to give it to you. Because I loved you and I wanted to make you jealous.'

She clapped her mouth. 'You what?' she screamed, and began raining his chest with blows.

'Ow! Ow! Stop! Stop! I deserve that but…ow!' Niru cried, doubling over, as Shweta continued raining blows on him. When she finally stopped, he looked into her eyes, pleading guilty. 'I'm sorry for everything. Forgive me?'

Shweta dropped her hands to her sides.

'Come here,' he whispered, spreading his arms. 'Please.'

She pouted and stood firm.

'Please?' he said, taking a step towards her.

She frowned, then relented, and stepped into his embrace. 'The better to see me with?' she said, as if she were Red Riding Hood, and he, the Big Bad Wolf.

Relief washed over him as she smiled at him. And he realised how badly he'd wanted her to accept him. Nothing made him happier than to see her happy. 'No, the better to eat you with,' he said, suddenly, grabbing her and growling. She laughed as he began tickling her and making chomping sounds while she begged him to stop.

Shweta savoured the fun moment. Finally Niru paused and their eyes met, his arms still around her.

He leaned in to plant a soft kiss on her forehead, moving to her eyelids and then to the tip of her nose. The kiss trailed to her lips and her breath quickened.

'I love you,' he said, his voice a whisper, before bringing his mouth to hers for an intense, sweeping kiss.

After all this waiting, this moment and the very essence of his words, the first of his true feelings for her, felt like everything she'd ever dreamed of.

Wanting to savour every inch of his closeness, her chest pressing against his, the rush of his hot breath, the fullness of his lips, she returned his kiss feverishly, hungrily matching his desire with hers, lip for lip, teasing, sucking, demanding, as if right there in that long searing kiss, she was fulfilling the yearning of a lifetime. Her body on fire as his hands caressed every inch of her, she groaned with pleasure until she could take it no more. They made love with an overwhelming sense of joy and abandon, trembling, rushing, fumbling, and finally giving in to the waves of passion and longing, breathless and hungry for more, their all-consuming desire and urgency at its zenith, as if this had taken way too long in coming.

When they finally pulled apart, it was only to slowly return to their dinner, which was cold by now, but neither of them cared. Shweta settled on Niru's lap and snuggled back into his arms as they fed each other the delicious biryani.

After dinner, they curled up on the couch to watch *DDLJ*, one of their old favourite movies. Laying her cheek against his, she enveloped him in a hug. He stroked her hair and cooed sweet nothings into her ears. And so they remained, laughing at their favourite scenes and reminiscing about the good old days.

In that moment, nothing else mattered. Shweta's heart was bursting with joy at being with the man she loved, and who loved her back.

As she revelled in the sensation, Shweta was sure this was what she'd wanted all along—this crazy, sweet, and dreamy moment— when everything around them ceased to exist.

EPILOGUE

A few months later...

MARRY ME?

The words, in beautiful, red, calligraphy, were piped on to a rectangular wedge of the mango panna cotta dessert that had just arrived at their table.

Shweta looked up from the breath-taking arrangement on the plate into Niru's twinkling eyes as she clapped her hands over her mouth. She had not seen this coming at all. There hadn't even been a hint of a proposal to her before this.

They were seated in Sector 7 Café in HSR. Niru was looking at exploring new and inspiring specials for his café's menu to add to its five-star ratings on Zomato, for which they'd been checking out new eateries over the weekends.

'Is he ever going to ask you to marry him or is he only interested in making you his unofficial, unpaid food-taster for life?' Keertana had kept asking for months. A lot else had happened too in the last few months. Shweta was now living in a PG away from home. So, all Keertana could do when she had life-changing questions like these was to either give her a call, or nag her when she went home over the weekends. If she wasn't out food tasting with Niru, that is.

Now she understood why he'd disappeared in the direction of the kitchen just a little while ago.

Her eyes misted. 'YES!' she cried. This to Niru and, in her thoughts, to her mother. Her ecstatic voice travelled across the room and every pair of eyes in the café turned towards them. 'I thought you were never going to ask,' she said smiling, her voice now down to a whisper.

'I was just a little wary of being rejected for being way too impatient, I suppose.'

His heart-warming gaze melted her insides. 'Aww!' Shweta touched his hand from across the table. 'This is such a beautiful setting too,' she couldn't help exclaiming, awestruck as much by the decor of the place he'd brought her to, as by the eye-catching dish in front of her. 'And this,' she pointed to the food and drooled. 'This leads straight to sugar heaven.'

'All the better to write heartfelt feelings on,' Niru said, smiling cheekily.

He was cheeky, she had to give him that, pulling a surprise on her like this. And she hadn't cared what her mother had thought all these months, because frankly, the no-wedding-bells-on-the-horizon moments with Niru hadn't bothered her. She was happy just dating him, so to speak, even if it was partly over work.

'Should I also find a ring buried in here somewhere?' Shweta laughed.

Niru chuckled, rather sexily. He looked dapper tonight, she noted, blushing, with the gel in his hair and a soft navy blue shirt that set off his eyes perfectly. She hadn't noticed all the effort he'd taken to make this moment so special. Until now.

As if that was the moment he'd been waiting for, he rolled up his sleeves and whipped out the ring from his pocket. It was so sleek and beautiful, with a tiny diamond heart set on the top.

She gasped. 'It's so pretty!' She couldn't take her eyes off it. She gave him her hand and he slid in onto her finger. It fit perfectly!

Post dinner, they left to celebrate with a round of club-hopping, and then went to her house to tell her parents. Yet another surprise awaited Shweta there.

Niru's mother sat in the living room talking to her parents.

When they walked in, three pairs of eyes fixed on them.

Savitri cleared her throat. 'I have something to say,' she began. 'It's about Shweta and Niru.'

A hush descended on the room. Savitri looked around at everyone. In a slow, deliberate voice she said, 'I only wish Niru had proposed to Shweta sooner. I have always wanted Shweta as my daughter-in-law.'

Shweta exhaled a big sigh of relief, now that she knew his mother approved.

Prabhu jumped in shock. 'What?! When did this happen?' Keertana's mouth fell open. 'Really?' she said.

Niru turned to Prabhu. 'Uncle, I'd like to marry your daughter.'

Prabhu pulled out his pipe and started filling it, taking his own time to reply. Keertana's eyes were welling up already. Exhaling a long plume of smoke, Prabhu turned to Shweta. 'Is this alliance acceptable to you, my dear?'

Shweta ran up to him and hugged him. 'Yes, Papa,' she said. 'He's the man I want to spend the rest of my life with.'

Her father pulled apart and held her at an arm's distance. 'Even if there's no US or UK in your future, or even if Niru's business is broke?'

She turned towards Niru before answering that question. The pale yellow light from the lamps in the room danced across his face. He looked so handsome she could kiss him right now. She'd never felt so happy in her life and so sure of what she wanted.

She turned back to her father. 'Very much,' she whispered, tears clouding her eyes.

Prabhu was also swept away by the mood in the room. 'Very good then,' he said. And he rose to shake hands with Niru. 'She's all yours,' he said, laughing. 'I can't wait to wash my hands off her.'

'Papa!' Shweta complained, sniffling.

'Shouldn't we ask astrologer Kini for an auspicious date?' Keertana said, all of a sudden.

'Yes, Ma,' Shweta said, teasing her mother. 'Please ask him if you'll be a good businesswoman too. You've already got some more purse orders.'

The whole family burst into laughter. Keertana sulked momentarily but quickly joined in the excitement over the happy news.

Laughter filled the room, and the parents were soon busy in an animated discussion about the wedding. Shweta and Niru took the opportunity to escape and stepped outside on to the porch, holding hands. Shweta rested her head softly on Niru's shoulders. He pulled her close and bent down to kiss her forehead. Up in the inky sky, the pearly full moon shone behind the silhouette of the mango tree. They spoke nothing, savouring the silence and calm of the moment. The world felt so perfect like this. And so did her life.

Gazing far away into the distance, Shweta sent out a silent prayer of gratitude to the universe.

For Niru.

THE END

Thanks for reading!

Reviews are worth their weight in gold to authors! If you enjoyed this book, please take a moment to post a review on Amazon, Instagram, Goodreads, your blog, or simply spread the word. Thank You! :)

Did you enjoy The Wedding Tamasha? Check out the story of Neha and Prithvi in Priyamvada & Co. Read ahead for a sneak preview

The Menon Women Book Two

PRIYAMVADA
& CO.

SUDHA NAIR

Author of the bestselling novel *The Wedding Tamasha*

PRIYAMVADA & CO.
PREVIEW

Prithvi just missed the car on the right, racing him to the last empty parking spot next to his new apartment in HSR, Bangalore.

"Hey," he yelled, slamming the brakes of his Ford Ecosport. He slid the window down and stuck out his finger at the red Maruti, which had grazed the right side of his car as it fled past. "Hey, you!"

But the reckless driver had already dived into the spot, parking badly, and was now jumping out to make a run. A woman, he realised, dressed all in white—white kurta, white dupatta and white churidar. As she sped past, his gaze snagged at the hard-to-miss, mismatched pair of slippers on her feet—one with a large yellow bow on top and the other with two thick lines of beads—before she became a blur. He craned his neck to catch the last of her, her long, unruly curls spilling over her shoulders as she whizzed through the gates of the very building he was going to.

In the back of the car, his mother, Vinodini, deep in slumber, stirred. "What happened?" she asked groggily, and promptly went back to sleep before he could answer.

He cursed and got out, his walking stick—the result of a recent injury—hitting the ground first. The silver paint on the right side of the car was streaked with three long gashes. "Fuck!" He kicked the tyre and scanned the street for an alternate spot, regretting that he hadn't thought to ask for his underground parking number.

On the opposite side, diagonally across, was a spot. If it were only him he'd have parked there and walked back. But with his mother and her wheelchair...he grunted.

A jarring honk from the back startled him and he clambered back in, still fuming. He put the car in gear, and moved it to the side of the road, so that the car behind him could get past. Then he got back out to unload his mother.

His mother was smacking her gums in her sleep as he got her wheelchair out of the boot. Her care-giver, Daisy, sat right beside her, snoring with her mouth open, her buck teeth on prominent display.

"Daisy!" Prithvi called to her. Daisy's mouth opened wider. "Daisy!" he shouted, louder.

The unflower-like Daisy sat up abruptly, wiped the spittle off her cheeks, and looked at him in a daze. "*Entha*, Kuttan Sir? What happened?" She called him "Kuttan Sir" because his mother called him "Kuttan." Daisy was the third certified nurse from the Red Cross in the last six months since his mother's fall. His mother loved the new nurse, the thirty-something, hardworking and honest Daisy, who, to Prithvi's annoyance, smelled oddly of raw fish and burnt coal.

The ten-hour, non-stop ride from Kochi to Bangalore, cooped up in the car with her in the back seat, had suffocated him. But finally, relief! He took in a breath of the cool, fresh air. "We've reached," he told Daisy. "Let's get Ma out. Give me a hand from the other side, will you?"

Prithvi scooped his mother out of the seat while Daisy hitched up her hips.

Vinodini, a one-time actress from decades ago, fluttered her eyelids open, in slow motion, and flashed him a gummy smile. "What was all the commotion?" she asked, smacking her gums, once again.

She reminded him of the old and skinny *Betaal* from the *Vikram Aur Betaal* TV show from his childhood. How much his mother had changed! Her skin was shrivelled, her nails mottled and bent. When he'd left India to study in the US twenty-five years ago, she was still a beauty. Now, a grey bob cut replaced the knee-length black tresses she used to have, and the arms that held on to him with a tight grip were wrinkly.

But she still hadn't lost her theatrical booming voice. "Get my teeth before people see me like this."

Daisy hurried out with Vinodini's precious dentures swimming in a leak-proof jar filled with water. In two thwacks, Vinodini had clamped them into place.

Prithvi slow-wheeled his mother across the street fringed with tall buildings and coconut palms. It was a quiet and green locality. Daisy followed him meekly, Vinodini's bag hitched on to her shoulder. The rest of the bags would just have to wait.

At the entrance to the building, another flight of half a dozen steps awaited them, and Prithvi grunted again. His foot was not that bad but it still hurt sometimes, especially after a long drive like this. Scooping his mother up once more, he made it up using his good leg while she hung on for dear life, her fingers digging into his collarbone. Daisy propelled the rattling wheelchair up the stairs behind him and helped Prithvi lower his mother into it when they finally reached the landing.

A crowd was already gathered at the elevator entrance and it filled up as soon as it came down. There was no space for him or the wheelchair. He waited for the next trip as the elevator went back up, stopped at the fifth and finally returned to zero, the door opening with a clang. A large group stepped out. Something seemed to be up at the fifth floor, where he too was headed. Luckily, the three of them were alone on the next trip.

On the fifth floor, the elevator door opened to the sight of hundreds of slippers, shoes and sandals scattered all over the corridor, from the direction of his neighbour's flat, number 502, all the way to the elevator's mouth.

What a warm welcome, Prithvi thought, cursing his luck, and edged his way out from behind his mother's wheelchair to kick the footwear aside. His gaze caught at a mismatched pair of slippers—one with a large yellow bow on top and the other with two thick lines of beads—stuck beneath a wheel. What the hell! *The one who'd scraped his car was here?*

"Ow!" his mother yelped, shaking violently as he rolled the wheel over the errant pair, crushing one's bow and probably cracking the other's beads.

Served the bloody slippers right for annoying the hell out of him! "Can't help it," Prithvi muttered. "I'm trying to get us through."

Once they were out, Daisy managed to banish the rest of the slippers out of their way.

Vinodini beamed at Daisy, showing off her perfect row of false teeth. "Thank you!"

They made it to their flat, number 503. Vinodini and her favourite nurse were busy discussing the new place as Prithvi unlocked the door and let them in. "What's going on there?" his mother wanted to know. "A lot of people…"

He looked to the right. The door to their neighbour's was open.

Inside, a big crowd was gathered. Laid on the floor in the middle, was a man, wearing a two-piece suit, a crisp white shirt and red tie. His dark hair was gelled and combed back, his eyes were shut and his nostrils and ears were stuffed with tufts of cotton. Swirls of grey from lit incense sticks formed a halo above his head. Sitting on the floor next to him, was a young woman, her face half-hidden. Probably his wife. The late morning light shone harshly on her troubled face. Her nose was red, her face blotched and puffy, and her eyes boring through the inert figure. She was sobbing and jabbing a handkerchief into her dark, teary eyes. She looked so torn and vulnerable, Prithvi couldn't help but shudder.

Suddenly, the woman's glance shifted to the door, to where he stood. She stared for a moment, her doe-like eyes swimming in a puddle of tears.

Then her expression changed. Those miserable, puddle-filled eyes turned fearful, almost horrified. Through her clamped mouth she let out a long, shrill wail. It was a baleful, banshee cry, one that turned all heads towards the door. The next moment, she fainted and fell into the arms of a woman behind her.

Stupefied, Prithvi backed away.

GRAB IT AT

MYBOOK.TO/PACO

Want More Stories?

Receive an exclusive short and sweet office romance story, LOVE OFFICIALLY (preview ahead), and news, updates, and more, when you sign up to receive my email. Find details at SudhaNair.com/newsletter. Let's keep in touch! :)

LOVE OFFICIALLY PREVIEW

Remember the time when you were young and life was full of confusing choices? What if you didn't know which was the right choice to make? What if your whole life depended on that choice? Take a nostalgic trip down memory lane. Read LOVE OFFICIALLY—a **sweet and short office romance story** *to find out how* **Meera** *faces the challenge of choosing the right man!*

'Hey, want to go out for coffee?'

Meera looked up from her messy desk.

Elbows propped on her office cubicle wall, Vivek beseeched her with puppy eyes.

She threw him a quick 'No!' and went back to rummaging for those client requirements that she'd jotted down after the customer call that morning.

'Oh, come on,' Vivek said, blocking her entrance, his hands spanning the width. 'You need a break.'

She rolled her eyes at him. Did he think she wanted to start the office gossip mills by going out alone with him?

'I was only suggesting a cup of coffee!' Then, 'Hey!' as he moved the tiny clay Ganesha idol out of the way before she could knock it down in her frenzied search. 'Want me to call Shabnam too?'

Shabnam—smart, well-dressed, and always the first to know what was going on in the office—was her bestie at work.

As if on cue, Shabnam came over. 'Hey there, you two!' Her face was flushed, and she couldn't help giving Vivek a flirty smile first. 'Guess what!'

Head bent back over her desk, Meera said, 'What!' Then, suddenly, she found those rogue documents she'd been looking for. 'There you are!' She put them right on top of her to-do box and turned to Shabnam.

'One of us will get that transfer to the US this month.' Shabnam bounced up and down. 'The boss is going to announce it in a couple of days.'

Meera's heart missed a beat. This was what she'd been waiting for. Please, please, let it be me, she said a little mental prayer.

'Well!' Vivek said. 'Another of his marketing ploys.' He turned to Shabnam. 'By the way, Shabnam, do you want to go out for coffee?'

'Really?' Shabnam shrieked. Some heads in the other cubicles turned towards them. Shabnam glanced around shamefaced, then went back to him, all smiles.

'With us?' Vivek's face broke into an amused grin.

Shabnam's face fell but she rebounded quickly. 'Sure!'

Vivek raised his eyebrow at Meera, then stuck out his hand to help her up from her seat.

Without thinking, she nestled her hand into his. Her hand tingled at his touch, sending spirals of warmth up her arm. She jerked it away as soon as she was up.

On the way to the cafeteria, the girls needed to use the restroom, so Vivek went on ahead.

'You see how he can't take his eyes off you!' Shabnam said, as she did an 'O' in front of the mirror and touched up her lipstick. 'You should give him a break.'

A smile played on Meera's lips. 'You want him? He's all yours.'

Shabnam pouted. 'I wish he'd shown the slightest bit of interest in me.' She brushed her hair till it shone while Meera waited. Then she lined her beautiful eyes with kohl. 'He's handsome, eligible and so hot!'

Meera didn't deny his hotness factor. It made her blush, every time she thought about him. He was also a great co-worker, kind, helpful. In other words, perfect! But, she'd decided, she wasn't going to let romance ruin her chances for the transfer that she'd been waiting for, for a long time. 'What I need is that transfer. Then I can get away from home and not have to meet men I don't like.' She let out a long sigh. 'I can't wait!'

'What you really need is a good man who loves you.' Shabnam pursed her lips. 'Like him.'

Meera smirked. 'How can I be so sure he loves me? For all you know, it's just a fling. It's only been two months since he joined.'

'He has eyes only for you,' Shabnam said. "You're smart, attractive and sweet. Only you don't know it yourself.'

'And you're the best friend in the whole world.' Meera squeezed her into a hug.

When they reached the crowded cafeteria, they found Vivek seated at a corner spot.

'I've already ordered three coffees, a masala dosa for Shabnam and two pav bhajis for us,' he said to Meera, as they took their seats at the tiny round table.

'How did you know I love masala dosa?' Shabnam looked up at him and fluttered her eyelids.

Meera loved to watch Shabnam flirt.

He played along. 'Because I have good memory.' Shabnam's slap at his hand made him grin.

The waiter arrived with their food and coffee.

'You shouldn't have ordered pav bhaji for me,' Meera said. 'It's too much!'

'Why? Are you on a diet?' Shabnam winked at her. 'Is someone coming to see you again?'

Vivek choked on his coffee. 'Aw!' His hands flew to rub the quick setting brown stain off his shirt.

Meera wished Shabnam would stop being such a blabbermouth. Vivek's face had grown darker. He was staring down at his coffee. She couldn't tell what was wrong with him all of a sudden.

Clueless, Shabnam egged her for more details.

'It's my parents,' Meera said, shrugging it off. 'I've tried but they won't stop calling suitors home to see me.'

'Do you know who it is?' Shabnam said.

For a moment, Vivek's ears perked up.

'All I could gather was that he works in the US.' She took a long sip of coffee, hoping that that would be the end of the discussion.

'So he can so be your ticket to the US?'

She glared at Shabnam. 'Don't be silly. As if I'd marry somebody just for that.' Then she slid a glance in Vivek's direction. He had gone back to his coffee.

'Talking of the US,' Shabnam started again, 'who do you think is going to get this transfer?'

I hope it's me, Meera thought. That way I can escape awkward meetings with suitors.

'It's going to be one heck of a great experience to work in California,' Vivek said, sounding excited. 'From what I've heard, the assignment will be for three years. I'd love to go but I'm new to this office. I'm sure you guys have a better chance.'

'Oh, you're smart,' Shabnam blurted. 'You do have a chance.'

They discussed a few more likely candidates, and all of their own chances, and then Shabnam had to go because she got a phone call.

'Shall we go too?' Meera said, looking around at the crowded cafeteria and wondering if she recognized anyone that she knew.

He leaned forward and smiled. 'But we haven't finished our conversation.'

She didn't know why but she felt like a deer caught in the headlights. 'What do you mean?'

He leaned closer and tucked a loose strand of hair behind her ear.

'Why are you so afraid of going out with me?'

'Stop that!' She swatted his hand away. 'Someone will see.'

'You're being paranoid,' he said, laughing. 'Just tell me you're not attracted to me like I am to you and I'll leave you alone.' His eyes shone like a baby's.

With how close he was leaning towards her, and his eyes daring her, she just couldn't think straight. *Uff!* 'Don't be so pushy!' She shoved his chest.

He caught her hand and wouldn't let go. 'You're this amazing woman that I want to know better. Won't you give me a chance?'

'Look, Vivek,' she said, wriggling her hand free. 'I don't want this…us to ruin my job.'

He let out a whoosh of breath. 'Okay,' he said, raising his hands in his defense. 'I know you have an independent streak. You're charming and incredibly delightful to talk to.' He ran his fingers through his hair. 'And here it goes.' He held her gaze as he said the words softly, 'I think I'm falling in love with you. All I'm asking is to give me a chance.'

The waiter came to take away their empty cups and plates, and she smiled to herself, watching how he was helping the guy along, impatient for him to leave. Twisting the end of her dupatta, she waited for them to be alone again.

After the waiter left, he looked at her, one eyebrow raised, waiting for her reply.

'I don't think romance at work is a good thing. So, either you'll have to quit or I'll have to.' She shrugged, faking the sassiness while inwardly scowling that both choices sounded terrible. *Did her self-imposed rule about office romance even make sense?*

His shoulders drooped. 'So, do people working together never fall in love?'

'They probably do. I'm just not one of them,' she was quick to retort.

'All this excuse about working together is BS,' he said, calling her bluff. 'You know you don't care about that—'

'I do!'

Just then the waiter sauntered over again with the bill. Vivek pulled out his wallet at the same time that Meera pulled out her purse.

The waiter went straight to him.

'Let me,' he said to her. 'Consider it my best wishes for the latest man who's coming to see you.'

Meera frowned at him.

'Though I really hope he's horrible.' He grinned. 'If you need more time to get to know me, I'm willing to wait.' He winked at her. 'Hopefully you'll change your mind before you or I are transferred out of here.' He chuckled to make light of it but Meera's heart beat so hard she could almost hear it.

Together they rose to leave, with Vivek coming up right behind her. As she took her first step, she felt a strong tug at her dupatta. It pulled her backwards and she fell straight up against his chest.

Strong arms held her steady. 'Sorry,' he said, his breath blowing across her ear, his baritone making her toes curl. Her throat went dry. There was a brief pause and the next moment, he lifted his foot off her dupatta and released her.

'Thanks!' Gosh! She felt her cheeks burn as she looked everywhere but at him. She so wished, after it was over, that she could have snuggled closer for longer.

Subscribe to my newsletter to get the full story at SudhaNair.com/newsletter. Hope to see you there :)

Acknowledgements

This debut novel is a labour of love, and while faced with one of my biggest fears, as with any new gargantuan project such as writing a novel, I've absolutely loved bringing this story to you. I hope that you, dear readers, will love and appreciate this work. I thank you for picking up this book, and if you've come this far, I hope the journey was worth it. Thanks so much for staying with me and I hope that my subsequent books will also bring you joy.

My stories have been about women and their dreams and aspirations. I'm inspired by women who've shown us that whatever we dream of is not only achievable but also very much within our reach. For teaching us that we must grab our opportunities as they come.

My first thanks to Abhijeet Nair and Nitya Nair, my angels, who boosted my confidence when I was just starting out, gave me feedback, and read and critiqued every word of my early manuscript.

Big thanks to my beta readers who pointed out the errors and gaps to fill. My honourable mentions for taking on this cringe-inducing and boring task include Priya Gopalan, Mrinalini Menon, Ashritha Thirumalai, and Priya Gokul.

Nikita Jhanglani is a very intuitive editor, who provided the most thorough and professional editing, offered valuable insight and advice, and also stayed with me till the very end, remaining available for every question I had at any odd time of the day, even after her job was done.

Thanks to my amazingly super cover designer, Manoj Vijayan, who brought the cover of this book to life incredibly more gorgeously and beautifully than I had imagined.

My partner-in-crime, crossword buddy, reading and writing companion, second-editor-in-command and proofreader—Devika Rajan. I'm lucky to have you in my corner. You've been invaluable to my writing life and I thank you from the bottom of my heart.

Thank you, Sanil Nair, for the professional photographs, and the funny and perfect title for this book, which I'm very proud of!

I owe huge thanks to Ruchi Singh, who I consider as my mentor. Ruchi is the most kind, generous, and affectionate person I have ever met. I am eternally grateful that you came into my life when I was desperately looking for someone like you. You are my biggest blessing!

Thank you, Sonia Rao, ML, Wrimo India. I feel your loving presence around me even when I don't seek you out.

Thank you, Kavita Nachnani, for explaining the technical aspects of stock trading, and Deepma Jadeja, for the once-over!

This book is dedicated to my dad, who is no more: I wish you were here to see this but I know you'll be beaming at me from above.

To my mom, who showed me that a woman can be a superwoman. Something I never came close to :) Thank you for encouraging me to never give up.

Thank you Dinesh Gopalan, Mrinalini Menon, and Priya Gopalan, for always having my back.

A big thank you to my near and dear ones for cheering me along the way. And to the many friends, fellow writers, and family who have been an important part of this book in myriad ways. You know who you are!

Lastly, but to whom I owe the most!

Dear God, I thank You.

About The Author

SUDHA NAIR won the Amazon KDP Pen to Publish contest for her debut novel, The Wedding Tamasha—a tale about love, family, values, and traditions. She loves writing stories and creating worlds where she lets her imagination run riot and has fun along with her characters. Sudha lives in Bangalore, India.

CONNECT WITH SUDHA ON:

WEBSITE: sudhanair.com
EMAIL: sudha@sudhanair.com
FACEBOOK: facebook.com/SudhaNairAuthor
INSTAGRAM: instagram.com/sudhagn